Frank Merriwell's Marriage
Inza's Happiest Day

BURT L. STANDISH

Author of the famous Merriwell Stories.

BOOKS FOR ATHLETICS

LONDON
IBOO PRESS HOUSE
86-90 PAUL STREET

Frank Merriwell's Marriage
Inza's Happiest Day

BURT L. STANDISH
Author of the famous Merriwell Stories.

BOOKS FOR ATHLETICS

Layout & Cover © Copyright 2020 iBooPress, London

Published by
iBoo Press House

3rd Floor
86-90 Paul Street
London, EC2A4NE UK

t: +44 20 3695 0809
info@iboo.com II iBoo.com

ISBNs
978-1-64181-918-3 (h)
978-1-64181-919-0 (p)

Frank Merriwell's Marriage
Inza's Happiest Day

BURT L. STANDISH
Author of the famous Merriwell Stories.

BOOKS FOR ATHLETICS

MERRIWELL SERIES
Stories of Frank and Dick Merriwell
Fascinating Stories of Athletics

A half million enthusiastic followers of the Merriwell brothers will attest the unfailing interest and wholesomeness of these adventures of two lads of high ideals, who play fair with themselves, as well as with the rest of the world.

These stories are rich in fun and thrills in all branches of sports and athletics. They are extremely high in moral tone, and cannot fail to be of immense benefit to every boy who reads them.

They have the splendid quality of firing a boy's ambition to become a good athlete, in order that he may develop into a strong, vigorous, right-thinking man.

Contents

FRANK MERRIWELL'S MARRIAGE.

CHAPTER I.

AT EAGLE HEIGHTS.

"I would give ten thousand dollars to know Frank Merri-well's secret," declared Wallace Grafter, sitting in a comfortable "Old Hickory" chair on the veranda of the Eagle Heights clubhouse and watching the Albany boat, which was passing on its way up the Hudson.

"It would be worth it, my dear boy," yawned Philip Phipps, a youth from Poughkeepsie, as he snapped a half-smoked cigarette over the rail and drew out his handsome watch, at which he casually glanced. "But do you think he has a secret?"

"Of course he has!" exclaimed the first speaker decidedly. "His record proves it. What time is it?"

"Ten-twenty," answered Phipps.

"He'll be here in forty minutes," said Grafter. "I'm curious to see him."

Farley Fisher, straight, square-shouldered, military in his bearing, not over twenty-four years of age, standing at a corner of the veranda, smiled a bit scornfully.

"It is amusing to me, gentlemen," he observed, "to think that any fellow can keep up a fake as long as Merriwell has."

"Fake?" cried Phipps, excitement bringing a touch of falsetto into his voice.

"Fake?" questioned Grafter, moving his chair to face Fisher more squarely. "What do you mean by that?"

"Just what I said—no more, no less. I am satisfied that Merriwell is a faker."

Inside an open window of the reading room, which was close at hand, Hobart Manton had been glancing over the pages of a magazine. The words of those outside reached his ears. He dropped the magazine and leaned on the window ledge.

"I agree with you, Fisher," he said. "Merriwell is the biggest faker in this country, and in many ways the cleverest. You know I'm a Yale man. At college I heard so much of Merriwell and what he had done while there that I grew sick and disgusted. He was successful in fooling almost everybody, it seems."

Grafter rose to his feet. He was a well-built fellow, nearly six feet tall, with splendid shoulders and carriage. He was the son of Mike Grafter, the well known Tammany politician, familiarly called "Reliable Mike" by his associates in New York. Although young Grafter had never been guilty of doing a day's work in his life, he had inherited a splendid physique from his parents and had made athletics his hobby, beginning with the days of his baseball playing on the open lots in Harlem. Like his father, he was generally well liked, although it was claimed that, with his sturdy frame he had also inherited some of old Grafter's ideas of winning in any contest by whatever method possible, either fair or otherwise. Like his father, he was also able to cover his tracks so completely that nothing crooked had ever been proved against him, and he was prompt to vigorously resent any insinuation or hint of unfairness.

"I presume," he said, "that you gentlemen have heard the saying of the late Abraham Lincoln that 'you can fool some of the people all of the time and all of the people some of the time, but you can't fool all the people all of the time?'"

"What has that to do with Merriwell?" asked Fisher.

"If he is a faker," retorted Grafter, "I swear it seems to me that he has succeeded in fooling all of the people all of the time since he started in to fool them at all."

"I'd like to know what any one means by calling him a faker," said Phipps.

Manton rose quickly from his chair and came sauntering out onto the veranda, followed by his particular friend, Denton Fisher, of the Harlem Heights A.A.

"Gentlemen," he said, a knowing smile on his smooth-shaven, bulldog face, "I think I can explain what I mean by calling Merriwell a faker. A faker is a deceiver—he pretends to accomplish things he does not actually accomplish. At college Merriwell won a great deal of glory as a football captain and a baseball player. Investigation will show that the football and baseball teams of those years were the strongest ever turned out at Yale. He obtained the reputation, while the men behind him did the work. It has been so ever since."

"Apparently," said Phipps, "you do not give Merriwell any credit for developing such strong teams."

"I place the credit where it belongs, with the coaches. Merriwell developed nothing. He happened to be fortunate in having such good teams to back him up, and he has lived on the reputation made at Yale."

"His career since leaving Yale——" began Grafter.

"What has he done? Personally, I mean. He has traveled round more or less, with an athletic team made up from the best Yale men of his day and a few clever outsiders. He still works the old game of living on the glory that should belong to others. But he is careful when he plays baseball teams to choose such teams as he can defeat in most instances. For instance——"

"The Chicago Nationals," laughed Grafter. "Didn't he win two games off them in California?"

"Fake!" laughed Manton, in return. "He has plenty of money, and he can afford to buy the rubber game, especially when it costs a big team nothing to lose it. That's another of his tricks. He goes round the country spending money freely. Who couldn't win at almost anything if he had plenty of money!"

Grafter shook his head.

"I have found out," he said, "that legitimate amateur sports are generally on the level. Amateurs, as a rule, cannot be bought."

"Well," said the Yale man, with a slight curling of his lips, "I presume you speak from experience."

Instantly Grafter flushed and his hands closed quickly.

"What do you mean by that?" he demanded, a threat in his voice. "You may have a reputation as a gentleman boxer; but you had better be careful with your tongue, for I don't fancy being insulted, even by you."

Manton looked like a pugilist toned down, or toned up, like a gentleman. He had a thick neck and the cast of countenance that one instinctively associates with pugnacity. He had taken part in many an amateur boxing match, and some of the contests had been "to a finish." It was his boast that he had never been "put out." It was generally known that his college career had terminated suddenly and unexpectedly because he had attempted to beat up one of the professors.

"You're touchy, Grafter," said Manton, with a slight shrug of his muscular shoulders. "What's the use? Can't you take a joke?"

"The right kind of a joke. I presume you're joking about Merriwell?"

"On the contrary, I'm in sober earnest. I meant just what I said."

"It sounded like a joke to me," said Phipps. "Why, I didn't suppose any one questioned Merriwell's standing as an athlete. Surely it is not questioned here, else he would not have been invited to take part in our meet."

"It is possible we may be able to show him up as the faker he is," laughed Manton. "Why, the fellow actually has the nerve to claim that he is the all-round champion athlete of this country."

"I don't think he made such a claim himself," said Grafter promptly. "The newspapers called him that after he made the best record at Ashport last week. That was a contest for the all-round championship of the country."

"At Ashport!" sneered Manton. "And where is Ashport, pray? A little country town somewhere on the Ohio River. Who did Merriwell meet there?"

"Amateurs from all over the country," answered Phipps. "According to all reports, it was one of the most successful contests ever held in this country."

"But it was not the regular meet of the Amateur Athletic Association of the United States. It was nothing but a country club affair, at most. Championships won at such tournaments do not count. It's a case of pure gall for Merriwell to set himself up as the leading all-round amateur of the country."

"Besides," reminded Denton Frost, "he was defeated there by a local man in a cross-country run a short time before."

"Who defeated him?" questioned Phipps.

"Oh, some unknown. I agree with Manton that he'll be shown up here if he ventures to take part. We'll have the leading amateurs in the East."

"Gentlemen," said Grafter, who appeared to have recovered his good nature, "if Mr. Merriwell enters for any of our contests, I'll give you an opportunity to win some of my money, for I shall bet on him."

"Better use stage money," advised Frost. "You won't miss it so much."

"Don't worry about me," flung back Grafter. "If I lose some real money, I can stand it."

"That's a good thing for you," grinned Frost, in a chilly manner.

"I think I heard you remark that you would give ten thousand to know Merriwell's secret," said Manton. "I'll tell you what it is, and it won't cost you a dollar. Pick out easy marks as opponents. In that manner you'll always be a winner."

"I don't fancy you think we have many easy marks belonging to this club or entered for the tournament?"

"No, not many."

"Will you name some of the events in which men are entered who cannot be defeated by Merriwell?"

"Ye-e-es; the standing long jump, the high jump, and the pole vault. The champions of the country are entered for these events, and Merriwell would be outclassed in any one of them."

"Perhaps he may be induced to take part in them."

"I doubt it. When he finds out the men who are entered, he'll keep out. Why, Jack Necker, the Hartford man, is going out for the world's championship, and he can jump some. My friend Frost is entered for the pole vault. He came within an ace of defeating Burleigh, the world's champion, last year, and he can vault eight inches higher this year than he could then. He'd make Merriwell look like a high-school kid at it."

"Perhaps we'll have a chance to find out very soon what Merriwell intends to do," said Phipps, rising and looking down the winding drive. "Here comes a carriage, containing Bert Fuller and two strangers. I fancy one of the strangers is Frank Merriwell."

The Eagle Heights A.A. was peculiar in many ways. It was a "country club" for amateur athletes, most picturesquely located on the Hudson, some miles above Peekskill. One of the qualifications for membership was that each and every member must belong to some other amateur club and must be the champion of his own club in some particular line. For instance, Bert Fuller, president of the Eagle Heights A.A., was the champion gymnast of the Madison Square A.A.; Wallace Grafter was the best shot putter of the Catskill Club; Horace Manton was the star boxer of the Albany University Club; George Branch was the leading long-distance bicyclist of the Century Club, of Boston; Philip Phipps was the champion billiard player of the Poughkeepsie Pastime Club, and Denton Frost, of the Harlem Heights A.A., was a candidate for the championship of the world at pole vaulting.

It will be readily understood that the Eagle Heights A.A. was an organization made up and maintained by rich young men, or the sons of wealthy men—gentlemen they were supposed to be, one and all. But wealth is not always the brand of birth or breeding, and, like other clubs, the Eagle Heights contained members who lacked the natural instincts of the gentleman, although they had a certain veneering, or outward polish.

The Eagle Heights A.A. was the outcome of the modern development of interest in athletics and sports. Ten years ago the organization and maintenance of such a club would have been impossible; and, indeed, the scheme seemed wild and visionary when first outlined at the Manhattan A.A. by Frederick Fuller, the father of Bert Fuller. Although plainly told that he could never carry the project through, Fuller, Sr., went about it in earnest, secured a site for the clubhouse, with fine grounds on every hand, started a fund, interested other men of wealth, and finally pushed the thing through. The Eagle Heights A.A. was nearly two years old and flourishing like a green bay tree. It was generally regarded as the acme of glory to be admitted as a member, and the time had already arrived when it was found necessary to make a finer discrimination in regard to admissible candidates.

As was natural, rivalry for honors among the club members of this remarkable organization was very keen. But not all the contests were held for the benefit of members only. Already there had been three open meets of various sorts, and now there was to be another, in which all athletes regularly registered in the A.A.A. of the U.S.could participate. Frank Merriwell, having reached the East after a tour of the country, had received a special invitation to be present and to compete if he desired.

Having learned that Merry would visit the club at a certain time, there was an unusually large number of members present on the forenoon of this midweek day.

Phil Phipps was correct in thinking that one of the two strangers in the carriage with the president of the club was Frank. The other was Merry's boon companion, Bart Hodge.

The carriage stopped at the broad front steps and Fuller sprang out, followed by his guests.

"Here we are, Merriwell!" cried the youthful president, with a wave of his hand. "What do you think of our location?"

Frank permitted his eyes to sweep over the beautiful prospect of fields, woodland, and hills, through the midst of which flowed the blue, majestic Hudson. It was a vision to delight the soul of any true lover of nature.

"It is grand, Fuller!" he answered, with enthusiasm. "With such a view outspread before you, you should be constantly spurred to do your level best at any undertaking. Surely it is an inspiration."

The face of Hodge betrayed his admiration, but he said nothing.

"My father chose the spot," said Fuller proudly. "He saw what could be done here. Although we are up among the hills, we have one of the finest athletic fields in the country. Let's go in. I know many of the boys are anxious to meet you."

"And I am one of them," declared Wallace Grafter, advancing to the steps.

He was introduced to Frank and Bart, shaking them heartily by the hand.

Phil Phipps and Farley Fisher followed.

"We have a Yale man here, Merriwell," said Fuller. "I know

you'll be welcomed by a son of Old Eli. Mr. Manton———"

He stopped short, for Hobart Manton, with Denton Frost at his side, had already turned away and was entering the clubhouse.

The president flushed. For a moment he seemed surprised and confused, but he quickly recovered, smiling a little, as he said:

"Evidently Manton's modesty prevented him from pressing forward at once. He intends to wait to meet you inside."

Frank nodded. He knew something was wrong, but he did not show it. He did not even return Bart's queer look of questioning.

They entered the building. In the parlor they met other members, all of whom were very cordial. In the reading room were still others.

Manton and Frost were there when they entered. The pair surveyed Frank and Bart with an air of indifference, and together, just before Fuller would have presented them, they sauntered away into another part of the house.

Fuller was furious, although he tried to conceal it.

There was no mistaking this repetition of the act.

It was a deliberate slight.

The president made a resolution to give Manton and Frost a prompt calling down, but, not wishing to leave Merry just then, he waited for another opportunity.

The visitors were conducted through the building until they finally came to the gymnasium, which they found lavishly fitted with the finest modern apparatus.

In the gym a number of fellows were at work. The only spectators were Manton and Frost. But now neither Fuller nor the visitors gave the two chaps the slightest notice, although walking past them within a few feet.

At one side of the room, and running the full length, was a string of flying rings.

Coming to the end of these, Hodge was seized by a sudden desire to test some of the energy he felt seething within. Giving a short turn, he sprang into the air, caught the first ring, swung to the second, from that to the third, and so on until he had traversed the complete line.

Manton and Frost left the room, laughing softly and saying something to each other about showing off.

Bart had not thought of "showing off," but he realized that his action might be regarded as the outcome of a desire to exhibit himself, and his face grew dark.

"When the time comes right, one or both of you chaps are going to get something from me," he thought.

They next inspected the billiard room, coming at last to the bowling alleys.

There they again found Manton and Frost, who seemed on the point of starting a string.

Now an odd thing happened. Manton stepped forward and spoke to Frank.

"You've been kept busy shaking hands with the rest of the boys," he said. "I'm not inclined to rush forward and overwhelm a visitor. I leave that to Grafter."

Fuller was relieved, and he immediately introduced both Manton and Frost.

"We're glad to know you, Mr. Merriwell," declared the gentleman pugilist. "I heard a great deal about you at college. You surely had all Yale hypnotized. Of course some of the things they tell of you are preposterous. I regard you as very clever in being able to secure such a reputation."

"I don't think I understand you," said Merry, disagreeably impressed by the fellow's words.

"Why, you know they seem to think in New Haven that you were a champion at any old thing to which you turned your hand. No man could excel at everything. That's out of reason. I presume you were fairly clever as a baseball pitcher, or something of that sort; but they seemed to fancy you were possessed of the powers of a god. For instance, although I was the champion bowler and sparrer, I was continually being told what Merriwell did when he was there. I grew sick of it. I longed for an opportunity to demonstrate to them that you were not the only person on earth. Of course I had no such opportunity. Had you drifted along at the proper moment, I'd taken special delight in showing you up on the alleys."

He laughed as he made this statement.

"Evidently," said Frank, "it was a good thing for my reputation that I kept away from New Haven while you were in college."

"As far as bowling or boxing was concerned."

"You're a fine bowler?"

"I am the champion of this club, although one of our members is the champion bowler of the White Elephant, of Paterson."

"I'm hardly in my best form as a bowler just now," confessed Merry.

Frost started to laugh, but checked himself.

"I presume not," smiled Manton.

"I have bowled very little during the last two months, having been interested mainly in outdoor sports."

"Don't be alarmed," said Manton; "I'm not going to challenge you."

"But I was thinking of challenging you," said Merry sweetly, his words causing the heart of Bart Hodge to leap with satisfaction.

14

CHAPTER II.

IN THE CLUB ALLEY.

"Oh, were you?" exclaimed the gentleman pugilist, with a touch of surprise. "Well, that suits me! If you're not in your best form, however, you had better wait, for I'll bury you."

"Even if you do that, it will give me pleasure to witness your skill," nodded Frank. "And I believe I am able to accept defeat gracefully. I've been compelled to do so more than once in my day."

"What's that?" cut in Frost, in his cold voice. "Why, from all reports I should fancy you had never been defeated at anything."

"You know reports are generally exaggerated."

"Well," said Manton eagerly, "if you're anxious to be trimmed, we'll get at it."

Merry calmly removed his coat and vest.

A colored boy had followed them into the room, and he had the pins all set up.

At this point Grafter, Phipps, and Fisher appeared, apparently looking round for the visitors. They were surprised and interested when they found out what was taking place.

"Just in time, Grafter!" cried Manton. "Have you plenty of the needful on your person? You know the sort of talk you were making on the veranda a while ago. Here's the opportunity to part with some of your filthy."

Grafter was not one to back down. They stepped aside and spoke in low tones.

"Bet you a hundred I beat him this string," proposed Manton.

Frank knew what was taking place, and he seized the opportunity to say:

"Mr. Grafter, I'm not in my best bowling form, and bowling is not a specialty with me."

"I'll go you, Manton," said Grafter, without paying the least heed to Frank.

The gentleman pugilist smiled with satisfaction.

"No need to put the money up," he said. "Then we won't break any rules. Here's where I begin to get into you. I hope Merriwell stays around until after the meet. I'll have you going to your old man for change."

"For conceit," returned Grafter, "you certainly take the cake. If you win my money, you're welcome to it."

Frost was smiling as they returned and Manton made ready for business.

Merry had been looking the balls over. They were a fine lot, but he weighed one after another in his hands, examined the finger holds and finally selected two of them as his favorites.

A coin was tossed to see who would lead off, and it fell on Manton.

He picked out a large ball, took his position on the right-hand side of the runway, bent forward, swung the ball at the end of his arm once like the pendulum of a clock, then ran forward and rolled.

He started the ball from the right-hand side of the alley, rolling it toward the head pin, which it struck quarteringly.

With a crash, every pin fell.

"Pretty, old man!" cried Fisher approvingly. "That's the way to start her off!"

"It's keeping it up that counts," said Grafter.

"Don't worry about me," advised Manton smilingly.

Now the strange thing of the affair was that Grafter, although he had bet on Frank, was inclined to believe Merry would be beaten. He knew Manton to be a wonderfully good bowler, while he was not at all certain that Merriwell had ever accomplished much at it. Having made betting talk on the veranda, however, he was not the fellow to let Manton back him down, and, therefore, he had ventured a hundred dollars on the result.

It is likely that Bart Hodge was the only person present who had perfect confidence in Merry as a bowler. Bart's face was grave and unreadable as that of a stone image.

Frank picked up one of the two balls he had selected. He was watched closely to note his "form" by all present. He poised the ball in front of his face, made a short run and a single swing.

Seven pins fell.

Denton Frost smiled chillingly.

Farley Fisher shrugged his military shoulders.

Manton managed to repress any exhibition of satisfaction.

Not a word of complaint did Merriwell utter. By his manner no one could have dreamed he was in the least disappointed.

He took the other ball and rolled for a spare.

Two pins went down and the one remaining tottered, swayed, and righted itself.

"Nine pins," said the scorer, as he made the record on the sheet.

"Hard luck, Merriwell," said Hobart. "You'll have to do better than that."

"I think I shall," admitted Merry. "Still I did my level best for that spare."

"Spares don't count when the other fellow is making strikes," observed Fisher.

"The other fellow may not make strikes all the time."

"It's plain you don't know Manton. I'm afraid he's roped you in as a mark, which was not very nice of him."

Fuller, who was scoring, looked disappointed, for he had hoped that his guest would do better.

The pins were spotted and Manton went at them again.

Boom! The ball went rolling down the polished alley.

Crash! Every pin fell.

"Another strike," said Frost. "It's the natural thing with him."

Frank had discarded the first ball used by him. He put it aside where it would not get mixed with the others.

At this point he assumed all the self-command possible, fixing his mind on the point where he wished the ball to strike. He was steady as a mill.

The ball was delivered perfectly, leaving his hand without the slightest jar as it touched the polished alley. With a soft boom it rolled straight to the point on which Merry had set his mind.

Crash!

"Strike!" cried Fuller. "That's the stuff, Merriwell! Now you are showing your style!"

"But he began a trifle late, I fear," said Frost.

"Don't let your fears trouble you," advised Bart Hodge. "The string is just started."

Grafter could not repress a smile of satisfaction. He did not like Manton, and it was his earnest wish that Merriwell would push the fellow hard, if he could not win.

"You're getting the range of the alley," he said. "Of course you were taken at a disadvantage, not being familiar with it. You should have rolled a few before beginning."

Frank nodded. He realized that Grafter was right, but it was too late to rectify the mistake.

"For one thing," he said, "I think I made a mistake in the first ball I used. The finger grip was not just right for me. The holes were a trifle too close together."

"That's odd," said Frost. "That's the pet ball of Spaulding, the champion of the Knickerbocker Bowling Club and the second best man in this club."

"Without doubt his hand is built differently from mine," said Merriwell. "It's a fine ball, but not suited to the breadth of my grip."

"When I fizzle I'll tell you why it happened," laughed Manton, in a most irritating manner.

Hodge felt like punching the fellow; but Frank remained in nowise disturbed.

The Eagle Heights man took his time when the pins were spotted. He chalked the soles of his feet, moistened his fingers the least bit with the sponge, chose his favorite ball, made his habitual swing and smashed down every pin for the third time.

"Thirty in the first box," said Fuller.

"Which leads Merriwell twenty-one," observed Fisher. "That's quite a handicap."

"It is when a man seems determined to make strikes right along," admitted Frank good-naturedly.

"I think I have my hand in your pocket, Grafter," chuckled Manton.

"Perhaps so," admitted the great shot putter of the Catskill Club. "But 'there's many a slip,' you know. Don't be too sure of anything in this world. It doesn't pay. I've found that out by experience."

"He's setting a hard pace, Mr. Merriwell," said Fisher, with affected politeness, yet plainly with the idea of rubbing Frank against the grain.

"He is," confessed Frank; "but that makes it all the more interesting."

"Your sand seems good."

Fuller shook his head at Fisher, but the latter pretended he did not see it.

Frank did not hurry. When he did deliver the ball he sent it once more to the exact spot he wished.

Nine pins fell.

Hodge uttered an exclamation of bitter disappointment, followed by another of exultation; for the tenth pin, which had been tottering, finally fell.

"That's great luck for you, Merriwell," declared Manton. "You got that strike by the skin of your teeth."

"It would have been a shame had he missed," said Hodge. "He struck the pins perfectly."

"Still you know such things happen and leave pins standing at times. I thought he struck a trifle too far to the right."

Fisher and Frost exchanged glances and moved closer together.

"This Merriwell is no slouch at it," said Fisher, in a low tone. "He's keeping right after Manton."

"That's right; but I don't believe he can crowd him very hard. He'll slip up pretty soon."

"It's not impossible for Manton to slip up."

"But Manton is not the kind to slip up in a case like this. He's a sticker."

By this time Manton was ready again. Again he did the trick, although, as in the case of Merry, one pin threatened not to fall.

"That would have been tough!" declared the Eagle Heights man, with relief.

"Of course you struck the pins just right," muttered Hodge.

"Yes, I did!" exclaimed Manton. "Any one could see that."

"It seems to make a difference who rolls the ball," said Hodge.

"Thirty in the second box for Manton, total of sixty," said Fuller, as he marked the score down.

When the pins were spotted Frank discovered two that were not set right. He instructed the boy to place them squarely on the spots, which was done.

"Better be careful," sneered Frost; but pretended to laugh.

Manton had made four strikes in succession. His friends fancied this would begin to shake Merriwell's nerve; but that was because they did not know Frank, whose nerves invariably became steadier when engaged in a trying contest of any sort.

Merry sent the balls into the midst of the pins.

Crash!

"All down!" exclaimed Fuller. "Thirty for Merriwell in the second box, with a total of thirty-nine."

"Which is a long distance to the bad," observed Frost.

Manton frowned the least bit. Merriwell was altogether too successful in following up with strikes.

"Why don't you quit it?" he cried, pretending to joke.

"I'm waiting for you to quit," retorted Frank.

"You may have to wait a long time."

"I don't think you'll go all the way through the string with strikes."

"I may."

"Of course. Still it is not probable."

Manton followed with another strike.

As he took his position to bowl, Frank discovered that the pins were spread slightly. He asked the boy about it, but the boy insisted that they were on the spots.

Merry started to go down the alley to investigate, whereupon the boy hastened to alter the positions of the pins slightly.

Immediately Fuller gave the boy a sharp calldown.

"You know what you're down there for," he said. "Put every pin up perfectly."

Frank struck the pins in his favorite manner, and they went down promptly.

"I don't believe he means to quit," laughed Fuller. "That gives him a total of sixty-nine in his third box."

"But Manton has ninety in the same box," reminded Frost.

"The string is half rolled, that's all," muttered Hodge.

Still it looked serious for Frank, as Manton was not the sort of fellow to let slip an advantage that he had fairly within his grasp—at least, that was what his friends thought. No one could have guessed by the face of the gentleman pugilist that he was worried in the slightest degree. He pretended to enjoy it. In his heart, however, he was growling over the persistence of his opponent, which was quite unexpected.

"Why don't you give up, Merriwell?" he laughed.

"I'm not quite ready to give up," was the quiet answer.

"I've heard that he never gives up, Manton," said Fuller.

"Some people never know when they are beaten," chipped in Fisher.

"That's a good qualification," said the president of the club.

"But it makes them appear ridiculous at times, don't you know."

This time the pin boy had every pin up correctly. Manton hesitated as he was starting, pretended that his shoes were slippery, and resorted to the chalk box.

"He's beginning to feel the strain," thought Hodge, in keen satisfaction. "He's getting shaky."

Fortifying his nerve, Manton rolled in his usual style.

Crash!

"All down again!" said Frost. "I think he's going through the string with strikes."

"Total of one hundred and twenty in his fourth box," announced the scorer. "That's a three-hundred clip."

"Now we'll watch Mr. Merriwell," observed Manton, sitting down with a satisfied air.

"Everybody watch," urged Frost.

"Lots of talking for a match," reminded Fuller.

"Oh, but this is not a regular match," said Fisher.

"But it's regular enough so that a stranger should have fair play," came in something like a growl from Grafter. "You know what is generally thought of men who try to rattle opponents."

"Merriwell has the reputation of never getting rattled," said Frost, with another icy smile.

Frank seemed giving their chatter no heed. With the same air of deliberation he smashed into the pins and cleaned the alley.

Frank had a total of ninety-nine in his fourth box, which left him still twenty-one pins to the bad.

"Well, here goes another strike," said Manton, as he selected his ball.

CHAPTER III.

SHIFTING WINDS.

anton seemed just as confident as ever, but apprehension was beginning to grip him. In his heart he was troubled by a slight fear that he might fail.

It is this feeling of doubt that defeats many a man in the game of life, as well as in other games. No person should ever attempt a task while troubled by the smallest shadow of a doubt. He should have such command of himself that his confidence in his ability to succeed cannot waver. Through years of training Frank Merriwell had brought himself to the point where he refused to doubt when in anything like his normal condition.

At the very moment of delivering the ball Manton was assailed violently by the doubt he had been unable to crush out of his heart. That doubt sent an electric shock along his arm to his hand, which quivered as he released the ball.

Instantly he realized he was not going to strike the pins properly. Still he prayed for a fortunate result, knowing by experience that pins often fell well when hit poorly.

In vain.

The ball cut through them, taking down only seven, leaving two on one corner and one on the other.

"At last!" thought Hodge exultingly; but not a sound came from his lips, and only the gleam in his dark eyes could have betrayed what was passing in his heart.

"Well, now that was rotten, hard luck!" cried Manton, in disgust. "The ball slipped."

"You've kept your promise, Manton," said Grafter.

"What promise?"

"You said that when you missed you would tell us how it happened."

Manton shot him a look of anger.

The pin boy had sent Manton's ball back. He took it from the return and stood inspecting the pins.

"There's a possible spare in it," said Frost.

Manton turned to inspect the score sheet.

"A spare will save me," mentally decided the Eagle Heights man. "If I can get those three pins with this ball, I'll never let him catch me."

He rolled with precision and determination. The ball went down the alley in beautiful style. It was his hope to send one of the two pins flying across to sweep down the single pin on the opposite corner, and he believed he was going to do it.

Fate was against him, however.

The ball took the two pins, and the head one shot across the alley, but it missed the single pin.

Manton clenched his fist and made a gesture of dismay, breathing an angry exclamation.

Fuller quickly jotted down the score.

"This is Merriwell's grand opportunity!" cried Grafter. "I have a finger and thumb into your pocket, Manton."

The Eagle Heights bowler turned away and sat down, mopping his perspiring face. Fisher stepped over and sat down beside him.

"Merriwell will slump, also," he said, in a low voice. "It almost always happens that way. If the leading man falls down, the one following takes a tumble."

"That's something no one can count on," muttered Manton.

"Great Scott!" gasped Fisher. "You're not giving up?"

"Hardly; but that was infernal luck."

It was almost certain that Denton Frost felt quite as bad about it as Manton, but he said nothing. His face was like a cake of ice.

"It's the golden moment, Merry!" muttered Hodge, in the ear of Manton.

Frank knew it. There was nothing mechanical about him, yet he was steady as a piece of machinery. Through life he had tried to grasp his opportunities. This was an opportunity he must not miss.

The pins were up when he stepped onto the runway. He picked up his ball and took his position.

There was a hush.

In the midst of it Frost turned to Grafter and whispered:

"He's shaking; he'll blow up now."

The whisper was loud enough for every one to hear, and Frost was rewarded by several hisses from the spectators.

Boom!—the ball sped down the alley.

"It's another strike!" exclaimed an excited watcher.

Crash!

A dozen persons shouted, for it was a strike.

"Still he's only one hundred and twenty-nine in his fifth, against your one forty-seven," murmured Fisher, in the ear of Manton.

"But his strike gives him the advantage on the next two boxes," muttered the gentleman pugilist huskily.

"He can't beat you if you get right down to it."

"I'll do all I can."

Fisher was disappointed in the manner of his companion.

Manton did try hard the next time, but two pins were left standing.

"I'm getting my whole hand into that pocket," said Grafter.

Manton clipped off the two pins with his second ball, and secured a spare.

"That may hold Merriwell," said Frost. "His turn is coming."

Apparently Frank struck the pins perfectly, but there was another shout when it was seen that he had left two standing.

"I told you!" said Frost.

A gleam of hope came to Manton's face.

Frank waited for the ball to be returned. Then he tried a difficult shot in the hope of getting a spare, but missed the first pin by the merest fraction of an inch. Fuller swiftly marked down the score, and a perfect roar filled the alley when the result was seen.

Merry had one hundred and fifty-seven in the sixth box and one hundred and seventy-five in the seventh, which tied Manton at that point.

In the eighth box he had one hundred and eighty-three, with the result of Manton's spare to be recorded in that box, which, without doubt, would again put the Eagle Heights man in the lead.

"You have him!" hissed Fisher, in Manton's ear. "Keep your nerve now and you'll beat him out easily!"

Frost smiled in his usual manner.

"Take your hand out of my pocket, Grafter!" cried Manton. "The wind has changed."

"Perhaps so," admitted the shot putter. "But it isn't over yet."

It was Manton's turn to roll his ninth.

"Put a strike on top of that spare, old boy!" urged Fisher.

The gentleman pugilist tried hard enough, but the ball swept straight through the centre of the pins, leaving one on either corner.

Manton stood with his hands on his hips, glaring at the two pins.

Grafter laughed.

"The wind seems to be full of flaws," he remarked.

Boiling with anger, Manton seized a ball and sent it booming along to take off one of the two pins.

"One hundred and ninety-three in the eighth box, and two hundred and two in the ninth," said Fuller.

"Ten ahead of Merriwell in the eighth," muttered Frost, clinging to hope. "Let's see what Merriwell will do."

Frank's turn came directly, and he went after the pins in a resolute manner.

He got them.

"Strike!" was the shout, as he swept them all down.

Manton seemed to turn green.

Grafter opened his lips to rejoice, but changed his mind and said nothing.

"Luck—nothing but luck!" said Frost freezingly.

Still Manton did not give up, for he knew there was a possibility that his antagonist might take a terrible slump in the last box.

"Keep after him, old man," urged Fisher. "You may pull out."

"Not much chance for it," confessed Manton; but still he tried hard, and swept down all the pins.

"Roll it off; it's your last box," said Fuller.

Manton repeated the trick twice more.

"A good string," observed Fisher.

"Not for me," muttered the gentleman pugilist, as he went for his collar and necktie.

"Eat 'em up, Frank!" urged Hodge. "Go after them all. The first ball counts."

Merriwell knew it. He betrayed no uneasiness, but he took the utmost pains.

There was a hush as he sent the huge ball rolling down the polished alley.

Crash! It was a strike.

Manton turned away. He could not speak, and his hands shook a bit as he buttoned on his collar and adjusted his tie.

Merry waited for the pins to be reset and his ball to be returned. Then he rolled again.

"Another strike!" exclaimed Hodge.

But it was not. Nine pins fell.

Fuller quickly added up the score which showed that Frank had defeated Manton by nine points.

CHAPTER IV.

SOREHEADS.

Hobart Manton was sore all the way through. Having put on his coat, he came over to Merriwell, who was betraying no exultation over the outcome.

"I presume it's up to me to say something pleasant," he observed. "You defeated me on the level, all right; but you couldn't do it again in a week."

"Perhaps not," admitted Frank, unruffled. "Still you know there is an old saying that the future may be judged only by the past. I'm not a champion bowler."

"You're not?"

"No, sir."

"Why, I thought you pretended to be a champion at everything you attempted to do."

"On the contrary, I make no pretensions whatever."

"He doesn't have to," chipped in Grafter. "His record speaks for him."

"Perhaps you'll have an opportunity to purchase his secret for ten thousand dollars," sneered Manton. "You are so flush with money."

"It wouldn't cost me quite ten thousand now," retorted the shot-putter. "Only nine thousand nine hundred. I have a hundred coming."

"That's right," admitted Manton; "but winning that hundred may cost you dearly before long. I generally get even."

"Welcome to try."

"If you linger until our open meet comes off," said Manton, again addressing Merriwell, "we'll try to find some one to defeat you at something."

"Jumping or pole vaulting, for instance," said Farley Fisher.

"In a club made up of specialists you should be able to defeat an ordinary all-round man," said Frank. "You know it is the rule that an all-round man seldom excels at any particular thing."

"He fancies he is the exception to the rule," said Frost, in his cold, chilling way.

"Gentlemen!" exclaimed Bert Fuller reprovingly; "don't forget that Mr. Merriwell is a guest!"

"Oh, never mind them," smiled Frank. "They're amusing themselves by seeking to get me on the string. It doesn't disturb me, and it may give them pleasure."

"He's too blamed cool and undisturbed!" growled Farley Fisher, turning away. "Makes me want to punch him! I know Manton is just boiling to get at him with his fists."

"Manton could show him up that way," said Frost. "Too bad he didn't challenge the fellow to put on the gloves. Then there would have been no question about the result."

The defeated bowler left the alley, accompanied by a few of his bosom friends.

Frank was congratulated by a number of the members, who told him plainly that they had not fancied it possible he could defeat their man at bowling.

"Well," nodded Merry, "you know there was nothing sure about it until it was over. Mr. Manton is a splendid bowler, but he takes defeat hard. He's a poor loser."

Grafter kept close to Merry. Before Frank left the club, he found an opportunity to say:

"I'd like to have a little private talk with you, Mr. Merriwell. Will it be too much bother?"

"Not at all, Mr. Grafter. I'm at liberty any time you may select."

"Where are you stopping?"

"At Elm Tree Inn, down below. Just going down for lunch now. Will you take lunch with me?"

"I should be pleased to!" exclaimed Grafter. "But why don't you stop here to lunch?"

"I invited him," the club president hastened to explain; "but he said he had some business that he must look after, and so he could not stay to-day."

"Oh, then I'll interfere with your business?" said the shot putter.

"Not at all. The fact is, I'm half expecting some of my boys to arrive at the inn, and I wish to be there when they show up."

A few minutes later Grafter was in the carriage with Merriwell, Hodge, and Fuller. Manton and his particular chums watched the four depart.

"Grafter makes me ill!" growled Manton. "He's ready to bow down and worship Merriwell. Seems to think the fellow has some wonderful secret method of becoming a champion. Oh, hang the luck! Why did I fail to defeat him to-day! I'll guarantee I can do it next time!"

"You should have challenged him for another string," said Fisher.

"I couldn't very well. I think I mentioned that one string would be enough. I said something of the sort before we began bowling. Besides, I was too hot over losing that string. I knew he would defeat me if we rolled another right away."

Dent Frost had his derby pulled over his eyes. He was humped on a chair, his feet on the window ledge.

"It didn't seem to bother you as much as it did me," he observed. "Wonder if Merriwell is coming back here this afternoon?"

"I understand he is. Why?"

"I'd like to run him up against somebody who could knock a corner off him. Who's the man?"

"There he is now!" exclaimed Fisher, as a young chap in flannels approached the house, followed by a caddie with a golfing outfit.

"Cleaves?" said Manton.

"The very fellow," asserted Fisher. "He's the golf champion of this club, and he could be the champion of the country, if he would give up business and turn his attention to golf."

Manton shook his head.

"It wouldn't satisfy me much to see Merriwell defeated at such a mild game as golf," he declared.

"I'd like to see him beaten at something that would hurt him— and hurt him bad."

"You're looking for revenge."

"That's what I am," was the confession. "I'm looking for it, and I'm going to have it!"

"Now you're talking," nodded Frost. "Rib him into the pole vault at our meet, and I'll give you a taste of it."

"Don't be too sure. I thought I could put it over him on the alley to-day. I'd like to smash his face!"

"Why don't you?" murmured Frost.

"I may—when I get a chance. Couldn't pick a quarrel with him here, you know. Hello! here's Necker."

A slender, blue-eyed chap approached.

"What's this I hear?" he exclaimed. "They tell me you've let a stranger down you at tenpins, Mant."

"So they're blowing it round?" snapped Manton, frowning. "I thought they would. Seem to take delight in it. I suppose there are fools around here who fancy it's an honor for a member of this club to be defeated by the great Frank Merriwell."

Necker whistled.

"Was that the fellow who did it?"

"Yes."

"Where is he?"

"Gone. He's stopping down at the Elm Tree. Grafter's mittened onto him."

"I've been wanting to get a look at Merriwell. What's up? Is he here to take part in the meet?"

"I reckon so. He'll expect to put it all over our bunch. You want to look out, Jack. You know he's a champion at everything."

Necker laughed.

"I'm not afraid of that kind of a champion," he declared. "Jack-of-all-trades and master of none, you know. I hope he does jump against me. It will add interest to that event."

"Don't you be too sure of defeating him," said Fisher.

"I'll defeat him all right if he jumps," assured Necker. "But he'll be too clever to let me show him up. He had better stick to his baseball. That's what he was cut out for. I'm sorry you fell down when you tackled him, Manton."

"I tell you he is a bad man at anything," said Fisher. "I didn't think it a while ago, but I believe it now. He's a chap with supreme confidence in himself."

"Sort of a swell head, eh? Goes round with his chest out and a chip on his shoulder?"

"That's what makes me all the sorer on him. He doesn't go round that way. He's too quiet and modest. Never'd know he considered himself anything in particular. Of course, that's all a bluff. I'll guarantee he's all swelled up inside, even if he doesn't show it."

"I'm growing more and more interested," smiled Necker. "If he can be induced to enter the jumping contest I'll make him look like a yellow dog with a tin can tied to its tail, I promise you."

"And I'm ready to do the same thing to him at the pole vault," said Frost.

"And I'm going to push up against him in another way if I find an opportunity," growled Manton, clenching his fist and looking at it earnestly.

"It seems to me," said Fisher, "that Mr. Merriwell will have his hands full of business if he lingers around here."

CHAPTER V.

THE SECRET.

Frank was a bit disappointed by the failure of his friends to reach the Elm Tree Inn that noon.

Grafter lunched with Merry and Hodge. They chatted pleasantly throughout the meal. The shot putter noted everything that Frank ate.

"Do you conform to a rigid diet?" he asked.

"Not exactly, although I do not eat the things I know are not good for me."

"Can you outline a diet that is proper for all athletes in training?"

"I might outline one that would be proper for most athletes, yet not for all. I have found by experience that human stomachs vary, and it is an old saw that 'one man's meat is another man's poison.' Still there are some rules that apply to every one. Certain things must not be touched by the fellow who proposes to become an athlete."

"For instance?"

"Tobacco, liquor, coffee."

"Don't you think a man may take a small drink with beneficial effect at times?"

"Never when in health."

"When not in health——"

"He's not fit to take part in athletic contests. Liquor may be used as a medicine when prescribed by a doctor who knows his business."

"How about the theory that liquor in moderate quantity is a food? You know that's the assertion of the most advanced doctors of the present day."

Frank nodded and smiled.

"It may be a food," he admitted; "but it is a most dangerous one. The person who uses it as a food must acquire an appetite for it. Half a pint of liquor a day might not seem to harm a strong and rugged man until he acquired the appetite and desire for it. In the end it might ruin him. It is something that cannot be tampered with. It should be let alone by all healthy persons."

"What's the secret of your remarkable success in becoming the champion amateur athlete of America, Mr. Merriwell?"

Again Frank smiled.

"Am I the champion of America?"

"So called by almost every one."

"Well, there is no great secret about my success. In the first place I began young. I have been working for years to make myself perfect physically without overdoing and breaking down. It's a delicate thing to know just how much hard work will be beneficial for one, for overdoing invariably weakens. I have been temperate, and I've tried to live properly. I have no vices that can weaken me. Petty vices are the ruin of hundreds of would-be athletes. I enjoy life thoroughly without seeking enjoyment in forbidden paths. All the while I have been training my body I've trained my mind also.

"Mind and body must work together. The chap who wishes to become a champion must be earnest, sincere, and determined. He must never slight his work. He must always keep himself keyed up to the finest possible point. The moment he grows careless or negligent he begins to slump and go backward. He must have unwavering confidence in himself. It's hard for a youngster to be confident in himself without showing conceit, and then every one wants to kick him. But there is such a thing as absolute and perfect self-confidence without conceit."

Grafter seemed a trifle disappointed.

"Have you told me your secret?" he asked.

"I informed you that there was no secret about it. The secret of success is generally hard work. Veterans will tell you so."

"But some fellows seem to succeed without working."

"No man has made great success in this world without working; but you know for many men work is play. The boy who enjoys work is certain to be a winner."

Grafter shook his head.

"I'm afraid," he confessed, "that I'll never be much of a winner at anything, for I do not enjoy work."

"Learn to enjoy it."

"How can I?"

"Put your heart into it. Get interested. That's the trick. Never do a thing with the simple desire to get it done quickly, but with the determination to get it done well."

"That's good advice, I reckon," admitted Grafter; "but can you tell me how it is that you happen to be an all-round champion, yet able to defeat fellows who have made a special effort to excel in one particular line?"

"I have told you the whole secret. Other fellows may have been content to perfect themselves in one or two lines; I have tried to become perfect in many lines. Some things I like better than others. If I attempt a thing that I do not like very well, I work at it all the harder. If I find some other fellow who can do it better than I, then I set out to do it better than he can, and I never stop until I succeed. Even then, I generally find still another chap who is my superior and keep on trying to beat him."

"But you were specially adapted to become a great athlete. You were athletic when a boy?"

"I made myself so. I was something of a weakling when born. My mother expected me to die. I remember hearing her say it was a shame I could not grow up to be strong and rugged. She even fancied I might have lung trouble."

"It doesn't seem possible!" cried Grafter, surveying Merry's sturdy figure.

"When I became old enough to think, I resolved that I would be strong. I sought to learn how to make myself strong. I discovered the way. Do you know it is a fact that almost all great athletes and strong men have been weak children?"

"I did not know."

"It's true."

"But it almost seems that you must hypnotize your opponents in matches. How is it that you defeat them time after time when they appear to have the advantage, the same as you did Manton to-day?"

"I grasp the opportunity."

"The opportunity? Why——"

"In almost everything there comes an opening, or opportunity, that may be seized with advantage. It came to-day when Manton failed to make his seventh straight strike. I always watch the other fellow to see when he weakens. At that point I try to put forth my best efforts. If he slumps and I succeed, he may lose his nerve. All through life a man must be ready to grasp the opportunity."

"And that," cried Grafter, as if his eyes had suddenly been opened, "is the secret of his success!"

32

CHAPTER VI.

A "GO" AT GOLF.

It was mid-afternoon when Frank and Bart again appeared at the clubhouse. They came walking briskly up the road, and were greeted by Fuller, who, with others, was waiting for them on the veranda.

"I suppose you're too tired after that climb to think of inspecting our field right away?" said the president of the club.

"On the contrary," smiled Merry, "that has simply whetted our appetite for more."

"Then come on."

A number of club members accompanied them. Fuller led the way along a broad walk and out through a small grove. They came upon a broad, level field, like a plateau. Round the field ran a fine track, inclosing a baseball diamond and football ground. At one side were long rows of open seats, rising in tiers. At one end of the oval was the trackmaster's house, which also served as a bathhouse and contained dressing rooms for the competitors.

Merry was surprised.

"Certainly I didn't look for this here," he confessed. "I was wondering where you could have a field up among these hills. This is splendid."

"Oh, my father knew what he was about when he selected this location!" laughed Fuller.

They walked along the track, noting its splendid condition.

"It must have cost a pretty penny to lay this out and build this track," said Hodge.

"It did," nodded Fuller; "but it's paid for, and we don't owe a dollar."

At the far end of the track they came to the golf links, where a number of enthusiasts were enjoying the sport.

At this moment, seemingly in an accidental manner, Ross Cleaves, the champion of the club, accompanied by Manton, Frost,

Fisher, and two or three others, came up to the teeing ground.

"Why, hello!" cried Manton, with attempted pleasantness. "Here's Merriwell. We were just speaking of you, Merriwell."

"Were you, indeed?"

"Yes; I was telling Cleaves he ought to challenge you for a round of the links. You have a knack of winning at everything, but we think Cleaves could take a fall out of you at this business."

"I concede the probability," said Frank.

This did not satisfy Manton at all.

"Do you dare try him a round?" he demanded. "He's looking for some one who can make it interesting for him.

"Then I'll recommend Hodge," said Merry, placing a hand on Bart's shoulder. "He's fairly good at it."

"It takes some one who is more than fairly good."

"Does it? Well, perhaps Hodge will prove good enough to keep Mr. Cleaves busy. If Mr. Cleaves isn't satisfied after it's over, let him come to me, and I'll try to give him satisfaction."

"He seems inclined to duck," said Frost.

Bert Fuller was annoyed beyond measure. He walked over to Manton and Frost, to whom he spoke in a low tone, his words being heard by no others.

Manton shrugged his broad shoulders and turned away.

"Well, I'm looking for some one," said Cleaves. "Mr. Hodge will do, if Mr. Merriwell doesn't feel like it this afternoon."

Without a word, Bart began to peel off, another golfer having offered his clubs for use.

Although he was not in golfing rig, Hodge was quite willing to do his best.

Cleaves teed carefully, addressed the ball in graceful form and led off with a long, beautiful drive. The ball did not rise high into the air, but went sailing away, away until it almost seemed that it would be lost to view.

In the meantime, Fuller had obtained a caddie for Hodge.

"There's a starter for your man, Merriwell," said Manton.

Frank spoke to Bart in a low tone:

"Beat this man if you can," he urged. "I am confident that you can make him hustle if you play half as well as you did in Ohio last week."

Hodge had won a golf trophy in Ohio.

Having teed, Bart selected a club, got the hang of it, and then addressed the ball. His form was faultless, and he made a drive that seemed fully as handsome as that of Cleaves.

"Well!" was the exclamation of Fuller; "he did that in style. I believe he drove quite as far as Cleaves."

The two opponents sauntered leisurely down to look for their balls, and it was found that Hodge had driven some yards farther than Cleaves.

It happened that both balls had lodged favorably. Cleaves sent his sailing toward the little flag that marked the first hole. Bart did the same. Then Cleaves made a handsome approach, lodging close to the hole. Hodge fell off somewhat.

"Cleaves makes it in four," said Frost. "Hodge will be one behind on the first hole."

Cleaves did make it in four.

Then Bart took his time, pulled some grass away from the vicinity of his ball, selected another club and astonished every one by dropping the ball into the hole.

"A piece of luck, nothing more!" exclaimed Fisher.

"All right, Bart," nodded Merry. "You have your eye with you to-day, and I'm satisfied that you'll make it interesting. I'm not going to follow you round the links. You'll find me at the clubhouse when you're through."

Bart nodded.

"Well, what do you think of that, Manton?" hissed Frost, as Frank turned away and, accompanied by Fuller, retraced his steps toward the athletic field. "He seems to consider the thing is settled. The crust of that fellow!"

"It is settled," said Manton. "Hodge had luck to start with, but Cleaves will put it all over him. What are you going to do? Shall we follow them round?"

"Let's."

"All right."

Something more than an hour later, as Frank sat on the veranda of the clubhouse, chatting with Fuller and others, George Branch came hurrying up.

"Well, what do you think?" he cried. "That was a hot one! They kept neck and neck all the way around. Neither one was more than a hole behind at any time. And then, at the finish, the last hole was made in two. It was amazing."

"Who won?" cried several.

"Hodge," answered Branch. "He——"

But he was checked by a shout of incredulity from several of the young men on the veranda.

"What are you giving us?" demanded one. "Hodge won? Hodge defeated Cleaves? Go on!"

"It's straight," declared Branch. "I don't blame you for being incredulous. Cleaves is sore."

Even then some of the club members fancied he was "stringing" them. They had fancied Cleaves invincible. The good start made by Hodge had seemed an accident; but they knew it could be no accident that the visitor had pushed Cleaves all the way round the course.

Others who had followed the contestants now appeared, and they confirmed the statement of Branch. Hodge had won.

Fuller turned to Merriwell.

"You must have had confidence in your friend all the time," he said.

"I did," nodded Merry. "I knew what he could do, for I saw him take the trophy at the St. Andrew's Club, of Oberlin, Ohio, last week. We were made honorary members of the club and urged to compete for the cup. Hodge competed and won it."

"Let's walk over to the trackmaster's house, Merriwell," invited Fuller. "We'll find them there."

They sauntered over together, followed by some of the others. Manton and Frost were talking with Cleaves in front of the trackmaster's house. Manton frowned at Merriwell as he approached.

"You did that very cleverly," he said. "I suppose you'll take the glory of your friend's clever accomplishment?"

Frank was more than annoyed.

"I fail to understand why you should suppose anything of the sort," he retorted.

"Why, you didn't dare go against Cleaves, so you pushed Hodge into it. You have the reputation of being a great all-round champion, but I've noticed that much of your glory comes from the accomplishment of your friends. If any one wishes to know your secret method, that is it."

"Evidently you're something of a sorehead," said Merriwell. "It's a remarkable thing that a club of this sort always has at least one sorehead among its members. I wish to remind you that neither Hodge nor I came here with the idea of butting into your club and showing what we could do. We were invited as guests. You have attempted to show us up. Blame yourselves if things have not gone to suit you."

"That's plain talk," said Bert Fuller. "I regret to see you exhibit such a spirit, Manton. At the suggestion of the social committee, I invited Mr. Merriwell and Mr. Hodge to visit us. They should be treated with proper courtesy while here."

It was a proper calldown for Manton. At first the fellow seemed ready to fly into a burst of uncontrollable passion. His face grew crimson and then turned ashen. He dared not make an insulting retort to the president.

"You're taking me in a literal sense," he finally managed to say. "Can't you let me chaff Merriwell a bit? It seems to be the only satisfaction we can get out of him."

"Unless he enters for some of the special events at the meet," put in Frost. "The broad jump and the high jump, for instance."

"And the pole vault," said Manton. "But I presume he'll put some of his friends in for these things."

"That will save him," nodded Frost.

Frank laughed.

"I'm not here to kick up trouble. Do you think your best men will engage in the events named?"

"Sure."

"Well, I had not thought of participating; but, just to please you, I'll agree to enter for the jumping and the pole vaulting."

"Good enough!" cried Manton. "I see your finish!"

Hodge had been washing up inside. He came out now, looking fresh as a daisy.

"Cleaves is a better man than they had in the St. Andrew's Club, Merry," he said. "I won by a lucky drive."

"I told you it was luck!" exclaimed Manton triumphantly. "I knew it!"

But now Cleaves spoke up like a man and declared there was not much luck in the persistent manner in which Hodge had kept him at his best all round the course. He confessed that he had done his level best to get a lead on his opponent, but had found it impossible to draw away from him.

"I expect he'll give me another opportunity," he concluded. "I shall then try to square the score."

"You shall have the opportunity," promised Bart.

Suddenly Manton assumed a different air. Laughingly he walked over to Frank, observing:

"Perhaps I've been a trifle hasty, Merriwell; but you can't blame us for feeling it when you and your friend come here and down us so easily. This is supposed to be a club of champions. If you were to defeat us at everything, the papers would make sport of us. As it is, some of the papers have been inclined to poke fun at us and call us a lot of bluffers. We think we're the real thing; but you've taken us off our guard. Were you ever taken off your guard?"

"Oh, yes, I fancy so."

"I've heard not. Why, I've even been told that no man could catch you napping and get the advantage of you. I don't believe that, you know."

"I presume not."

"No, it's ridiculous," said Manton, pretending to turn away and stepping behind Merry.

Quick as a flash he clasped Merriwell round the body, pinning his arms at his sides.

"There," he said, "you see how easy it is to prove the falsehood of the statement. I have you foul now."

"Do you think so?" asked Frank.

"I know it. You can't do a thing."

Merry was angry, but he kept a check on his temper. He resolved to teach the fellow a lesson.

Instantly he dropped to the ground, coming down on his right knee. At the same instant, Manton's arms having slipped up round his neck, he seized the man's right wrist, pressing on a certain muscle in such a manner that it caused a sharp twinge of pain. He pulled forward sharply, turning Manton's wrist to the right. Thus, in a twinkling the fellow found himself jerked over Frank's back and losing his balance. As Manton was falling, Merriwell rose sharply to his feet, and the fellow was hurled flying through the air, to fall flat on his back ten or twelve feet away.

It was done so swiftly that few saw just how it happened; but all realized that the gentleman pugilist had been tricked and grassed at a moment when he had fancied he was demonstrating the ease with which Merriwell could be taken off his guard.

Manton was dazed. He sat up, his face expressing bewilderment, chagrin, and rage.

"What—what——" he muttered hoarsely.

Then he turned his head and glared at Frank. He saw Merry standing quietly, with his hands on his hips, smiling the least bit.

"I trust you are not harmed, sir," said Frank politely. "As you had secured a grasp on me from the rear, it was necessary to be a trifle violent."

"Good land!" gasped Bert Fuller.

Manton rose to his feet.

"You tried to break my neck!" he grated, his face livid.

"Oh, no," denied Frank. "Had I tried, you would have a broken neck now, I assure you of that."

The gentleman pugilist felt of his arm and shoulder, which had been severely wrenched. He saw some of the witnesses smiling, while others were regarding him with pity. That was enough to infuriate him beyond restraint.

"I'm disgraced if I do not thrash that man!" he thought. "I'll do it here and now!"

Having arrived at this determination, he tore off his coat.

CHAPTER VII.

THE FIGHT.

hat are you going to do, Manton?" sternly demanded Fuller, stepping forward.

"I'm going to put a few dents in the face of that chap!" was the savage answer. "He may be able to bowl and throw people round with his Japanese tricks; but we'll soon see if he can fight!"

"There'll be no fight!" exclaimed Fuller. "You got what was coming, for you tried to impose on him. You have only yourself to blame."

"Mr. Fuller," said Merry, in the quietest manner imaginable, "in case Mr. Manton insists, I trust you will not interfere. It seems to me that he is determined to force a personal encounter upon me, and we may as well get at it without delay."

His fighting blood was up at last, and still he smiled. Bart Hodge was the only one who realized how dangerous Merriwell really was when he smiled in that manner.

"It will disgrace the club!" exclaimed Fuller.

"No need for it to be generally known if Mr. Manton will step down here a short distance behind the trees."

"I'll step anywhere you say," panted the pugilist; "but don't you try to run away!"

"You don't know him!" muttered Hodge, whose eyes were gleaming. "You'll be better acquainted with him in a short time."

Fuller was regretful, but he finally agreed to let Merry and Manton settle the trouble if they would retire to the spot designated by Frank.

They did so, the witnesses accompanying them. Frost urged Manton on.

"Smash his face!" hissed he. "Spoil his beauty! You've got to do it!"

"Leave it to me!" growled the pugilist. "If I don't beat him up I'll commit suicide!"

On their way to the spot Frank stripped off his coat and vest and removed his collar and necktie, giving these articles to Bart.

Fuller tried to apologize to Merry, but Frank checked him.

"You're not in the least to blame," he said. "You can't be responsible for the behavior of every member of the club."

"Manton will be expelled."

"Oh, I wouldn't do that! Don't do it on my account. I can look out for myself."

"He's a great fighter. He was the champion boxer at Yale in his day."

"Don't worry, Fuller. I'll try to take care of myself."

The moment they reached the spot chosen Manton advanced on Merry. There were no preliminaries and no delay. They were at it in a hurry, crouching, sparring, circling, seeking an opening. No rules had been mentioned. It was a fight to the finish in such a manner as they chose.

Manton feinted with his right and tried for Frank's jaw with his left.

The blow was parried, and Merry came back with a cross counter that landed and staggered his enemy.

Frost ground his white teeth together and swore.

"Get at him, you fool!" he snapped.

Manton responded by coming back at Merry and landing a body blow; but for this he received one on the mouth that split his lip and loosened a tooth or two.

The fight grew faster and more furious. They came together and Manton clinched, but Merry uppercut him and forced him to break. As he leaped away he was touched lightly by Frank, who followed him closely.

Hodge was standing with his hands in his pockets, watching every move.

"Give him a little more jujutsu, Frank," he advised.

But Merriwell shook his head. He had seen opportunities to practice the Japanese tricks on Manton, but was resolved to give the fellow his medicine in his own way. Manton considered himself a fine boxer, as, in truth, he was. To defeat him at his own game, and do it twice in one day, ought to settle his hash.

Manton side-stepped skillfully as he got away from Frank, then came under Merry's guard and delivered another body blow, seeking for the solar plexus.

"That's his game!" muttered Hodge. "Look out for it, Merry. It's dangerous."

Frank was quick to discover that his enemy was working to get a heavy one into his wind, and after that he guarded the spot with greater care.

Time after time the pugilist tried to get another one in on Frank's body. In fact, Frank led him into making these attempts, and each time he punished the fellow by cutting up his face.

In a few moments Manton was bruised and bleeding, but he seemed just as fierce and determined as when he began.

"He's a hog for punishment," decided Hodge.

Dent Frost was quivering with excitement.

"Manton will be a sight, no matter how it ends," he thought. "Merriwell is marking him all up! I don't believe he's touched Merriwell's face."

Then he uttered an exclamation of delight, for his friend had blocked a lead and landed on Frank's forehead, sending his head back.

"That's the way!" he hissed. "A little lower and Merriwell would have a fine black eye to care for."

Fuller looked on with his blood stirred, although he was very sorry that the affair had occurred. It was a savage fight, and soon both men began to show the strain, although Manton was breathing much more heavily.

Frank's lips were pressed together, but his face wore that same smile. It enraged the gentleman pugilist, who was determined to "knock the smile off."

Manton came in with a rush, and Frank went under his arm, rising and turning in time to get in a blow.

This very thing was repeated a few moments later.

Then they grappled again, and Manton succeeded in blocking as Frank sought to uppercut him as before.

"No you don't!" he panted. "You can't do that all the time!"

Merry smashed him on the kidneys, making him wince a little.

Then Manton sought to get in a blow in the break away, but it was blocked.

Manton's eyes were beginning to puff up, his nose was bleeding and his lips cut. Blood stained his white shirt.

"He'll be a spectacle to-morrow," thought Hodge.

Dent Frost was looking for his friend to get in the "wallop" that would settle the fight. Three times Manton had tried for it and missed.

Again he tried, and missed.

Merriwell came back with a blow that sent him to the ground.

He rose at once.

Frank permitted him to get onto his feet. In fact, Merry waited until Manton resumed the attack.

"It can't last much longer," said Bert Fuller.

Frank seemed seeking another opening. In a few seconds he found it and his fist shot out.

Smack! The blow landed squarely. Manton went to the turf. He rose more slowly, but he forced himself to get up, although the ground was unsteady beneath his feet.

"He's done for!" groaned Frost, as he saw his friend stagger.

He leaped in and caught Manton by the arm.

"Quit it!" he said. "You're out!"

"You lie!" snarled the gentleman pugilist, flinging Dent off and seeming as steady as ever. "I've just begun to fight!"

Once more Frank waited until his enemy closed in. Then he took his time and knocked the fellow down for the finish.

Manton lay still a moment, tried to rise, struggled to his elbow and fell back.

"He's out!" cried Frost huskily, as he lifted Manton's head.

CHAPTER VIII.

A PAIR OF KNAVES.

bout four miles from the Eagle Heights club lived Joel Bemis, a farmer. On the afternoon of the day following the events just recorded in the best "spare room" at the Bemis farm sat a young man whose eyes were covered by a bandage and whose face was cut, bruised, and discolored in places.

A step sounded outside the door, and the man on the chair started and lifted the bandage from his eyes.

"Frost!" he exclaimed, as Dent Frost entered. "Well, you've been a devilish long time coming!"

"Came at the first opportunity, Manton," declared the visitor, eying the other. "Say, but you're a sight! You did let that fellow cut you all to pieces!"

"You don't have to tell me!" snarled Hobart Manton. "I've looked in the glass."

"That must have been to-day. You couldn't see out of your eyes last night."

"What are you trying to do—rub it in?"

"Oh, no; but I'm sore because you let him hammer you up that way."

"Not half as sore as I am. I'd like to kill him!"

"Why, I thought you could fight!"

"I can."

"It looked that way!" sneered Frost coldly.

"I can," repeated Manton; "but he can fight better. I hate to acknowledge it, but I have to."

"He certainly made a holy spectacle of you."

"I'll get even! You wait!"

"I don't know how you're going to do it."

"I'll find a way! I've thought of a hundred ways. I haven't had anything else to do. Tell me, what do they say at the club? I suppose they know all about it? Of course Merriwell and Hodge had to blow about it."

"I don't believe they have said a thing. I told everybody who asked questions that you were called to the city on business. I think Fuller succeeded in inducing Merriwell and Hodge to keep still for the present. Cleaves hasn't said anything. He doesn't like those chaps."

"But he's wishy-washy; he doesn't hate them. I didn't hate them to begin with. I counted Merriwell a big case of bluff, and I wanted to show him up. This is the result!"

Manton was bitter enough. He realized his mistake, but felt deeply the disgrace he had brought upon himself. It made no difference that he was wholly to blame for the whole unpleasant affair.

"Well, what are you going to do?" asked Frost, taking a chair.

Once he had regarded Manton with considerable respect; but now his respect was gone and he found it difficult to hold in check a feeling of contempt for the fellow.

"What is Merriwell doing?"

"He's getting ready to participate in the meet."

"Getting ready—how?"

"Practicing jumping and pole vaulting. Some of his friends have arrived at the Elm Tree. There's a field near the inn. I watched them through a field-glass this forenoon. Merriwell is a pole vaulter, sure enough; but I don't believe he'll press me close."

"Don't you?"

"No."

"Let me tell you something, Frost."

"Go ahead."

"I've changed my mind about that fellow. He's a winner if given anything like a square show. If you defeat him, you'll have to do it through a trick of some sort."

"Rot! Just because he happened to get the best of you, you fancy he can beat the world. Get over it!"

"All right; but you wait and see. Unless you find some method of preventing him by a trick, he'll show you up, just as he did me."

"You make me sick!" snarled Frost angrily.

"Oh, do I?"

"Yes, you do!"

"You'll be sicker after you go against him."

"You're completely whipped. All the spirit has been taken out of you."

"I've learned something. You've got your lesson to learn."

"How can he be defeated by a trick?"

"I don't know now. If I find a way, will you try it?"

Frost hesitated.

"It's tom-foolishness," he declared. "I'd rather beat him on the square."

"Go ahead! Go ahead! Have your own way and be sorry about it afterward."

They were silent some moments. At last Frost slowly said:

"If you could tell me of any method that would work I might consider it—that is, if it wouldn't be detected."

"I'll devise a method before to-morrow. I've got nothing else to think about. Come round to-morrow and I'll have a plan. I hope I can get my face into shape so I'll be able to attend the meet without causing comment. I'll have to stay shut up here a day or two longer, though."

"Well, I'm going back," said Frost, rising. "I'll come round to-morrow. So long."

CHAPTER IX.

THE GREAT DAY.

It was the day of the Eagle Heights meet. The morning was misty, but by eight o'clock the sun drove the mists flying down the river toward the sea and shone forth from a cloudless sky of blue.

Never at any country club for amateur athletes had there been such a gathering of "swell" followers of sport for sport's sake. Contestants came from various parts of the East, and people of wealth, who were interested in open-air sports and who could attend, appeared to witness the events.

Frank Merriwell and a number of his friends reached the clubhouse at nine o'clock in the forenoon.

They were welcomed cordially. Frank met a number of young athletes whom he knew and was given the "glad hand" by all of them.

"I presume you're going to give the rest of us a show here to-day," laughed one. "You're not going in for all the honors?"

"Hardly," he answered. "I'm entered for three events, and no more—the broad jump, the high jump, and the pole vault."

"That's a relief! Let's see, who are the principal men you're up against in those things?"

"Jack Necker seems to be the jumper they count on."

"Necker? Oh, yes; he's from Hartford. Well, by George! He's a corker! And in the pole vault?"

"Denton Frost is the representative of this club. They say he is a wonder."

"Yes, I know about him. He's a good man, too. Here's hoping you have luck."

Bart Hodge had been wandering around. He came back to Merry after a while.

"Manton is here," he said, in a low tone.

"Is he?"

"Yes. He's looking pretty well, too. Shows scarcely a mark."

"Well, I'm looking for no further trouble from him."

"I don't think he'll tackle you personally, although I have no doubt that he would enjoy cutting your throat."

A little later Wallace Grafter, accompanied by a thickset, florid-faced, baldheaded man, came upon Merry.

"Mr. Merriwell," he said, "I want you to meet my father."

"Is this the boy ye told me about, son?" cried Reliable Mike, as he grasped Frank's hand. "Well, it's a fine-looking lad he is, to be sure. And ye say he has good fighting blood in his veins? He looks clever, but not at all dangerous. I'm proud to know ye, Mr. Merriwell."

"Thank you, Mr. Grafter; I'm very glad to meet you, too."

"Whist now! Do ye think ye can win at the pole vaulting?"

"It's impossible to say. I shall do my best."

"Do. Me boy has a dollar on ye. That chap ye had some trouble with when ye first came here kept after Wallace. He wanted to bet ye wouldn't win the pole vault. He even offered odds. Betting is bad business for a young man, but Wallace couldn't stand it, and he took the chap for the limit."

"I'm sorry he bet on me," said Frank; "but under any circumstances I shall do my level best. I agree with you that betting is bad business for a young man—or an old man, either."

"Aw, it's not so much harm for us old bucks who have learned the ways of the world. It runs away with the young fellows. If they win, they blow the money. If they lose, they can't afford it. We'll watch ye, my lad."

With another hearty shake of Frank's hand, Reliable Mike drifted along in company with his son.

Dick Starbright and Dade Morgan were there, and they enjoyed more or less popularity as the friends of Frank Merriwell.

When Merry reached the track he was astonished at the size of the gathering. He had not expected half as many people would be present.

The various committees and officials were at work, athletes were moving about over the field, and there was a general air of eagerness.

Great numbers of people were present in carriages. They were the relatives of competitors, and the handsome turnouts told that their stations in the world were not humble ones.

At one side was a double stand, part of which faced the track and part the field. The seats were uncovered.

The early events of the day were to take place on the track, and, therefore, the portion of the stand fronting the field was unoccupied, while the other section had begun to fill up.

A remarkable number of girls and young ladies were there. They were dressed in summer garments and added color and beauty to the scene.

Frank and Bart entered the stand just as the starter's pistol barked and sent off fourteen clean-limbed young chaps for the mile run.

The day's events were begun.

The run proved to be an interesting affair, three of the runners fighting for victory right up to the last foot of the finish. One represented Eagle Heights, and he strove as if his life depended on it to start the day with a victory for the club.

But Martin Sayers, of the Knickerbocker A.A., won by not more than a yard, although he fell over a moment after he breasted the tape.

The mile run was followed by a bicycle race, which was won by George Branch, greatly to the satisfaction of all Eagle Heights.

Then came the eight-hundred-and-eighty-yards run, and this was won by a man from the Bison A.A., of Buffalo.

Dade Morgan found Frank in the stand.

"See here, Merry," he said, "I've just learned something that may interest you. Young Grafter has bet a thousand dollars that you will win the pole vault this afternoon. Hobart Manton is the man he's betting with."

Frank frowned.

"It might teach Grafter a lesson if he lost," he said.

Morgan gasped.

"What?" he cried. "You don't mean that you'll let Denton Frost defeat you?"

"Frost is not the only other man in the pole vaulting."

"But he's reckoned as a sure winner, cutting you out. That tough, Manton, seems to believe he is, anyhow. I don't understand why he should be so positive. Watch out for treachery, Merry."

"I don't see what can be done to spoil my chances in the pole vaulting."

"Fellows like Manton will resort to anything. I want to see him lose his money. It will hurt him. He has taken advantage of your generosity in keeping still about the fight, and now he's blowing that you are a faker."

"That was his first claim when I appeared here. I fancied I had taught him something different."

"He's your bitter enemy. I feel that he will try to injure you before the day is done. Watch out."

CHAPTER X.

THE HIGH JUMP.

The events of the forenoon left Eagle Heights five points in the lead of any other club, and there was rejoicing at the clubhouse during the interval of intermission at midday.

The first contest of the afternoon was jumping.

Merriwell came out in a suit with a large, white M on his breast. The letter stood for his club, but Frost and Manton, who were with the judges, commented on it and declared it marked Frank's egotism.

There were nine contestants entered for jumping honors. Each club was permitted to enter two men, if it wished; but only two clubs had taken advantage of this.

One was the Merries. Dade Morgan had entered.

This proved something of a surprise to Frost and Manton, who had not known about it.

They seemed to regard it as a joke, however, for they laughed and said that Merriwell might enter his whole club without having a show.

The running broad jump was started by Tom Willis, of Jersey City, who cleared nineteen feet and one inch.

The next man fell an inch short of nineteen.

Then came a long-limbed chap who sailed through the air and planted his heels five inches ahead of Willis' mark.

He was wildly cheered by a little group of friends.

Morgan and Merriwell were standing close together and watching.

"That's pretty fair, Dade," said Frank. "Do you think you can beat it?"

"I believe I can," nodded Morgan.

The fourth jumper could not reach the mark made by the long-limbed chap.

Then it was Merriwell's turn.

A cheer went up as Frank stripped off his sweater and made ready. Every one seemed to expect something great of him.

Hodge and Starbright were watching from the stand.

"Merry will show them a trick now," said Bart. "I can jump some myself; but I'm not in it with him. I don't see why Morgan went into this."

"Frank wanted him to."

"Oh, he did?"

"Yes. You know Morgan was a wonderful jumper at college. Merry was the only man who ever defeated him, and that was by not more than an inch or so. I think he's in perfect form. Our trip has done him good. He was run down when Frank took hold of him in New York last fall; but he has built up wonderfully. He says Merry saved his life."

There was a hush now, as Merry walked out to the starting point.

"'Rah for Merriwell!" cried an enthusiast.

"That's Grafter!" laughed Manton, turning to look at the stand. "He expects to win a thousand off me to-day. I knew better than to bet on the jumping, and I have him caught on the pole vaulting, for he loses no matter what happens, if Merriwell does not win. Merriwell may have a broken neck before the day is over."

"I hope he gets it," said Frost, in his cold-blooded manner.

"You can't hope so any more than I do."

"He's going to make his first trial. Watch."

Frank toed the starting line. He crouched and seemed to gather himself. Then he sped along the run, every muscle tense, a look of resolution on his handsome face. He came up to the mark in perfect stride and launched himself into the air.

The manner in which he sailed over the ground caused more than one witness to gasp with surprise and admiration. His feet were drawn well under him, and at precisely the proper moment he launched them forward. He struck perfectly and came up without a "bobble."

The crowd shouted.

They knew he had made the best jump thus far.

Dent Frost whistled in dismay.

"Manton, he's a wonder!" he muttered. "I think he wins!"

"Don't you believe it. Necker is the man."

"If Necker beats that, he'll beat his own record by several inches."

The measurers were running the tape under the eyes of the judges.

In a moment this was done, and a judge announced in a loud voice:

"Frank Merriwell's distance, twenty feet, eleven inches and a half!"

There were some Yale men in the stand, and the Yale cheer went up instantly.

"Merriwell wins!" was the cry that was repeated over and over. "That can't be beaten to-day."

The next contestant seemed disheartened by the stunt, for he fell far short of nineteen feet.

It happened that Necker was the eighth man on the list, while Morgan was ninth.

When Necker's turn came Merriwell held the record by eight inches.

Necker had plenty of friends to cheer him. He looked panther-ish in his jumping rig. He was thin, but his muscles were like bands of steel covered by pink velvet.

Necker caught Manton's eye as he walked out to the starting point. He nodded and smiled the least bit.

"He's confident," said Manton; "and he knows what he can do. I believe he'll beat Merriwell."

"Never!" retorted Frost. "It won't be done in this event."

Necker balanced himself, made a start, went flying to the mark, and leaped.

"He's 'way behind!" growled Frost.

"He has three tries, if he wishes to take them."

"I know he has. Merriwell didn't try but once."

"He didn't have to."

Necker's first jump was not measured, for he had not made more than eighteen feet.

He took his time about returning and starting again.

The Eagle Heights men seemed to think he had little chance to defeat Merriwell, although they knew he could do much better than he had at first.

The second time he tried it was seen that he meant to do his level best. He flew over the ground in strides which gathered impetus steadily, and he came to the mark in a perfect manner.

Through the air he shot, his feet gathered beneath him. When it seemed that he must drop to the ground he kept on, flinging his feet far out, landing on his heels and coming up with an out-swinging of his arms.

Hobart Manton gave a yell.

"He's done it!" he cried. "I believe he's beaten Merriwell!"

"Keep still!" warned Frost; "they may put us off the field if you make too much of a fuss."

"How does it look to you?"

"He's tied Merriwell, at least, and he has still another trial. If he can tie him, he can beat him."

The stand was buzzing with excitement. Two persons in the stand were very anxious. They were Hodge and Starbright.

"What do you think, Dick?" asked Bart.

"If I'm not mistaken, he's beaten Merry a bit."

"It can't be possible!"

"I'm afraid it is."

The measurers ran the tape. They took care. Then they consulted with the judges.

One of the judges turned toward the stand.

"Mr. Necker will not jump again," he said. "His record is twenty-one feet and one inch."

The Eagle Heights men howled with satisfaction.

Their man had defeated Merriwell by an inch and a half.

Bart Hodge looked ill.

"Why didn't Merry try more than once?" he muttered huskily. "He could have done better! Now he's lost his chance!"

"Wait," said Starbright. "Let's see what Morgan will do."

"Oh, Morgan isn't in that class! It's a shame!"

Still Dick clung to hope, thinking it possible Morgan might do something that would surprise every one.

Necker was satisfied. He knew he had done his handsomest and that he would fall back if he made another attempt. He had added some inches to his own best record, besides defeating Merriwell.

Dade Morgan, slender, graceful, and electric, walked toward the starting point.

"Who is he?" was the question asked by many in the stand.

"Oh, he's one of Merriwell's team," was the answer. "He won't cut much ice."

In all his body Morgan felt the current of life running strong. He believed himself physically at the top notch. He was full of confidence.

In his college days he had never covered twenty-one feet, but something told him he was a better man than he had been in those days. He was matured; his powers were at their flood.

Crouching, he set his teeth and gripped his hands. He started slowly and surely, gathering speed and power. When he reached the take-off mark he was flying. Into the air he went, shooting forward like a bird on the wing. On and on he sailed. It was all over in a moment, but the spectators rose.

They knew Morgan had landed almost in the tracks of Necker.

Denton Frost actually staggered.

"What do you think of that?" he gasped. "I fear he has tied Necker!"

"I fear he has beaten him!" grated Manton.

"Impossible! Who is this Morgan? Whoever heard of him?"

"Oh, he was a rattler at college until he began to dissipate. Then they said he broke down and lost ambition. I've been told he was the most dangerous rival Merriwell ever had at Yale."

"If he has beaten Necker——"

"It will be a bitter pill to swallow."

"They are going to measure. He isn't going to jump again! By the great Harry! he's beaten Necker, or he would try again. He's the last man and——"

He checked himself and waited.

The tape was stretched. Again the measurers took the utmost care, watched by the judges.

The crowd waited.

Then one of the judges turned and held up his hand.

"Dade Morgan's record is——"

He paused. The hush of great expectancy seemed to keep every one from breathing. He finished:

"Twenty-one feet and three inches! Morgan wins the broad jump."

Two more disgusted men than Frost and Manton it would have been hard to find.

They had not dreamed the broad jump would be won in such a manner.

Of course, Necker was also disgusted, but he tried to conceal it and appear a good loser.

The high jump followed.

Ten men were entered for this, both Morgan and Merriwell being of the number.

Necker resolved to retrieve himself.

Manton found an opportunity to speak to him and urge him to try, as if his life depended on it.

"You were too confident," said Manton.

"That's right," admitted Necker. "I thought I had it easy. I might have tried again."

Frank congratulated Morgan.

"You came in like a dark horse, Dade," he smiled.

"I was rooting for you inside when you came up to the mark. Necker's chest has collapsed a great deal. He's a great jumper, but it doesn't do for such fellows to get too chesty. It ruins them every time."

Morgan was delighted with himself.

"I owe it all to you, Merry," he said. "Remember when you found me in that bum hotel on the Bowery?"

"Yes."

"I was pretty near all in then. Never expected to be much of an athlete after that. You took hold of me and straightened me out. I won't forget it."

"Do. It's what any friend would do for another."

"Oh, some day I'll get even with you!" threatened Dade, with a smile.

In a short time everything was ready for the high jump.

The first man made five feet and ten inches on three trials.

The second man could not clear the bar at five feet eight.

Morgan was third on the list this time. He was cheered as he squared away for the start.

He had the bar placed at five feet ten. Over it he went, drawing his feet well under him and flinging them round sideways.

"This man wins the high jump, too!" hissed Frost.

"That is better than it would be to have Merriwell win," said Manton.

"Not much better."

"But some."

Dade had the bar moved up to six feet.

Then he went at it, but barely touched it with his heel as he went over, which displaced it.

"Ha!" cried Manton. "That's too high for him!"

Morgan walked back to the starting point. He signaled for the bar to be placed the same as before.

When it was up he seemed to hesitate. He paused a few seconds, then settled himself and started.

Up, up he went. As he reached the highest points he gave a twisting movement of his body and flung his feet sideways over the bar, coming down without grazing it.

"Six feet for Morgan," announced a judge.

"'Rah for Morgan!" whooped an enthusiast. "He's the real hot stuff!"

"I believe Necker can beat that," said Manton. "It's great jumping; but Necker is keyed up now, and he'll stretch himself for all he is worth."

Necker was seventh on the list.

When his turn came no one had reached Morgan's mark. Could he do it?

He had the bar set at five feet ten for the first trial. Over it he went.

"Why, that was easy!" exclaimed Manton. "He can go higher than that, all right!"

"I believe he can," nodded Frost hopefully. "Morgan is a better jumper than Merriwell. There is no danger from Merriwell if Necker can defeat Morgan."

The bar was next placed at six feet.

"Go it, Necker!" cried some one in the stand. "You can do it, old man!"

He did do it, although the least fraction of an inch was to spare as he passed over the bar.

Morgan was tied.

"Put it up an inch and a half," said Necker quietly.

Hodge heard him in the stand.

"He can't make another inch," he said. "He barely cleared the bar at six feet. He'll dislodge it this time."

"It's more than even chances that he will," nodded Starbright.

But Necker made that jump as if his life depended on it. He rose handsomely and cleared the bar without brushing it.

Then the Eagle Heights crowd cheered, for their man led in the high jump by an inch and a half.

Necker turned away smiling, giving Manton a look. Manton motioned for him to come nearer.

"You might have won the broad jump just as easy," said Manton.

"I know that," agreed Necker. "It was my fault. I thought I had it won."

The men who followed made a sorry showing beside Necker.

Then came Merriwell.

Manton grinned sneeringly, and Dent Frost laughed coldly.

"This day the great champion is not doing so much," said the gentleman pugilist. "Grafter won't be offering so much money for his secret method. Secret method! Bah!"

"Has he a method?"

"Oh, that's rot. He's a mark. He's just a little better than ordinary athletes, and he poses as the greatest wonder in the whole world."

At the very start Frank had the bar placed at six feet.

"Never!" exclaimed Frost. "He can't do it!"

"Let him knock it down," whispered Manton.

Frank did knock it down. He did not get away just right, and his heel touched the bar as he was going over.

Manton laughed outright, but checked himself.

Frank spoke in a low tone to the judges.

Then many persons uttered exclamations of astonishment, for he had ordered the bar raised an inch and a half!

That placed it at the height of Necker's best jump.

"Never!" repeated Frost.

In the stand several persons uttered cries of joshing.

But they were destined to receive a shock, for Merry shot at the bar, leaped into the air, and went over it in beautiful style.

Then the Yale men broke forth into that fine cheer.

Necker seemed dazed.

"He must have springs in his shoes," he finally growled.

Frost was speechless with rage. Manton managed to recover enough to say:

"That only ties you."

But Merriwell had ordered the crossbar up an inch and a half more, making six feet three in all.

"Not in a thousand years!" cried a voice in the crowd. "It's impossible!"

"He'll show you!" exclaimed Bart Hodge.

Frank settled himself, measured with his eye the distance he had to run and the height to the pole, and then started.

Up and over he sailed.

He had beaten Necker by an inch and a half, and the following contestants declined to make an effort.

CHAPTER XI.

FAILURE AND DISGRACE.

he pole-vaulting contest came late in the afternoon, and Denton Frost set a stint at the very outset that appalled the greater part of the contestants.

Man after man failed to come anywhere near the mark he had made.

Frank Merriwell's turn came at last.

He had his own pole, which no one else was allowed to use.

Farley Fisher had joined Hobart Manton, Frost remaining with the other contestants.

"Look here, Fisher," said Manton, in a low tone; "you want to keep your eyes open now. You're going to see something."

"What do you think I'm going to see?" inquired Fisher. "Do you fancy Merriwell is going to win? Why, I've heard you bet a dollar or two to-day that he would not defeat Frost."

"So I did, and he won't. You haven't any use for Merriwell, have you?"

"Not a bit."

"Well, you know I haven't. Watch him—watch him close!"

Frank was about to make his first attempt. The crossbar was placed and, gripping his pole, he started.

Up, up into the air he swung. It was a beautiful sight. The crowd was breathless.

At the proper moment Frank lifted himself higher on the pole to fling his body over the bar.

As he did this the pole suddenly broke beneath him.

Cries of terror came from the spectators as they saw him falling from that height, for it seemed that he was destined to strike on his head and shoulders and sustain serious, if not fatal, injuries.

One thing Frank had learned while practicing the Japanese art of self-defense was to fall in such a manner as to sustain the least injury. Usually a person who finds himself falling becomes rigid and stiff, so that when he strikes he is jarred in every part of his body. The Japanese fall limply, with their muscles relaxed. In this manner Frank fell.

Although he struck on the back of his neck and his shoulder blades, he came up in a moment, rising to his feet, as if wholly unharmed.

Seeing this, Manton uttered a curse of anger and dismay.

"The devil protects the fellow!" he hissed. "His neck should have been broken."

The judges and others gathered around Frank, all seeming to feel sure he must be injured. He finally convinced them that he was not. Then one of them told the people in the stand, and there was a cheer. This cheer became a roar when, selecting another pole, Frank prepared to vault.

At his first attempt he cleared the bar, tieing Frost. Next time he disturbed it; but he tried again and flung himself over it a full foot higher than Frost had done.

It was the best vault made.

Frank won, and Manton lost a snug little sum of money.

But that was not all Manton lost. Investigation revealed the fact that Merriwell's pole had been tampered with and weakened in such a manner that it could not fail to break. This discovery stirred up the Eagle Heights people, and a rigid inquiry followed. Fuller did some detective work, with the result that he finally got hold of the chap who had tampered with Merriwell's pole. This rascal was badly frightened, and he made a confession, in which he told how he had been given fifty dollars by Hobart Manton to do the job.

Manton was expelled in disgrace from the Eagle Heights A.A., and his membership in the A.A.U. of the U.S. was annulled. His days as an amateur athlete in good standing were ended.

CHAPTER XII.

THE PLAN OF MELVIN M'GANN.

Two men sat talking in the room back of the Hotel Imperial bar, New York City. The slim, dark-eyed man, with the tiny mustache, was Melvin McGann, until recently a partial owner of the Philadelphia Athletics. The stout, sandy man, with the red face and red necktie, was Robert Gowan, at one time interested in the New York Giants.

"I'm afraid it's a wild scheme, McGann," said the latter, in a husky voice, which seemed choked and somewhat smothered in the speaker's thick throat. "You're looking for revenge, regardless of consequences, that's what's the matter."

"I'm looking for revenge," admitted McGann; "I admit that. But I'm no fool. The plan is practical. Hurley convinced me of that. We can't lose much, and we may open up a field that will revolutionize baseball."

"I'm not a revolutionist," wheezed Gowan. "If there's money in it, I may be interested, not otherwise."

"Well, there's a prospect of money in it. It might mean the forming of a new league, with you and me at its head."

"Huah!" grunted Gowan noncommittally.

"Why not?" exclaimed McGann. "You know, as well as I, that every year the big leagues 'try out' a lot of good men who are not kept simply because there is not room for them. These men are held until after the season is fairly under way and then are dropped. They go to the minor leagues and to independent teams. Many times they are fast enough for the major-league teams, but they fail to land because old-stagers pan out and hold their jobs for another season. I'll guarantee that this year the two big leagues will drop enough cracking good youngsters to form another fast six-team league. It has been done already."

"And most of the men have secured positions on minor leagues."

"I'm not talking about forming a league—this year. I'm talking about getting together one team, made up of outcasts, that can trim anything playing baseball."

"Can it be done?"

"Sure."

"You'll have to show me."

"Wait till Hurley comes," nodded McGann, looking at his watch. "He should be here now. He'll tell you what men he can get hold of."

"He's a sorehead."

"Yes, he's sore, and you can't blame him. He had every reason to suppose he'd make the Cleveland team. He's one of the greatest stickers in the country. Not even Lajoie can swat the ball harder or oftener. And he's a great first baseman. As an organizer and captain he ranks with Collins."

"Then why didn't he get there?"

"Jealousy—that's what he says."

"That's what he says," wheezed Gowan. "They all have some such tale to tell after they're dropped."

"I happen to know he tells the truth. He came on from the West and spent all the spring getting into condition. He seemed to have a cinch. There was talk of farming him, and holding him over for next year, but a certain power prevented, and he suddenly found himself out in the cold, cold world. Jersey City wants him; Los Angeles wants him; Fort Worth wants him. But he wants revenge. He was the man who talked me into the idea of getting together a team of outcasts and showing up some of the big teams."

"How do you propose to show them up?"

"Beat them at their own game."

"That's easy enough—to talk about."

"It can be done."

"They won't play you. At this time of the year they are pretty busy among themselves, with no open dates."

"You forget Sundays. Sunday baseball is not played in Boston, New York, and several other places. Every Sunday a number of big-league teams rest, while others play. On week days we can get games with the best independent teams."

"And lose money right along."

"No. Hurley says he knows a dozen men who have been dropped, and who will go into the scheme heartily if they see a chance to get up against one or two of the big teams, so they can demonstrate what they can do. These men are enthusiastic, and they'll play for expenses up to the time that the team makes money. They will sign with the understanding that they are to be paid certain salaries if the receipts justify it. You see there is no probability of any great loss, and there is a possibility of big profits."

Gowan meditated.

"After showing me that a team of fast players can be made up," he finally wheezed, "you'll have to show me that such a team can get at least one game with some of the majors."

"Will you take hold of it then?"

"I—I may," answered the stout man cautiously.

"Well, here, I have a pull with two managers who will favor me. Look at these letters. Here's one from Collins, of Boston, and this from McGraw. Both promise to give me a game if I get the team and they find an open date."

Gowan adjusted a pair of spectacles and examined the letters placed before him, while McGann lighted a cigarette.

"All very friendly and fine," admitted the stout man, as he refolded the letters; "but neither man makes a definite promise."

"As far as possible, both do. I know they'll keep their word. I'll guarantee to get a game with one of those teams, if we can make up a bunch that is fast enough. I can get the field in Hoboken for almost any Sunday if I arrange for it in advance. We can draw a mob. I tell you, Bob, we'll make money, sure as fate. If we succeed with one team made up from outcasts this year, we can keep our little scheme quiet, and next season we can begin early to make arrangements, and we can spring the Outcasts League, which will come pretty near rating with the National or the American. Of course we'll be outsiders for a season; but we may be able to show the country some baseball that will make the National Association recognize us. In two or three years, if we plan properly and carry out our schemes, we may be pushing the two top-notchers for leadership. That would give me all the revenge I want for being crowded out in Philadelphia."

"It's a visionary scheme, Mel. I doubt if it can be done this year with a bunch of outcasts. I'd like to hear what Hurley has to say. Why doesn't he show up?"

"Here he comes now," said McGann.

Hurley was a well set-up young chap, with a businesslike air. His face was pleasant yet grave. He had the chin and nose of a commander, while his eye was quick and penetrating. He advanced and greeted Melvin McGann, who shook hands with him and then introduced him to Gowan.

The stout man shook hands without rising. There was little polish about him.

"Hope you've not been waiting for me a great while, gentlemen," said Hurley. "I've been talking with Mat O'Neill, who was just thinking of starting for Hartford, where he has a chance to get into the Connecticut State League. I induced him to stop over until to-night. Told him there was something in the wind, and outlined enough of the scheme to interest him, without letting him into all the details. I had to do it, for O'Neill is just the man we want. You know him, Mr. McGann. He pitched in the Northern New York League last season and made a wonderful record. Collins picked him out, and gave him a trial in New Orleans. He lost the game, and he hasn't been given another chance. The other pitchers panned out, and Collins dropped him. He had hard luck in New Orleans. If they'd tried him again I'm sure he would have opened their eyes. I'd like to run him against the champs."

Hurley was a man of enthusiasm. He expressed it in his manner of speech, yet there was that about him which indicated that he was not headstrong and reckless.

"Sit down, Hurley," invited McGann. "Tell us who you have on the string."

The ballplayer took a chair and the three drew close together around one of the little tables.

"Is it a go?" asked Hurley. "Can you raise the backing, Mr. McGann?"

"If Mr. Gowan sees that the prospect is encouraging, I think he will come into the deal with me."

"Good! He won't regret it. There's money in it, as sure as you're a living man. If we don't last more than three weeks, we can make money while we do last, providing, of course, that you're able to keep your part of the agreement, and get a game in Hoboken with one of the three big-league teams we've mentioned; either New York team or the Boston champs. Why, we can pack 'em into the field over at Hoboken like sardines in a box!"

"I know I can make good what I've promised."

"Tell us what players you can gather up, Mr. Hurley," urged Gowan. "I'm rather skeptical in regard to the strength of the team."

"Don't you be skeptical for a moment. Listen. I have O'Neill for the principal pitcher, with Boliver Bimm for change pitcher and the outfield. The Athletics let Bimm go because their sore-armed men came round all right and their list of pitchers was complete. Bimm can hit at a three-hundred clip, and they were dopey over in Quakertown when they let him slide. I can get Bill Brackett, who came so near making the Brooklyn team. He's a good utility man, as well as a fair pitcher. We can keep him on the bench and use him in the box against ordinary teams. He can pitch three games a week right along—four, if necessary. How is that for a pitching staff?"

"Huah!" grunted Gowan, in his usual noncommittal manner. "Go on. Who's behind the plate?"

"Cy Swatt."

"Why, I thought he had signed with Chicago."

"He's been cast adrift on the cold world."

"I don't understand why!" exclaimed McGann.

"Nobody else. I've got him on the string. We can land him, and he'll make 'em go some. He's one of the handsomest throwers to bases I ever saw. I played with him out on the Coast two years ago."

"Go on," wheezed Gowan, showing some signs of interest.

"I'll be on first."

"And that corner of the diamond will be well covered," nodded McGann.

"Thank you," said Hurley quietly. "We'll have Jack Roden at second. The Yankees gave him a show in one game. He accepted seven chances without an error and made a three-bagger out of three times at bat. He drew a pass once and was hit by a pitched ball once. He stole two bases. But there wasn't room for him on the team, and he never got another show."

"Sounds pretty good, doesn't it, Gowan?" asked McGann.

"Uh-huh," grunted Gowan.

"For third," continued Hurley, "I can land Hoke Marcey, who threw his arm out in practice while the Giants were on their Southern trip. His arm is back in shape again, but that accident lost him a chance to make the team."

"Marcey's my own particular pet," wheezed Gowan. "I recommended him to McGraw. Mugsey didn't treat him right."

"He'll be with us if we start right away," declared Hurley. "In the outfield, besides Bimm, we'll have Cal Grimley, of Detroit, for left, and Tip Creel, who's been benching it with the Washington Americans, for centre. Now, gentlemen, if that aggregation can't play ball I don't know a thing about the game. I believe I can make a bunch of hustlers out of them. Give me a week of playing with independent teams, and I'll be ready to tackle anything in the two big leagues. I'll show you some chaps who will work for every game as if their lives depended on the result. I'll get them working together in a week."

"Do you know for sure that you can land every man you have named?" wheezingly inquired Gowan.

"Well, I have the promise of almost every one of them. If we get the backing now, I'll have them together and practicing so soon it will make you gasp."

"You haven't named your shortstop," reminded McGann.

"Haven't settled on the man for the position. Can get any one of three. Don't worry about that."

"What do you say, Gowan?" asked McGann. "Are you ready to go in with me to back this team on the terms stated?"

"Yes," answered the stout man, "I'm with you."

* * * * *

Shortly after this the baseball world was given a sensation. McGann and Gowan's Outcasts made their first appearance in Ridgewood, N.J., easily defeating the locals. The next day they played in Hoboken and secured another easy victory. Their first Sunday game was with the Jersey City team of the Eastern League, and the score was eight to five in their favor. Then followed five games with the strongest independent teams in the East, and five more "scalps" were garnered to their glory. On the second Sunday they played the Giants of New York in Hoboken before a mob of people that simply overran the grounds. The score was three to one in favor of the Outcasts, and their reputation was made. They sought games with the New York Yankees and the Boston champs, but the managers of these two teams seemed attacked with a sudden severe case of "cold feet." Although they had given McGann reasons to believe they would play his team, this happened before the Outcasts were organized and had made such a bewildering record. After this happened they couldn't seem to find any open dates. Manager McGann challenged any and all teams in both the big leagues, the winners to take the entire gate receipts after expenses were deducted.

The Outcasts had arrived.

CHAPTER XIII.

THE FALL OF THE GIANTS.

On a fine Saturday afternoon late in June the wonderful Outcasts met the redoubtable colored baseball team known as the Cuban Giants. The game was played in Newark. The baseball cranks of Newark, Elizabeth, Jersey City, and New York were interested in the game, and a great crowd turned out to witness it.

The colored boys knew they were up against the "real thing," and they played like fiends from the start, hoping to be the first to break the winning streak of the new stars. The Giants had a great team, every man of them being a rattling good ballplayer, and they started off like winners, getting two runs in the first inning, one in the third, and shutting out their opponents for five straight innings from the start.

Bill Brackett had opened the game as twirler for the Outcasts, but in the midst of the third inning, after the colored players had made their third run, with the bases filled and only one man out, Bill was sent to the stable and Mat O'Neill took his place on the slab.

O'Neill promptly stopped the run-getting of the Giants by striking out the first batter to face him and causing the next one to put up an easy infield fly.

"Should have put him in before, McGann," wheezed Bob Gowan, who was sitting on the bleachers back of first base, in company with Melvin McGann and several acquaintances.

"Oh, it's all right," assured the manager of the Outcasts. "Hurley knows his business. I let him run the team on the field. We'll fall on that coon pitcher pretty soon and hammer him all over the lot."

"I don't know about that. He's a corker. These colored gents may change your luck."

"That's right," put in "Reliable Mike" Grafter, who was present.

"Your streak is busted, Gowan. The dinks done it."

Bob Gowan's confidence in his team was colossal. There was now no wavering uncertainty about him.

"Bet you a hundred we win this game, Grafter," he promptly wheezed, producing his money.

"Go you," said the Tammany man, diving into his pocket.

A stakeholder was agreed upon, and the money placed in his hands.

"Just because you happened to beat the New York Nationals you seem to think you can't be downed," grunted Grafter.

"I know something about baseball, Mike," retorted Gowan, with unusual animation. "I know we have the team to beat anything in the country."

"That's right," nodded McGann. "Every year the big leagues throw over enough clever youngsters to make another league. Out of the discards a champion team can be selected by any man who knows his business. I give Hugh Hurley the credit of knowing his business. He knows a baseball player by instinct. He picked up this team. If we were in either of the big leagues we would be pennant winners. Look how ourboys work together. They are like the individual parts of a perfect machine. Every man seems to have brains, and brains count in this game. We didn't get all the good men discarded. We tried for Josslyn, the young wizard twirler that Collins of the Bostons was chump enough to hand over to Providence. If we'd landed him, we'd had two of the greatest youngsters in the business. You know what Josslyn has been doing. He shut out Newark six to nothing in the first game he pitched for Providence, and he's been making batters blink and fan ever since. Still Collins is called one of the shrewdest managers in the American League. They all make mistakes of this sort. He hung onto a certain old-stager on account of his reputation, when Josslyn could pitch right round the old boy any day in the week. I'd like to get against the great bean-eating champs. Oh, say! we wouldn't do a thing to 'em!"

Grafter grinned.

"You have a bad case of it," he said. "Better have your head clamped before it gets any bigger."

"Results count," retorted McGann. "This will make our fifteenth victory, without a defeat."

"You seem to be one of those chaps who count chickens before they are hatched. Everything is against you to-day. You've made one clean hit off the coon pitcher."

"We'll find him before we're through. Just keep watch."

In the sixth inning the Outcasts resorted to a new trick. The first batter bunted and beat the ball to first.

The next man bunted toward third, laying down a "dead one" just inside the line. In the confusion that followed the batter reached first in safety.

Bob Gowan laughed.

"Now you see how they do it!" he exclaimed.

"I don't see that they've done anything yet," said Grafter.

When the next batter tried to bunt and popped up a little fly that was taken by the third baseman on the run and shot across to first for a double play, Grafter held onto his sides and roared.

"No use," he said. "The coons have you. You can't get away from them to-day."

Gowan looked somewhat disappointed, yet pretended to be not a whit less confident in regard to the result.

The next batter electrified every one by lacing the ball to deep centre for three bags and bringing in a run.

"I knew it!" wheezed Gowan. "It was bound to come."

"That's one run," grinned Grafter. "You'll get no more this inning."

"We have a man on third."

"Can't help it. Two out."

Grafter was right. The clever colored twirler caused the next batter to fan.

The Giants whooped joyously as they capered in to the bench.

In the seventh inning, however, the Outcasts fell on the pitcher and hammered out five handsome singles, which gave them two runs and tied the score.

In the first of the eighth the Giants made a desperate bid for a run, succeeding in pushing a man round to third, but he died there, O'Neill showing what he could do in a pinch and striking out two of the heaviest and surest batters who faced him.

The last of the eighth delighted the admirers of the Outcasts, for they got after the colored pitcher in earnest and "sent him on an aërial voyage." The result was three more runs.

"I told you, Grafter!" wheezed Gowan. "I knew what would happen! Why, our boys have been fooling with the nigs! They can't be beaten by anything outside the big leagues, and we know they can more than hold their own with the big fellows. There isn't an independent team in the country that can take a game off this bunch."

A young, healthy-looking, smooth-faced fellow had approached just in time to hear this remark.

"What do you think about that, boy?" asked Grafter. "Gentlemen, this is my son, Wallace."

"I think the gentleman is mistaken," said Wallace Grafter quietly. "I am confident that I know an independent baseball team that can wallop the Outcasts to a whisper."

"You have another think due you!" exclaimed McGann warmly.

"Two more," said Gowan.

"Are you in earnest, son?" inquired old Grafter.

"You bet," nodded Wallace.

"I've been betting," admitted his father, with a grin. "Bet Gowan a hundred his team would lose. It's plain I'm a hundred short."

"You can make it up and some more with it, if Mr. Gowan has the nerve to back his team against an independent team I'll name," said the politician's son.

"I'll back the Outcasts against any independent team in the country for a hundred—or a thousand," rasped Gowan.

Grafter and his son exchanged glances; the young man nodded.

"I kinder think I'll have to take you on that," said Mike Grafter deliberately.

The roaring of the spectators drowned his voice. O'Neill had just struck out the third Giant in the ninth, ending the game, the Outcasts winning by the score of six to three.

"What'd you say?" asked Gowan, as the shouting subsided and the great crowd, having risen, was beginning to move to leave the grounds.

"I said I'd take you—for a thousand," answered Grafter.

"Got it with you?"

"Always have that much loose change."

"Same stakeholder do?"

"Sure."

"Put up."

"All right. Cover."

Right there, before leaving the bleachers, the bet was made, Gowan backing the Outcasts against any independent team Wallace Grafter should name.

Not until the wager had been made did Bob Gowan ask:

"What team is this you're betting on, Grafter?"

"I don't know," answered the politician. "What team is it, son?"

"It's Frank Merriwell's team," said Wallace. "I think there will be no trouble about arranging the game on any kind of reasonable terms."

CHAPTER XIV.

ARRANGING FOR THE GAME.

On an open lot within sight of the Harlem River Frank Merriwell and Bart Hodge were practicing. Merry was working to see what he could do with the "spit ball," which he had found to be extremely difficult to control.

"You have it all right, Merry," declared Hodge. "Great Scott! doesn't she take a sharp shoot!"

"Always feel like I'm going to lose control of the ball when I deliver it," confessed Frank.

"You seem to have more speed when you spit on her."

"The ball leaves the fingers with greater speed. I suppose the sharp shoot is caused by the banking of air against the wet surface. You know air will bank heavier against the wet surface of a moving object than against a dry surface. About all the spit-ball pitchers have one way that they deliver the ball. I've been trying various ways. Watch this."

Merry swung his arm in a peculiar manner and the ball was delivered with his hand high in the air. It sped downward toward the outside corner of the stone which served as a plate. Suddenly it took a queer upward swerve.

Hodge grabbed at it and was nearly upset.

"What the dickens——" he cried, and stopped.

Merry was laughing.

"Do that again," urged Bart, returning the ball.

Frank complied.

"That beats!" gasped Bart. "Why, the ball seems to come down from your hand on a straight line toward the outside of the plate. Four or five feet before it reaches the plate it swerves upward with a combined rise and incurve, passing over the inside corner. It's marvelous!"

"It's something like an outdrop reversed—turned bottom up," said Frank.

"That's just what it is; but I can't see how you make it rise so much. Merry, can you control that?"

"I don't know. I've found out how to throw it. I presume control will come with practice."

"If you can control it, I'll guarantee you can strike the best of 'em out with it. It will be even more effective than the double shoot. It's marvelous! If you could start it toward the inside corner and give it the other sweep it would be magic."

"Let me see," said Merry, taking the ball in his hand and studying over it. "How could that be done?"

He tried several times, being rather wild, but finally Bart gave a shout.

"That's it! You did it then!"

"It seemed to be it," nodded Frank. "Wonder if I can repeat that?"

He kept at it until he did repeat it, not only once, but a number of times.

"Talk about sorcery!" cried Bart. "Certainly you are a sorcerer with a baseball!"

"I think I shall keep after that until I can handle it," said Merry. "I'd like to see what batters could do with it. I'll try it in the next game we play."

"Who are these men coming this way?" said Hodge, scrutinizing two persons who were approaching across the lot.

"I believe I know one of them."

"One looks natural to me."

"We met him at the Eagle Heights club the other day. It's Wallace Grafter."

"Sure enough!"

Grafter it was, and he was accompanied by Melvin McGann.

"How do you do, Mr. Merriwell!" cried Grafter cheerfully. "How are you, Mr. Hodge. We've had some trouble finding you."

He shook hands heartily with them, and then said:

"Let me introduce Mr. McGann, manager of the Outcasts, a baseball team you may have heard about."

"I should say we had heard about it!" exclaimed Frank. "Every one who takes the least interest in baseball must have heard of it by this time. So you are the manager of the Outcasts, Mr. McGann? Well, I congratulate you, for you certainly have a great team. I know good judges who declare your team is faster than anything in either of the two big leagues."

"You are correct in pronouncing men of that opinion to be good judges," said McGann. "We think we have the real thing. But, by the way, I have heard a little something about you and your team."

"Which has interested him somewhat," laughed Grafter. "He's after you, Merriwell. He's out for all the scalps he can gather."

"After us, is he? I suppose he is looking for a game with our team?"

"That's just it," nodded McGann. "We have an idea that you will be fruit for us, although we hope you'll be strong enough to make the game fairly interesting, in case you are not afraid to play us."

Hodge muttered something under his breath. It always irritated Bart to have any one insinuate that the Merries were afraid of anything on the diamond.

"It's a fine thing to have a good opinion of yourself," smiled Frank. "Evidently you are not troubled by modesty, Mr. McGann. Considering what your team has done, I don't know that I blame you."

"Will you give us a game?"

"We'll be delighted."

"You bet!" put in Hodge.

"Of course," said McGann shrewdly, "we'll give you a fair deal. We'll furnish the grounds, pay all expenses of advertising and pay you a hundred dollars for a game next Saturday afternoon. We can play in Hoboken if I engage the ground to-night."

"Such generosity is altogether surprising!" said Frank, with bland sarcasm. "Aren't you afraid you can't afford it?"

"I thought that would be satisfactory," said McGann. "I understand you chaps are playing for sport. Have you any salaried men on your team?"

"No."

"Well, you see——"

"We might play you for nothing!" interrupted Frank. "In Hoboken, too. There will be eight or ten thousand people out to the game, if the weather is good. Eight thousand paid admissions will mean two thousand dollars in gate money, if only twenty-five cents is charged. Mr. McGann, I am overwhelmed by your generous offer of one hundred dollars!"

"Oh, but you know expenses will be heavy. We must pay a round sum for the grounds, to say nothing of advertising and other expenses. Besides that, our players are high-priced men— all under salary. It costs like fire to run the sort of team we have."

"I've heard that you started out with every player under an agreement that your men should not be paid unless you made money. You took small chances at the outset. You have made money hand over hand. It's been a great thing for you. I don't wonder, if you pay the teams with which you play as liberally as you have offered to pay us!"

Frank's sarcasm was biting now, and McGann squirmed under it somewhat.

"Well, what do you want?" he asked sharply. "We have the reputation. The people will turn out to see us play."

"Oh, I think our team has some drawing power," retorted Merry. "We haven't failed to get out fairly good crowds wherever we have appeared. No, Mr. McGann, we'll not play you in Hoboken on the terms you have offered."

"You can say what you want, can't you?"

"Yes."

"Well?"

"We want all we can get. Although we enjoy the game, we're not easy marks."

"I didn't take you for easy marks, Merriwell," said McGann. "You misunderstood me."

"I hope I did."

Bart was smiling in a grimly satisfied manner.

"What is your idea of what is right in the way of terms?" asked the manager of the Outcasts. "Will two hundred dollars satisfy you?"

"Hardly!"

"Then what?"

"Not less than fifty per cent of the net receipts."

"Oh, that's no square deal! Why, we furnish the grounds and do the advertising."

"I said the net receipts. Expenses to be taken out before the money is divided."

"We couldn't think of it," said McGann decisively. "We have the reputation to draw the people. I'll make all the arrangements. We'll pay you fifteen per cent."

"I don't think we'll play," said Frank. "You'll have to look after other marks."

He seemed to consider the matter settled.

"We're anxious to play with you," protested McGann.

"You seem to be!" laughed Frank.

"We really are. You're the fellows we want to beat next Saturday. Some people actually seem to think you can make us work hard for the game."

"If you play us, you won't do any loafing," cut in Hodge. "That is, if you keep in the game for a minute."

"Fifty per cent is unreasonable," said the manager of the Out-casts. "I'll tell you what we will do. We'll give you twenty of the net."

"No go," said Frank. "Two-thirds to the winners, one-third to the losers. How does that strike you?"

McGann objected. He admitted that he felt as if the Merries would be getting too much if they received one-third of the net receipts.

"Oh, but we'd get two-thirds under that arrangement," declared Hodge.

"Would you?" sneered McGann. "Then what do you say if the winners take all the money?"

"That suits me very well," said Frank promptly.

The manager of the Outcasts gasped. Of a sudden, he fancied he saw how he could get out of it without paying Merriwell a dollar.

"Are you in earnest?" he asked.

"Certainly."

"You'll sign an agreement to play on those terms?"

"Yes, sir."

"It's a go!" cried McGann. "Let's make out the agreement and sign it right here. I'm afraid you'll change your mind."

"Don't worry in the least," said Frank. "Go ahead and write the agreement."

The manager of the Outcasts brought forth a large notebook. On one of the pages he wrote in the briefest manner possible the agreement, to which he signed his name. Frank read it over and promptly added his signature. Then Grafter and Hodge signed as witnesses, and the affair was settled.

Grafter was relieved, and he betrayed it.

"I was afraid you two would blow up over it," he confessed. "I want to see the game pulled off. I believe it's going to be the hottest kind of a tussle."

"Then there is another reason," said McGann. "But I fancy your old man would be far better off if no game took place."

Then it came out that, at the advice of Wallace, old man Grafter had bet that the Merriwells could defeat the Outcasts. He had done this without knowing what team he was backing, which demonstrated his implicit confidence in the judgment of his son.

"That's how I happened to bring Mr. McGann to you," laughed Grafter the younger. "Now I hope you can show the old man that my confidence in you was not misplaced."

Frank knew it would be useless to express his view in regard to gambling. Wallace Grafter had been brought up in the full knowledge of his father's ways, and to him gambling was something forbidden by cranks who knew nothing of the real pleasure in venturing the winning on a contest of skill or a game of chance.

It is remarkable how some men close their eyes to the bad results of gambling. They have tasted the pleasurable excitement of it, and they regard it, if not as a means of revenue, as a pastime in which the strong-minded may indulge without harm to any one.

But gambling has ruined more men than drink. It is a vice that may be practiced secretly, and, unfortunately, it seldom leaves its branding marks on the boy or young man who becomes its victim. When a man begins to drink hard his features tell on him, even though he is clever enough to refrain from getting drunk. His changed face warns his employer, who may take precautions in regard to the victim of drink. But there are no telltale signals hung out on the face of the young gambler who follows the races, the pool rooms, or occasionally plunges heavily in stocks. His employer is unwarned until the crash comes and the young man flees, a defaulter, or blows out his brains, disgraced and dishonored.

Are there not men who gamble mildly, without harm to any one? No!

The man who does a wrong thing sets an example before others. Even if he has such perfect control of himself that he may never indulge to excess, his example may lead some weaker soul into the crooked path that leads through fields of pleasure and pain to the gate of Purgatory.

Frank Merriwell was one who believed that a man should be judged not alone by the company he kept, but by the example he set. He believed that some of the world's best and greatest men had associated with the meek and lowly, but had exalted and uplifted others by their exemplary behavior.

He who keeps constantly in mind the desire to set a good example before others, cannot very well go wrong himself.

"It's pleasant to know some one has such confidence in our team," nodded Merry; "but, of course, you are aware that we'll be doing something remarkable if we break the winning streak of the great Outcasts."

"I know; still I think you'll break it. Some one will. It can't keep up."

McGann laughed.

"We wouldn't think of letting Merriwell's team defeat us," he said. "We shall take extra precautions. Every man will be in the best condition possible, Mat O'Neill will pitch, and we'll try to shut the mighty Merriwell bunch out."

"You'll succeed!" exclaimed Bart Hodge; "I don't think!"

"You may think," chuckled McGann. "Wait until after the game. Why, you don't know what you are going up against."

"By the way, Merriwell," said Grafter, placing a hand on Frank's arm, "have you seen anything of Hobe Manton lately?"

"I haven't seen him since the day of the meet at Eagle Heights."

"I have. Ran across him yesterday by accident. He stopped to speak with me, although I fancy he dislikes me now almost as much as he does you. He's a dangerous chap, and you want to keep your eyes open for him."

"Why, I fancied he was pretty well cooled down."

"Not at all; he's pretty well warmed up. He hasn't forgotten that he, the great 'gentleman pugilist,' was soundly thrashed by you out behind the cedars at Eagle Heights. And that is why he is determined to get even with you some time. He stopped me yesterday to tell me that he was going to square up the score. He said he had been keeping track of your movements, and he meant to catch you alone and off your guard. You want to be careful, Merriwell. There is no telling what he may try to do."

"Oh, I think he's not nearly as dangerous as he would have people believe."

"I don't know about it. He felt most keenly the disgrace of being kicked out of Eagle Heights."

"He brought it on himself."

"He thinks you were the cause of it all. He doesn't blame himself. At least, he doesn't seem to."

"Well, I'm much obliged for your warning, Grafter. I'll keep my eyes peeled."

Grafter and McGann now took their departure, bidding Frank and Bart good day. The manager had secured Merriwell's address, so that he might communicate with him if he should desire to do so before Saturday.

"Well, Bart," said Merry, as the manager of the Outcasts and the shot-putter of the Eagle Heights A. A. were disappearing from the lot, "how do you like the prospect?"

"It's great!" answered Bart. "Merry, if it is in us, we must defeat those chaps. I'd rather beat them than any team we have met this season."

"It would give us more glory."

"Glory is not all. I can tell by the way McGann talked that they believe themselves the only ones on earth. He fancies he has a snap in the arrangement that the winning team shall take all the gate money. He's chuckling in his sleeves over the fact that you refused his offer and then stepped into a trap by which we'll get nothing at all. His manner made me sore. I'd rather take that game than any ten common games."

"We'll go after it hard, Bart. If I can get the new curve down pat before that game, I may be able to bother some of the batters with it."

"Some of them! I'll bet you'll bother every one of them."

"Let's try it some more."

They resumed practice, and both saw that Merry made progress in handling and controlling the new curve. Bart also advanced in the way of receiving it, for he grew accustomed to the sharp upward shoot of what seemed to be a falling ball.

Finally they stopped and picked up their clothing, which lay on a pile of lumber near by.

Frank had begun to adjust his collar when Bart said:

"Look here, Merry—look quick! Who are these fellows?"

Behind the cover of the lumber pile nine young men had approached. As soon as they realized that they were seen by Bart, they started on the run for the two youths. In their hands some of them carried heavy clubs. They had the manner of thugs.

Merry took a look at them.

"Great Cæsar!" he exclaimed, not wholly without dismay. "It's Hobart Manton and a bunch of toughs! They're after us, Bart, and we're in for trouble!"

Both Frank and Bart thought of taking flight. It seemed folly to stop there and face nine ruffians who were armed with clubs. Bart caught up his coat and vest and started. As he ran something fell from his vest.

"Dropped my watch," he exclaimed, stopping and turning back for it.

It was a valuable watch in a certain way, being a present from his mother. He thought a great deal of it. Instantly Frank stopped and turned back.

They did not find the watch at once. Just as Bart picked it up the thugs came rushing round both sides of the lumber pile and were upon them.

"Yah!" snarled the leader, who was very well dressed, yet who had a face that seemed flushed with drink. "We have ye! Don't try to run!"

It was Hobart Manton himself.

"Manton," muttered Merry.

"Yes, Manton!" cried the fellow.

"And Frost!" came from Bart, as he pointed at another of the gang. "There's Frost!"

"And Necker, also," said Merry, nodding toward a third chap.

"Yes, we're right here!" grated Manton, who was plainly the leader. "We've caught you just where I've been wanting to get you, too!"

Merry surveyed the remaining six members of the gang, and he decided that they were genuine young loafers and desperadoes.

Manton saw Frank surveying the gang, and he laughed harshly.

"Oh, they're scrappers, every one of them!" he cried. "They know you can fight, and they're here to beat you up. You'll get all that's coming this day!"

"What a fine, brave fellow Manton is!" grated Hodge.

"You'll get yours, too!" declared the leader of the thugs. "Next to Merriwell, it will give me pleasure to knock the wind out of you!"

"So this is really the sort of ruffian you are!" spoke Merry cuttingly. "You were called the 'gentleman pugilist.' Gentleman, indeed! Why, you're just a common ruffian!"

"Go ahead!" cried Manton. "The more you talk like that the more delight I shall take in beating you up."

"You proved yourself a sneak at Eagle Heights. You brought disgrace on your own head."

"Yah! I was a member in good standing until you came."

"And then, out of a desire to show off, you led yourself into the most disreputable business. But I'm surprised to see Dent Frost and Jack Necker with you. I hardly looked for them to be in such company. Is it possible that they are chaps of the same caliber?"

Frost frowned, while Necker looked a trifle ill at ease.

"Oh, I have something to settle with you, too!" asserted the pole vaulter.

"I ought to have!" exclaimed the jumper.

"Well, you are fine sports, to be sure!" scornfully flung back Frank. "You were fairly and honorably defeated, and now you come here to beat me up for it! I understood that the Eagle Heights A.A. was made up of gentlemen! I don't understand how you ever got into it."

"Manton is our friend," said Frost.

"That's it!" Necker hastily cried. "He has been treated in a shabby manner, and you are the cause of it. He is our friend."

"You should be proud to own him as such!" sneered Bart.

"Another one for you!" growled Manton. "Come on, fellows."

"Wait a moment!" exclaimed Frank, flinging up his hand. "What do you think will be the end of this? If you don't kill us here and now, I promise to land you three in prison for assault with intent to kill. I mean you, Manton, you, Frost, and you, Necker. I know you. You were fools to come here with your thugs. The evidence against you will be overwhelming. You'll go to prison, every one of you!"

"Bah! He's trying to frighten you, boys," said Manton. "He thinks he can bluff us."

"I promise the remainder of the gang that I shall make it pretty warm for them. I seldom forget a face I have once seen, and I've been looking them all over. I'll spend a year, if necessary, in running this gang down and giving each one the full strength of the law."

"Don't pay any attention to him!" howled Manton. "He always makes a bluff. Fly at him!"

The thugs muttered among themselves and advanced, gripping their clubs. They spread out to intercept Merry and Bart if the intended victims sought to run away.

"Got to fight 'em, Merry!" hissed Hodge.

"Got to, Bart!" was the answer.

They placed themselves back to back, in order to defend themselves as best they could.

Jack Necker was hesitating. Manton appealed to him.

"Come on, Jack!" he cried. "Get into it!"

Necker threw down his club.

"Not I!" he exclaimed. "I've changed my mind."

"What?" snarled Manton. "What ails you?"

"I've changed my mind."

"You're afraid! You're a quitter!"

"I'd rather quit than go to the jug, and Merriwell can send the whole bunch up if he tries."

Frost seemed to hesitate. Plainly he was inclined to follow the example of the jumper.

"Don't you quit, Dent!" rasped Manton. "You've been telling what you wanted to do to Merriwell. Don't be a coward!"

Thus urged, Frost reluctantly joined the others, and Manton gave the word for them all to prepare for a grand rush.

"Make ready!" he cried. "We'll jump on 'em all together when I give the word. Now! One, two, three—go!"

A shout of warning came from Necker.

"Skip," he yelled. "Here comes a bunch of cops! You'll all be pinched!"

Then he took to his heels, running as if his very life depended on it.

Some of the ruffians had leaped in to get at Merry and Bart. Others, including Manton and Frost, heard the warning words of Necker and did not charge. They cast frightened glances around, saw three policemen, with drawn clubs, followed by two other men, coming at a run, then promptly took flight after the manner of Necker.

Manton was one of the very first to run, and he ran as if his life depended on it, while Frost followed him closely.

Merry managed to leap on one of the ruffians, tripping him and flinging him to the ground.

Hodge seized another and had a sharp fight with him; but the fellow staggered Bart with a blow of his club and broke away.

When the officers came up it was seen that Wallace Grafter and Melvin McGann were with them.

The ruffian Frank had held was promptly seized and subdued.

"I know him," said one of the policemen. "It's Hug Murphy, and he's wanted for some flat work. He'll get a vacation."

"We saw those chaps as we were leaving the lot," explained Grafter. "They were holding a consultation behind the board fence over yonder. I recognized Manton and knew there was mischief brewing. Then we hustled to find some officers; but we arrived just a moment too late."

"Or a trifle too soon," said Frank. "If they had tackled us in a bunch it's likely your approach might not have been noticed. In that case you might have nabbed more than one. I am very grateful to you, Grafter. It's certain enough that the thugs, armed as they were, would have hammered us up only for you."

"Don't mention it, Merriwell, old boy!" cried Grafter.

"Did you recognize any one in the gang besides Manton?" asked Frank.

"No."

"Two other chaps who are well known to you were there."

"Who?"

"Dent Frost for one."

"Impossible!"

"It's true."

"Why, Denton Frost is a gentleman!"

"How about Jack Necker?"

"He's regarded as one. You don't mean to say——"

"He was the other one."

"Well, this affair shall be reported at Eagle Heights!" exclaimed Grafter warmly. "I don't care to associate with ruffians of that cast. If they are not asked to resign from the club, I shall hand in my resignation."

He was in earnest and highly indignant.

Frank and Bart left the lot in company with the officers and the others. They saw nothing of the members of the gang who had taken flight.

"You see my warning was one to be heeded, Merriwell," said Grafter, as he was about to leave Frank. "Hobe Manton is vicious, and he'll do everything in his power to injure you. He'll stop at nothing. Better swear out a warrant for his arrest and put the police after him."

"I'll consider it," said Merry. "It would give me some satisfaction to settle the matter with him personally. I have a strong desire to show him that he received nothing but a mere taste when we had our little fight at Eagle Heights."

"I don't blame you, Merry!" cried Hodge earnestly. "I always like to settle such matters myself! I'd like to have a turn at him. He thinks he's a fighter; but I wouldn't mind meeting him on even footing."

"It seems to me that your friends are fighters, Grafter," said McGann.

"You'll think so after the game next Saturday," retorted Wallace.

CHAPTER XV.

GRAFTER GROWS UNEASY.

The game that was to be between Frank Merriwell's team and the great Outcasts was thoroughly advertised. Much was said about it in the sporting columns of the New York papers. The sporting writers were one and all inclined to doubt the ability of the Merries to check the triumphant career of the Outcasts.

One well-known sporting writer demonstrated in his paper, to his own satisfaction, at least, that it was utterly impossible for Merriwell's team to defeat the fast nine formed from the very best of the "timber" left over from the big leagues.

It must not be fancied that Frank himself felt certain of winning. He knew the sort of a "proposition" he and his comrades were going up against. It aroused all his sporting blood and determination. It likewise aroused the others. Hodge was the only man on the team who seemed confident of victory, but all were resolved to play for their very lives.

At least, it would be no disgrace if they met defeat. They practiced faithfully, and each day Merry worked at his new curve.

"Bart," he said, "I hope I can fool those chaps with that ball. I hear they are wonderful batters. I have been told that they have found a man who throws something like the double-shoot, and they have been practicing batting with him as pitcher. They expect to fall on me when I hand them up the double-shoot and hammer me to the four winds."

"You'll fool them, Merry," nodded Hodge positively. "If they get a single hit off that curve I shall be surprised."

"You've seen what the papers are saying about our prospects. We're called fast enough to make it interesting for college teams, but several degrees too weak to hold down the Outcasts. Henshaw, of the Universe, says the chances are more than even that we'll not score if O'Neill is used against us. Anderson, of the

Standard, says it would be a shame to use O'Neill and give us no chance; he urges Manager McGann to put in Brackett. Pulsifer, of the Evening Dispatch, thinks we are going to lose the reputation we have made on our trip this season."

"And they all make me tired!" cried Bart. "We'll give them a chance to sing another song in their Sunday columns."

The boys took care of themselves, lived properly and sought to come up to the game in the pink of condition.

Frank kept his eyes open for Hobart Manton, but once more Manton seemed to have disappeared completely.

From Wallace Grafter he learned that charges had been preferred at the Eagle Heights A.A. against Frost and Necker, as having attempted to assault an honorary member of the club. Merriwell had been taken into the Eagle Heights A.A. after his success at the meet in defeating two of its champions.

Saturday proved to be a fine day. The boys were in a glow of enthusiasm. When they thought of the coming struggle in Hoboken they tingled all over.

The game was to be called at 3 o'clock. At 2.30 Frank and his team reached the grounds and found a river of people crowding in at the gate. Evidently the game would be witnessed by an immense crowd.

They hurried to the dressing rooms and quickly got into their suits.

When they came out onto the field they found the Outcasts practicing.

The appearance of Merriwell's team produced a stir and caused many of the spectators to applaud loudly.

Melvin McGann hastened to shake hands with Frank. He was beaming in a most satisfied manner.

"Look at this mob!" he exclaimed. "I'm afraid we'll have hard work keeping them off the field. We've stretched ropes, but ropes won't hold a crowd back if it gets too large. Here is Captain Hurley. Mr. Hurley—Mr. Merriwell."

Hugh Hurley shook hands with Frank.

"Glad to meet you Mr. Merriwell," he said. "You may have the field for practice."

Frank sent his players out at once.

Bob Gowan and Mike Grafter were sitting together. Wallace Grafter joined them as the Merries trotted onto the field.

The Tammany man surveyed the youngsters in blue in a doubtful manner.

"Is this the team you told me to bet on, son?" he asked.

"Sure, dad," nodded Wallace.

"Rather immature, some of 'em. Look like boys."

"They are all men in years, although they do look rather boy-ish," said Wallace.

"Hum!" grunted Mr. Grafter doubtfully.

Gowan grinned.

"I've got ye!" he wheezed. "Your money is mine! The kids won't be in the game for a minute."

The Merries seemed rather nervous. In fact, they were too anxious, and they began practice by several bad fumbles and throws. Hodge was one of the offenders. He made a high throw to second.

"Whip it down again, Bart," said Frank.

Bart obeyed, but this time his throw was too low.

Immediately Frank took the ball and threw to second, taking pains to make the throw good.

It was a case of showing exactly what he wanted done.

Hodge set his teeth and resolved that every throw should be perfect after that, and it was.

To some it may have appeared that Merry was showing off. Instead of that, he was impressing Bart by force of example.

As Grafter watched the Merries practice he became more and more uneasy.

"I didn't kiss that thousand good-by," he said; "but I think I'd better have done it. I'll never see it again."

Again Gowan grinned.

"Oh, don't squeal so soon, dad!" cried Wallace, annoyed. "The trouble with you is that you have been reading the papers and you've got cold feet."

"The trouble with you," growled the old man, "is that you're stuck on Frank Merriwell, and you think the whole of his bunch just as good as he is. They're not. They're 'way below him."

"He'll do the pitching to-day."

"Pitching alone can't win a game."

"And he'll be up against Mat O'Neill," reminded Gowan. "O'Neill will show him up."

"Look here!" exclaimed Wallace. "I have a hundred or two on me that I'll risk. I'll wager that more hits are made off O'Neill to-day than off Merriwell."

"Put up as much as you dare," invited Gowan. "I'll cover all you have."

The bet was made.

There was some delay over beginning the game. Captain Hurley informed Merriwell that he was waiting for one of his players.

Finally the crowd in front of the gate parted, several policemen making an opening for a handsome landau, which was drawn by a spirited pair of white horses. The carriage swung up toward the bench of the Outcasts and came to a stop. From it sprang a small, compactly built, swarthy chap in a baseball suit.

At sight of this person Merriwell and several of his companions uttered exclamations of surprise.

"Do my eyes deceive me?" cried Frank. "That fellow looks as natural as life! I must be dreaming!"

The newcomer hastened across back of the home plate, his face wreathed in smiles.

"Once more," he cried, "once more I feast my optics on the only and original Frank Merriwell, my old college chump and side partner. The spectacle causes my throbbing heart to swell with emotions too turgid for utterance. Allow me to grasp your dainty digits, Frank."

"Cap'n Wiley, as I live!" laughed Frank, as he shook hands with the person who had made his appearance in this spectacular manner. "Why, cap'n, I fancied you had faded from this terrestrial sphere."

"Nay, nay, Pauline! I am here—very much here, as you will find to your sorrow before the game of to-day has passed into history."

"You are playing with the Outcasts?"

"Am I? Ask me! I am their mainstay and support. My fielding is about nine hundred and ninety-nine per cent. and my batting a trifle better than five hundred per cent. I was too fast for the Concord team of the New England League, and so they had to let me go. You see the other players didn't have any chance to shine with me in the game. I played all round them. Not only did I fill my own field at shortstop, but I often gamboled out into the extreme gardens and picked flies and line drives right out of the fingers of the fielders. I covered all the sacks from the initial corner round to the home plate, and often I backed up the catcher. The populace stood aghast at my strenuosity, and the players became jealous and pea-green with envy.

"These envious individuals formed a combine against me. They put their caputs together—caput is French for head—they put their caputs together and formed a combine. They decided to quit in a body unless I was released. The manager had no alternative. He pleaded with them with tears in his eyes and his fists doubled up, but they would not hearken unto reason, and so he was compelled to release me with honors. I immediately received offers from Boston, New York, Washington, Chicago, and Oshkosh. But

I decided to throw my fortunes in with the noble Outcasts, and here I am.

"I'm sorry for you, Merry, old boy, but you haven't a show with me in the game against you. Your double-shoot will not save you on this salubrious afternoon. You will remember that I acquired a spasm of the double-shoot myself, and I have had the boys batting against it for the past four days. Every man on the team can hit the double-shoot with his eyes shut. Just hand it up to them and regret it to the end of your tempestuous career."

"So you are the chap who has been training them to bat against me? I heard some one was doing it."

"I confess with all due humility and abnegation—abnegation is a good word, but I don't know what it means—I confess that I am the guilty party. I had to do it. You see we haven't been beaten thus far in our seething career, and we don't propose to have our immaculate record sullied by defeat. The boys knew I could hand out the double-shoot. When they learned that the game with your team had been arranged, they led me forth like a lambkin to the slaughter and bade me promulgate the sphere through the atmosphere after the manner in which you are wont to do. Then they took their little bats and learned to hit it. I warn you in advance that they can connect with the ball even though you make it travel like a writhing snake through the ozone. It will grieve my tender heart to see you batted all over the lawn, Merry; but I fear exceedingly that such will be your fate."

"What do you think of that?" exclaimed Hodge, who had never entertained any great liking for Wiley. "He has been teaching them to bat your pet curve, Frank."

"My loyalty to my own team led me to do so," protested Wiley. "Even though I love Frank Merriwell more than a long-lost brother—more than a drink after a drought—I am ever loyal to my own team. Don't use the double-shoot to-day, Frank! Preserve your reputation by keeping it tucked safely up your flowing sleeve."

"The same old Wiley!" laughed Frank. "Don't worry about me, cap'n. If you bat me out of the box to-day, I'll take my medicine."

The sailor then shook hands with some of the others and hastened to join his comrades, Hurley calling sharply to him.

As the Outcasts took the field, the sailor cantered out to the position of shortstop.

"Now, O'Neill," he cried, "unbend your wing and waft the crooked ones over the corners. Remember that I am behind you and fear not."

Mat O'Neill laughed. He was a slender chap, with long arms.

He glanced round to make sure the players were in their positions and then toed the slab.

Ready was in position to bat.

O'Neill shot over a high inshoot that seemed to curve round Jack's neck.

"Avast, there!" shouted Wiley. "Permit the ruddy-cheeked blossom to have a passing glimpse of it."

The umpire pronounced it a strike.

"That was sizzling hot, Mat!" exclaimed the catcher. "It burned in the mitt. You have your speed with you to-day. I don't think they can see the ball."

Ready had nothing to say, which was quite unusual for him. He gripped his bat and waited for the next one.

It looked wide, but came in and passed over the outside corner of the plate.

"Two strikes!" cried the umpire.

Wiley did a hornpipe.

"It's a shame, O'Neill!" he declared. "You should blush at your own perfidy. How can you do it? Don't you see you have the poor boy shaking like a sheet in the wind! Just toss him one and let him strike at it."

"He makes me sore!" muttered Hodge. "I always did hate the sound of his tongue."

O'Neill pitched again. This time the ball looked altogether too high, but it dropped past Ready's shoulders.

Jack did not strike at it, but the umpire promptly declared him out.

The wizard pitcher of the Outcasts had struck Ready out with three pitched balls, and Merriwell's man had not tried to hit one of them.

CHAPTER XVI.

CLEVER PITCHING.

Oh, me! oh, my!" cried Wiley. "How could you be so careless, Jack? I fear your reputation will sink into ignominy. At least, you could have shut your eyes and fanned once. You did not even agitate the atmosphere with your wand."

"You seem to be agitating it altogether too much with your tongue," flung back Ready, as he retired disconsolately to the bench.

Morgan stepped out to take his place.

"Who is this sedate youth?" inquired the sailor. "To me his classic countenance is strangely unfamiliar. I wonder if he will pass away in a trance, like his predecessor."

Mike Grafter had turned on his son as Ready was declared out.

"What do you think of that, boy?" he demanded. "That fellow didn't seem to know what he was standing up there for."

"He did appear doped," admitted Wallace; "but I think this one will wake up."

He was right, for Morgan smashed the first ball delivered. It hummed along the ground in the direction of Wiley. The sailor leaped for it and it struck his hands, bouncing out. Like a cat springing on a mouse, Wiley pounced on the ball, caught it up and whistled it across the diamond in time to put Dade out at first.

"Too easy to get it the first time," he said. "In order to show my superb style, I had to drop it and pick it up again. Bat them all to me. It's the easiest way you can get out."

Buck Badger, grim and sturdy, strode forth to the plate.

"A gent from the wild-and-woolly, unless I have been incorrectly informed," said Wiley. "Whoop! Yi, yi, ye-ee! Yow! Notice the coyotelike melody of my voice. Give him a slow one."

"About like this, eh?" said O'Neill, as he delivered a "dope" ball.

Badger had noted the speed of the pitcher, and he struck too soon.

"One strike!" called the umpire.

"Behave! behave!" exclaimed Wiley. "Why, he really tried to hit it before it left your hand, O'Neill."

"Confound that fellow!" grated Hodge. "He's getting on my nerves."

"Don't let him do that," advised Frank. "It's a part of his game. He always tries to worry the opposite side."

Buck had better luck with the second ball, for he sent a little Texas Leaguer over the infield and easily reached first.

"What do you think of that?" cried the sailor. "O'Neill, you're getting careless. You make me blush for you. Note the rosy color that suffuses my dimpled cheeks."

As Merry picked out his bat and walked to the plate he was given a round of applause.

"Ahoy there, my old college chump!" hailed the sailor. "Waft an energetic one in this direction and permit me to demonstrate my dexterity by placing my diligent digits upon it."

Frank seemed to obey, for he smote the ball full and fair on the trade-mark and sent it sizzing through the air straight at the speaker. Wiley seemed to have no more than time to put up his hands. The ball struck them and bounded off toward second base. Roden went for it as Badger came down the line. He could not get it in time to tag the Kansan, but he made a sharp throw to first and Frank was declared out.

"Score an assist for me!" cried Wiley. "I think I've lost a mitt, but I want to be credited with an assist. I'll never ag'in invite him to bat the ball in my direction."

"Why didn't you dodge it?" cried a spectator.

"I didn't have time," confessed the Marine Marvel, as he designated himself.

Mike Grafter had his face screwed up in a dozen hard knots.

"They got one hit, but it didn't amount to anything," he said. "I'll wager something the Outcasts do better than Merriwell, son?"

"If I had any money left, I'd go you, dad," said Wallace. "I thought you had good sporting blood. You seem to have a bad case of frosty feet."

"Can you blame him?" wheezed Gowan.

"Oh, they didn't do so bad after the first man," declared Wallace. "The others hit the ball."

"Only one of them hit it anywhere, and that was an accident."

"It was more of an accident than anything else that Merriwell didn't get a safe one. He nearly took the hands off that rattle-tongued chap at short."

Merriwell entered the box, and Creel, the centre fielder, smiling and confident, walked out to bat.

At the very outset, Hodge called for Frank's new curve.

"Oh, he's going to deliver the salivered sphere!" cried Wiley, as he saw Frank moisten the ball. "Hit one of those and it will travel at the rate of a mile a second."

"Cease thy idle prattle, cap'n," implored Ready, who was in position near third. "You are giving the tympanum of my ear a sensation of ennui."

"Hey?" gasped the sailor. "What's that? Ong wee? Is that proper pronunciation? I thought it was enn-you-eye. Ong wee! That sounds good to me. I'll use it at the first opportunity."

Frank delivered the ball. It swept downward from his hand toward the inside of the plate, but curved and swept upward and outward, crossing the outside corner.

Creel had looked for the usual drop of the spit ball, and he struck under.

"Strike one!"

The batter looked surprised. He knew the ball had taken some kind of a queer shoot, but he did not know just what had happened.

"Hit it where you missed it, Creel, old boy!" urged Wiley. "Look out for the double-shoot. He'll hand one up in a minute, and you will have an opportunity to demonstrate the ease with which we can project it to yonder fence."

Frank pitched again and tried the other sweep.

The ball seemed to start toward the outside of the plate. Suddenly it swept upward and inward, and again Creel missed.

"Strike two!"

Creel gasped.

"What's that he's throwing?" he muttered.

"Oh, hit the ball!" chuckled Hodge. "It's easy enough!"

"I'll hit the next one!" growled Creel.

"Bet you don't."

"I will if I swing at it."

"Bet you don't."

"Don't talk to that catcher, Tip," commanded Hurley sharply.

Creel was silenced. He set his teeth, gripped his bat and waited. At the same time, although ready to strike, he more than half expected Frank would "waste" one or two balls.

Merry saw the fellow was ready to swing if the ball came over. Again he delivered it a trifle wide, but it swept in and upward, being caught by Hodge almost directly behind the batter's shoulder. In fact, it seemed to pass under Creel's arm as the latter swung at it.

"You're out!" announced the umpire.

"I'd like to know what sort of a curve he used on me!" muttered Tip Creel, as he reseated himself on the bench. "It had a mighty queer twist."

Hurley was watching closely.

"It wasn't the double-shoot Wiley has been teaching us to hit," he said.

"If it was," said Creel, "Merriwell throws it entirely different from Wiley."

"Look here, cap'n," demanded Swatt, "have you been deceiving us?"

"Not on your autograph;" answered the sailor. "He has not yet promulgated the double-shoot through the sunny atmosphere. Perchance I made a mistake in admitting to him that we intended to bat it with extreme vigor the moment he passed it out to us. But linger yet a while and I prophesy that he will hand it forth."

Marcey, the third baseman, now came up. He did not attempt to hit the first ball pitched, for it seemed too wide. It swept in over the outside corner, however, and the umpire, who had a good eye and knew his business, declared it a strike.

Marcey flung down his bat, sprang onto the plate and glared at the umpire.

"What's that?" he snarled.

"Rotten! rotten!" howled a man on the bleachers, who sat in such a position that he could not tell to save his life whether the ball came over the plate. "Put him out! Get a new umpire! Put him out! He's roasting you! I've got some money on this game, and I want to see a square deal."

"Shut up!"

"Sit down!"

"Choke off!"

"Keep still!"

"Go die!"

These and various other cries came from the crowd, the most of whom knew the umpire.

The umpire ordered Marcey back into position. The batter grouchily picked up his bat and prepared to strike, muttering sullenly all the while.

Frank proceeded to whistle over a high one that was declared a ball. Then he used a "dope," at which Marcey struck too soon.

"He's no fool of a pitcher," muttered the captain of the Outcasts. "I'm afraid he's going to be a hard man to hit safely."

This opinion he did not express to the others.

Marcey was finally fooled with Merry's new curve, striking out.

"Come on, Bimm!" urged Hurley. "Put us into the game. Don't try to knock the cover off the ball. That pitcher is easy enough if you don't swing your head off trying to hit."

Bimm was one of the best batters on the team, even though he was a change pitcher. He stepped out fully determined to show the crowd that it was not such a difficult thing to hit Merriwell safely.

"I'd give something to get a two-bagger or better," he thought.

Still he did not try for a long hit. Instead of that, he shortened his hold on his bat and swung to meet the ball squarely, if he could.

He fouled the first one.

"Feeling of him, Bimm, my boy!" cried Wiley. "You'll find him soft and easy. Swat her to the so'west corner of the inclosure and steer your course around the diamond."

Bimm did his best, but, like the two before him, he fell a victim of Merriwell's skill and struck out.

Hurley looked round for McGann as he started for the field. He was beginning to think that Merriwell would prove a hard nut to crack.

On the bleachers Wallace Grafter was smiling with satisfaction and his father was feeling decidedly better.

"What do you think about it now, dad?" asked the young man.

"Can he keep that up, son?" asked the politician.

"Of course he can't!" wheezed Gowan. "Those men of ours are great batters, and they'll fall on him hard before long. When they do, you'll see him go up in the air."

"How about that, son?" inquired Grafter.

"Don't you worry, dad," advised Wallace. "I didn't urge you to bet on the Merries without knowing what I was doing. I've found out all about Frank Merriwell. Mat O'Neill is a rattling good pitcher, but he's met his match in Merriwell."

Bob Gowan laughed, holding onto his fat sides.

"All boys are alike," he said, "and your son is no more than a boy, Grafter. He has lots to learn."

"All boys are not fools," retorted Wallace. "I fancy that before the game is over to-day you'll confess that you have learned something."

Wallace was just a trifle disrespectful in his language. He was the young city man of the day, up-to-date, breezy, and assertive.

Mat O'Neill realized that Merriwell had made the best record in the first inning, yet he was confident that the youth could not keep it up. O'Neill had picked up his baseball in the rough-and-ready school of the independent and minor league teams, and he thought little of college pitchers, as a rule. Merriwell he considered in the class of the best college pitchers. Of course he was forced to admit that some college twirlers panned out well, for he knew what Clarkson, Matthewson, and others had done; but he thought them exceptions, and he believed Merriwell would be playing in one of the big leagues if he was fast enough.

Still O'Neill's pride had been touched, and he felt a desire to demonstrate that he, too, could strike out three men in succession, if he desired. This desire led him to begin the second inning with the determination to do his handsomest.

Bart Hodge was the first man to face him. Hodge had a grim face and businesslike air.

O'Neill handed him a high inshoot. Bart struck and missed.

"That's the woods!" cried Wiley. "Whisker cutters for him. He never finds 'em."

Following this two balls were called. Then O'Neill caught Bart on a drop.

Hodge seemed anxious, so the pitcher tried to pull him on a wide outcurve.

Bart let it pass.

"Three balls!" declared the umpire.

"Oh, you vill haf to got der plate ofer der pall, Misder Bitcher!" cried Hans Dunnerwurst from the bench.

O'Neill decided on a fast rise past the batter's shoulders, and his control was perfect.

Nevertheless Bart met the ball fairly, giving it a fearful crack.

O'Neill muttered an exclamation of chagrin.

Out on a line went the ball. Wiley made a wild leap into the air, but he could not reach it by two feet, at least.

"That's the high sign!" cried the sailor. "My arm was too short. I'll have to use my patent arm-stretching attachment to get those."

"The fielders will have to use their leg-stretching attachment to get them," laughed Dade Morgan, as he ran down to the coaching line. "Take second, Bart!"

Hodge obeyed, easily reaching second base before the ball could be fielded into the diamond.

"Now, Gamp—now!" urged Morgan. "It's just as easy. O'Neill will have his troubles to-day."

"I pelief you vos correctness, Dady!" cried Dunnerwurst, as he joined Morgan. "His troubles vill haf him to-day. Mofe dot pag away from, Partley! Got a good sdart und make a roppery. You vos der pest ropper in der punch. Id peen easiness vor a pase to steal you."

"These boys seem to bat some, Mr. Gowan," observed Wallace Grafter. "If they ever get to bunching 'em on O'Neill they will put him to the stable."

"One hit in an inning doesn't count," gurgled Gowan. "I've noticed that O'Neill knows how to scatter the hits."

"Son," said old man Grafter, "when it comes to baseball, you know a thing or two. I'm satisfied now that I have a chance for my money, and so I won't kick if I lose it."

"All right, dad," smiled Wallace. "I'm thinking we'll both win our bets."

Joe Gamp, long, gangling and awkward, stood up to the plate.

"Get back a little!" sharply commanded O'Neill.

"What fuf-fuf-for?" innocently inquired Joe.

"I'll show you what for!" grated O'Neill, as he sent a ball over with burning speed, keeping it so close that it barely missed the tall chap.

"Let him hit you," cried Wiley. "You'll never know it, and your funeral will occur to-morrow."

Gamp seemed alarmed, for he stood off from the plate; but as O'Neill delivered the next ball, he stepped up to it.

Just as Joe had expected, the ball was over the outside corner.

Gamp hit it, having stepped near enough to reach it with ease.

O'Neill had tried to fool him, but, instead of that, he had fooled O'Neill.

The hit was a safe one to right field.

Hodge went flying over third, being sent home by both Morgan and Dunnerwurst.

"Agitate your Trilbies, Boliver!" yelled Wiley. "Get your dainty fingers on the horsehide and hurry it hitherward! There is something doing!"

Bimm did his level best to cut off the score. Getting the ball, he made a splendid throw to the plate, but Hodge slid home safely.

Swatt, who was sometimes called "Crackson," on account of his batting, realized that he could not get Hodge, so he lined the ball down to Roden, hoping to catch Gamp, who had pranced toward second on the throw.

"Slide, Choe!" screeched Dunnerwurst.

Joe slid.

Roden put the ball onto him, but Gamp lay with his hand on the bag, and he was declared safe.

Old man Grafter laughed heartily.

"Gowan," he said, "the boys are playing all round your great Outcasts."

Gowan had nothing to say.

"This is criminal!" cried Wiley. "They should be ashamed! I don't believe they have any shame in them! I'll die of heart disease if this merry-go-round isn't checked right away."

"What's the matter, Mat?" asked Hurley.

"Nothing," answered the pitcher savagely.

"They're hitting you."

"I'll stop it."

"You'd better. We can't stand this."

Although he was angry, O'Neill was not rattled. He pitched with greater skill when Browning faced him. The big fellow made a number of fouls, but O'Neill finally struck him out.

Starbright followed.

"Another Goliath," said Wiley. "But the giants are easy. This one will fall like the other."

Starbright tried hard for a hit. Like Browning he made several fouls. Finally he put one into the air, and Crackson Swatt got under it and smothered it.

"Their last chance to do further damage has evaporated," announced Wiley, as Harry Rattleton stepped out. "This fellow will fall like golden grain before the shining sickle of the reaper. He never made a real hit in all his life."

Harry had little chance against the clever work of O'Neill. At the same time, he let none of the good ones pass without swinging. It did no good, for in the end he struck out.

The Merries had secured one run in the second inning.

CHAPTER XVII.

CASSIDY DEMANDS HIS MONEY.

In the midst of the great crowd on the bleachers back of third sat three persons who wore the clothes of laborers, but whose hands were not those of workingmen. They were Hobart Manton, Denton Frost, and Jim Necker. These chaps had ventured to witness the game together, but Manton refused to attend in the company of the others unless they wore a semi-disguise, like himself.

The "gentleman pugilist" was keenly interested in the game, for he confessed that he had bet money on the Outcasts, regarding the chance as a "snap."

"I've seen the most of Merriwell's bunch," he told his companions, "and they won't be in it for a minute. If you can find any marks who are willing to back Merriwell, bet every dollar you have. It will be just the same as finding money."

Frost and Necker had taken this advice. As they watched the beginning of the game they commented on the amateurish practice of Frank's team.

"I told you what to expect," chuckled Manton. "The only thing I'm sorry about is that I didn't have more ready money to wager. I've bet every dollar I could get together."

"Then," said Necker, "if you should happen to lose, you would go broke."

"I wouldn't have a whole dollar left," acknowledged Merriwell's enemy. "But there is not one chance in a thousand that I will lose. I can't lose. It will give me some satisfaction to see the great Merriwell properly beaten, but I'm sorry that I'll have no hand in the beating."

"You didn't give him much of a beating the last time you met him," said Necker, with a grin.

"All on account of that confounded slob, Grafter!" growled Manton. "If he hadn't seen us and brought the coppers we'd fixed

Merriwell so he would be in the hospital to-day, instead of playing baseball."

"And only for me," reminded Necker, "we might be in the jug, instead of here to witness the game. I saw the cops coming and gave you the alarm."

"We have something to settle with Grafter," hissed Frost, in his chilling way. "He's doing his level best to get us kicked out of Eagle Heights."

"And he'll succeed if you don't appear and answer to the charges preferred against you," said Manton. "I was kicked out, even when I did try to defend myself."

"Say," broke forth Necker, "did you pay that bunch of sluggers?"

"What bunch?"

"The ones you engaged to help us hammer Merriwell and Hodge."

"Pay them? Why should I? They didn't do anything, did they?"

"No; but you agreed to give them something, anyhow."

"Well, they've got all they will get."

"One of them got something," said Frost. "Hug Murphy was given a year for flat robbery."

"Next to Pink Cassidy," said Manton, "he was the ugliest man in the bunch. Pink was the leader."

"Speak of the devil," hissed Frost, "and you'll see the print of his hoof! There's Cassidy now."

"Where?" anxiously asked the other two.

Frost pointed out a chap with bright red hair.

"Yes, that's him," nodded Manton; "and he's spotted us. I'm sorry, for he'll come around."

He was right. "Pink" Cassidy, a sullen, stocky young thug, had seen them, and it was not long before he came forcing his way up over the bleachers and reached them.

"Set over, you!" he growled at a man who was beside Manton. "I wanter set wid me frien's."

"Go on!" retorted the man. "There's no room here, Mr. Buttinsky."

"Den I'll make some room," said Pink, as he grasped the man by the collar and gave him a jerk that flung him over the line of spectators below and onto the heads of the next row. "Allus move when a gent asks ye to."

Saying which, he calmly took the seat thus made vacant.

This action caused considerable commotion and enraged both the fellow who had been thus handled and those upon which he had landed; but Cassidy minded it not in the least, laughing and retorting to their angry words.

"If any of youse is lookin' for trouble," he said, "you can have all yer want. Better set still an' enjoy der game. Der gent wid the smashed dicer can git him a new one for der price. He needs it. Dat lid is all outer date."

"What do you mean by coming here and making all this row?" growled Manton. "You have half the bunch on this side rubbering at us."

"Oh, be calm, be calm," advised Cassidy serenely. "Let 'em rubber. Dey won't bite er northin'. I seen youse here, an' I took a fancy to set wid youse. You owe me money."

"What do you mean?"

"Dere, dere, don't gimme any o' dat! It don't go wid me. You know wot I mean. Dere's somet'n' comin' ter me, an' dis is me day fer collectin'."

"You can't get anything out of me. I'm broke."

"Nay, nay; I'm too wise ter swaller dat. A gent like youse never goes busted. Come down wid der long green."

"Shut up that talk!" grated the gentleman pugilist. "There's nothing due you."

"Den dere's somet'n' due youse, me boy! If youse don't settle I'm goin' ter tie you in a double hard knot."

Manton was enraged. He was not afraid of Cassidy as a fighter, but he feared the fellow would succeed in attracting the attention of Merriwell and thus get them all into trouble.

"See here," he whispered, "do you want to follow Hug Murphy?"

"I ain't t'inkin' of doin' dat."

"Well, you will if you kick up a disturbance here. Merriwell will spot you, and he'll push you, too."

"Speakin' one ter yerself, I t'ink," sneered Pink. "Wot would he do ter youse if he ketched ye?"

Manton and his companions were genuinely alarmed.

"Pay him, Manton!" hissed Frost. "Get rid of him somehow."

But Manton had wagered all his ready money on the game and had nothing left with which to pay the thug. He resolved, however, to get rid of Cassidy, if possible.

"Wait until after the game," he said. "I'll have some money then."

"How's dat?"

"I've bet all my ready money on the game."

"Tell it ter somebody else!"

"It's straight."

"How did you bet?"

"On the Outcasts."

"Den yer will have money, fer dey'll win in a walk. Yer won't be able ter make no squeal arter der game."

"No danger of that. I'll pay you then."

"All right; I'll stay wid yer till I git me coin."

That did not suit Manton, who had no liking for the company of Pink Cassidy.

"You move!" he exclaimed. "I'm taking no chances. Merriwell may spot you."

"If youse t'ink yer goin' ter git rid o' me dat way, ye're makin' a mistake," said Pink. "I'll move, but I'm goin' ter watch ye close, an' I'll nab yer der moment der game is over. You won't dodge me in der crowd."

"I shan't try. I may want you some other time, and I'm willing to do the right thing."

"Dat soun's good, but I t'ink ye're willin' 'cause ye can't help it. I'm onter your curves."

"Think anything you like, but slide out of this."

Repeating his promise to see Manton after the game, Cassidy moved.

Manton, Frost, and Necker breathed easier.

"He's a dangerous ruffian," hissed Frost. "You can't tamper with him, Hobe."

"I'll tamper with him!" growled Manton. "If I wasn't worrying about being spotted by Merriwell, I'd give him all that was coming, and don't you forget it!"

"Are you going to pay him any money after the game?"

"Not on your life! Not a dollar to that thug! When the game is over and the crowd begins to move I'll take chances. If he bothers me, I'll give him a sleeping slug on the jaw."

CHAPTER XVIII.

ON AN ERROR.

rost and Necker were disturbed when the Merries secured their run in the second inning.

"What do you think of that, Hobe?" asked Frost. "It begins to look bad to me."

"Oh, don't worry!" returned Manton, although he was a trifle disturbed himself. "This is just the beginning of the game. Merriwell can't keep up the pace he has set. Those fellows will get onto his style of pitching after a while, and then you'll see something happen to him. Those chaps behind him would go to pieces if the Outcasts began hitting."

"I hope they'll begin," said Necker, a trifle dolefully; "but I'm afraid they won't."

"Merriwell's men must be good batters," said Frost. "They've made three handsome hits off O'Neill. Nobody seemed to think they could do much with him."

"O'Neill hasn't settled down," declared Manton. "After he does he'll keep them from hitting."

"Here goes Merriwell into the box for the second time," said Necker. "Now watch. I hope they find him."

Captain Hurley was the first batter to face Frank in the second inning. He was resolved to set an example for his men to follow. Being a new hitter, he felt confident that Merry would find trouble in fooling him.

Frank knew Hurley's reputation, and he took no chances. The first ball pitched was the new curve, and it swept over the inside corner of the plate.

Hurley fouled it lightly, but the ball landed in Hodge's mitt and remained there.

Then Frank pitched two that seemed very wild. Hurley wondered if he had lost control. He was wondering when another of those queer corner cutters came over the outside edge and he struck at it.

"Two strikes!" cried the umpire, as the ball spanked into Bart's big mitt.

"Ye gods and little fishhooks!" moaned Cap'n Wiley, resting his head on his hands. "Is our noble leader going the way of dew before the morning sunshine? Will he likewise evaporate and fade away? Such a calamity would be too excruciating to endure."

Hurley was puzzled. He could not understand why he had missed the ball, but he realized that he had not fathomed the curve Frank was using.

"I'll get the next one!" he vowed.

Frank tried the inside corner, and for the third time Hurley missed.

"You're out!" declared the umpire.

The captain of the Outcasts looked very much chagrined as he retired to the bench.

"What's the matter?" asked Crackson Swatt. "Is the whole bunch hypnotized?"

"Something is the matter for a fact," admitted Hurley. "Try to bunt it, Swatt. We've got to find a way to get our bats against the ball."

The entire team had great confidence in Swatt. At the beginning of their career the Outcasts had batted with Swatt in the eighth position, like most professional teams; but his stick work had been so good that it was found advisable to move him up directly behind Hurley.

"Do project the ball somewhere, Swattsie!" implored Cap'n Wiley. "This continued agitation of the atmosphere without visible results is a weariness to the flesh. It will retire me to the bughouse before long."

Although four of his companions, all good batters, had failed to get a hit off Frank, Swatt was confident.

"He can't fool me," he told himself. "I'll hit it somewhere."

The first ball pitched by Merry passed behind Crackson's back, which caused him to laugh.

"Keep spitting on it," he said, "and you'll throw it over the grand stand before the game is ended. You can't control it. Better stop wetting it and pitch your usual way."

"Thank you for the advice," smiled Merry. "If I throw it over the grand stand I may decide to follow your kind suggestion."

But he kept on wetting the ball.

Crackson went after the second one pitched, but he was deceived like the others, missing it cleanly.

"Come! come!" cried a man on the bleachers. "I thought you fellows could hit a little. You don't seem to amount to shucks when you get up against a real pitcher."

Hurley was frowning and watching Merriwell's movements. He also tried to follow the course of the ball after it left Frank's hand.

Merry made another wild pitch, and the ball got past Hodge. This did no damage, however, as there was no one on the bases.

Among the spectators Hobe Manton brightened up a little.

"It will come in time," he said. "Merriwell can't keep it up. He's losing control now. What if the Outcasts had happened to have a man on third then? Why, he would have cantered home easily."

"But if they don't do better they'll never get a man on first," said Frost, with an icy sneer.

"They'll get one there pretty soon," nodded Manton.

"They can't hit Merriwell."

"They won't have to if he keeps on growing wild. They'll all walk."

But the next ball pitched looked good to Swatt, and again he swung at it.

He missed.

"Well, wouldn't that bump you violently!" cried Wiley, an expression of pain on his swarthy face. "Wait till I trip out there and put the marble over the fence. Then the gaping multitude will rise up and call me blessed."

Swatt had a puzzled look on his heavy face. Like those who had batted before him, he could not understand why he had failed so completely, although he realized that the ball had taken some kind of a freakish shoot.

"Make connections there!" yelled Wiley. "What ails you? Have you been smoking dope? Hit it anywhere and pray as you run. Don't be trying any fancy stunts at placing the ball. I know that old tar in the box, and he can throw everything from a high ball to a fish ball. You won't make a record trying to place your hits."

Swatt gave Wiley a look. Then he gripped his bat and waited.

Again the ball delivered by Frank looked good to him, and again he struck at it.

Again he missed.

"Boys," said Hurley, rising to his feet, "that man Merriwell has invented a new curve, and we'll have to wake up and hustle if we get any safe hits off him to-day."

"And all my labor in teaching this bunch to hit the double-shoot was wasted!" moaned the sailor. "When I think of that it makes my arm wearied and weak. I am fain to confess that Merriwell is too astute for a mortal of common clay."

Crackson Swatt sat down gloomily.

"I've batted against spit-ball pitchers before; but I've never seen one with that kink in his delivery," he admitted.

"You didn't bunt," said Hurley.

"I tried it once and missed. When I can't get my bat against a ball that curves fair over the plate the pitcher is a wizard or I have lost my batting eye."

Roden was next, and he attempted a bunt. He was the first to make anything like a success at hitting the ball, but his bunt went into the hands of Ready, who came rushing in for it.

Jack had plenty of time to throw Roden out, but he made a bad throw to Browning. The ball went over Bruce's head and into the crowd.

Wiley yelled like a maniac.

"Twinkle your Trilbies!" he howled, his eyes bulging. "Dust along the chalk mark! Scurry through the atmosphere! Take second."

Bruce got the ball and snapped it to Merry.

Roden had reached second in safety, and the crowd awoke, for at last it seemed that the Outcasts had done something.

Yet these two bags had been made on Ready's error, no hit having been secured off Frank.

On the bleachers Bob Gowan woke up and wheezed forth a cheer.

"Here is where we start!" he gurgled. "I knew it was sure to happen!"

"Oh, rot!" said Mike Grafter. "It was a great accident, and you know it, Gowan. They haven't touched Merriwell for a hit, and they may not."

"They'll touch him up now," asserted Gowan. "He'll go to pieces as soon as there is a runner on a base. These youngsters go to pieces easily."

"Bet you even money the next man don't reach first," proposed Grafter.

"Go you for a hundred!" promptly said Gowan.

Wiley was on the coaching line.

"Divorce yourself from that sack, Roden!" he whooped. "Dig your toes into the turf and be ready to burglarize that third cushion. Get off! Don't anchor there! Watch the swing of his propeller and move up on it every time. He won't throw down there. He thinks he'll strike Grimley out. Ha! ha! and ho! ho! I'd drop dead if he ever struck Cal Grimley out! Send the ball on a voyage,

Grim, old salt! Let her clear for a foreign port!"

Grimley hit viciously at the first ball, but, like all the others, save Roden, he missed.

"Open your eyes when you strike!" shrieked the sailor. "How could you miss it? That's criminal! Do your sleeping nights! It's too easy to hit that sort of a ball. Put it over the fence! Drop it out of the lot! Get away, Roden! You're hugging that sack as if you thought it a pretty girl. Forget your affection for it and break away!"

Grimley checked his desire to hit the ball hard. Steadying his nerves, he tried to meet it squarely and secure a safe hit.

He fouled it the next time he struck.

"Too bad!" howled Wiley. "Came near doing it then, Grim. Just a trifle more to the starboard. Steady now. You'll do it. You can't help it. Be ready to put on full steam ahead, Roden. You'll tie the score right here!"

But Grimley proved just as easy as the others for Frank, and Wiley groaned as the batter struck the third time and missed.

"It's a shame!" he muttered, as he cantered out to his position. "We can't keep on throwing away these chances. My reputation will be ruined if we lose this game."

Mat O'Neill used his head in the third inning. He mixed 'em up, using a change of pace that was very bothersome. Although two of the Merries hit the ball, not one of the first three reached the initial sack.

It was now Wiley's turn to strike.

"Do you think you'll hit it?" shouted a man on the bleachers.

"Think?" cried Wiley, in his peculiar manner. "How can I miss it? Watch the fence and see me drop it over with the utmost ease."

"Oh, yah!" cried Dunnerwurst derisively. "You vill drop der fence ofer der pall with Vrankie bitching—I don'd think!"

"Stop talking so carelessly," advised Wiley. "You get your tongue all tangled up so it falls over itself."

Twirling his bat as if it was a light cane, the sailor advanced to the plate.

"I am sorry for you, Merry," he said jauntily. "I have to do it. I believe in setting a good example, and I'll have to show these dopey dubs how to hit the ball. Once on a time I made a seven-base hit. I galloped round the diamond and came home while the fielders were chasing the merry sphere as it went dancing elusively away. As I reached the plate I heard one of the opposing players inform the umpire that I had failed to touch second sack with my dainty tootsie. I knew it was true. I likewise knew the umpire loved me now and would gladly claim he had seen me cut the cushion. Therefore I started round the diamond again and reached third before the ball was thrown in, thus making seven bases on the hit. I'll be satisfied with four off you, Frank. It will be a great sufficiency."

No one save Wiley would have ventured to spend the time to relate such an incident before striking; but the sailor did most things after his own particular fashion, and no one seemed inclined to object.

"I'm glad you think you'll feel satisfied with a four-base hit, cap'n," said Frank. "Go ahead and get it."

Surely the Marine Marvel tried hard enough when he swung at the first ball delivered to him. The bat flew from his hands and went whizzing through the air.

"Duck!" he yelled.

Ready "ducked" just in time to let the bat go over him.

"I pray thee be cautious," said Jack, as he straightened up. "What hast thou against me?"

"You're too handsome," answered Wiley. "I hate to behold a man who is handsomer than I."

The bat was returned to him, and he again took his place in the batter's box.

"Is that the way you hit it?" derisively called a spectator. "I don't think you'll drive it very far."

"Think again, Willie," advised the sailor. "You have one more coming, but you don't look to me as if you could stand it. Your thinking apparatus must be strained to its full capacity to grind out one whole thought a day."

Then he turned to Frank.

"We're old college chumps, aren't we, Merry?" he inquired.

"Sure," nodded Frank.

"Then give me a straight one right over the plate. I don't like that new kink you're pitching. It's like a foreign language to me. I'll make it all right with you if you give me one I can hit."

He smiled in his bland manner and seemed to think Merry would comply.

"Here it is," laughed Frank.

It seemed like a straight one, and the sailor swung hard a second time.

He struck under it several inches, for the ball swerved upward and outward in the same remarkable manner that had bothered every batter to face Merry.

"Two strikes!" declared the umpire.

"That's criminal, Merry—criminal!" exclaimed Wiley reproachfully. "How could you deceive your bosom friend like that? I thought guile and deception was not to be found in your heart, but now, alas! I realize that you are like other mortals of common clay."

Wiley now became the butt of ridicule for the crowd, but he did not mind it in the least. In fact, the more they tried to josh and guy him the more he seemed to like it.

He declined to swing at two coaxers.

"Nay, nay, Merry!" cried the sailor. "I am onto your tricks now. You would betray your bosom comrade. You'll have to put it over before I wiggle my wand again."

"I see you are onto me," said Merry. "It is useless for me to try to fool you, so I'll give you one straight over. Here it is."

Merry threw his peculiar "dope ball." Even though Wiley himself was a pitcher, and he often used a slow ball, he was fooled this time. It seemed to come up as large as a balloon, and he struck at it.

He hit it, too.

But he simply popped a tiny little fly into the air, and Merry sprang forward and caught it.

The spectators roared and shouted, asking the sailor if that was his wonderful four-base hit.

Wiley shook his head sadly.

"Never again as long as I tread this terrestrial sphere shall I trust human nature," he declared, ambling toward the bench. "I have been basely betrayed. But wait—my revenge is yet to come, and it shall be deep and terrible."

O'Neill longed to make a safe hit, but he was another of the batters that Merry fanned easily.

Then came Creel, and he bunted.

Again Ready got the ball in time to throw the man out, but once more he made a poor throw.

Browning was dragged off the base, and Creel reached it in safety.

Instantly Wiley appeared on the coaching line and opened up merrily.

He gave Creel the signal to try to steal second.

"May as well take chances," he muttered. "We'll never get a score any other way."

So the runner attempted a steal on the first ball Frank pitched to Marcey.

The ball came whistling into the hands of Hodge. Bart seemed to pause a moment and watch Creel on his way to second. Then he made a throw that sent the ball down on a dead line and straight into the hands of Rattleton, who was waiting.

Creel slid, but Harry nailed him, and the third inning was over.

CHAPTER XIX.

A GAME WORTH WINNING.

ell, what do you think of it, Gowan?" laughed old man Grafter, as the seventh inning closed with the score still one to nothing in favor of the Merries.

McGann had joined Gowan. He showed that he was worried.

"Think?" wheezed the corpulent backer of the Outcasts. "I think it's something unreasonable. I believe Merriwell has bought the game!"

"No, no!" said McGann, shaking his head. "You're wrong, Bob."

"Then why don't they bat that fellow?"

"He's using a new curve, and they can't hit it. Hurley says it's something absolutely novel."

"Well, are they going to let this fellow hold them down and break their streak?" wheezed Gowan angrily. "I have money bet on this game. Wake them up and get them into it. They've got to win!"

Mike Grafter laughed.

"No use to squirm, Gowan, my boy," he said. "We've got you."

"If they lose this game, McGann," said Gowan, "I lose a thousand dollars."

"That's not all we lose," said McGann. "I have a contract with Merriwell by which the winners take all the gate money."

"What?" gasped Gowan.

"That's right. He sort of forced me into it. Refused every other offer I made."

"Oh, no!" exclaimed Wallace Grafter. "You forget that I was present, Mr. McGann, when the arrangement was made."

"Well, he refused every reasonable offer."

"Not at all. He was willing to play with the understanding that the winners should have two-thirds and the losers one-third. He even offered to split the receipts even."

"Well, was that reasonable?" snapped McGann. "Here we have

the reputation, and a youngster like him wants to split even with us."

"It might have been better for you than the arrangement you made. If you do not get a dollar, you'll have no one but yourself to blame."

"They must win!" growled McGann.

He left the bleachers and hurried to the bench, where he waited to speak with Captain Hurley.

In the first half of the seventh the Merries fell on the ball hard, three men making long drives to the outfield, but the fielders were able to catch each one, and so there was no danger of more scores for Frank.

"We must do something, Hurley!" exclaimed McGann, as the captain of the Outcasts reached the bench. "If we lose this game, all the gate money goes to those chaps."

"How is that?"

McGann explained.

"That's bad," admitted Hurley. "We've been doing everything in our power. The boys can't bear the thought of being beaten by those chaps, but we can't seem to hit Merriwell. That new curve of his is a puzzler."

McGann implored Hurley to do something, but again he was assured that everything possible was being done.

However, there was some excitement in that inning. The Outcasts had found they could hit Merry safely only by bunting. Marcey, however, was an easy out at first. Bimm followed with a bunt that rolled foul, then struck a pebble and rolled fair again.

Merry got it and snapped it to Browning, who muffed it.

Bimm crossed first in safety.

The Outcasts began to whoop things up. They had many sympathizers in the crowd, and a great uproar arose.

Hurley followed with a bunt that landed Bimm on second.

The captain of the Outcasts was thrown out at first.

Swatt longed to "lace" the ball, but Hurley was positive in his signal for a bunt and he obeyed.

The bunt was sent down the line toward third.

Bimm raced for third as he saw Ready come off for the ball. Morgan covered the sack and Ready snapped the ball to him, instead of throwing to first. In his haste, Jack made a bad throw, and Morgan barely touched it with his fingers.

"Up!" yelled Wiley, who was on the coaching line. "Up and sail for port! Hooray, the score is tied! Now we'll win! I knew the disgrace of defeat could not fall on us!"

Bimm scrambled up and scooted for the plate, while the spectators rose and watched, some yelling for joy.

Bob Gowan yelled as loudly as his wheezy voice would permit, at the same time slapping Grafter on the shoulder.

"It's our game, after all!" he said. "Right here is where we win it!"

Among the spectators another man was highly elated. He was Hobe Manton, who whooped lustily.

"That's the trick!" he shouted. "I thought my money was gone, but now I feel it in my pocket with some more to keep it company."

Of course Melvin McGann was delighted.

But suddenly something happened to change the tune of the rejoicing ones. Apparently no one had observed that Buck Badger had worked in from the far outfield until he was not a great distance behind third. He happened to be in the right place to get the ball with little delay. Bimm was halfway from third to the plate when Badger threw.

Hodge was on the plate. He saw the ball coming, but did not put up his hands until it was quite near. An instant after he did put them up the ball spanked into them.

Bimm had not been warned, and he had made no effort to slide. Bart stepped off instantly and met him, tagging him with the ball.

There was silence—then another roar. This time the Merriwell admirers shouted.

"What's this?" gasped Cap'n Wiley, looking round in amazement. "Who threw in that ball?"

The umpire declared Bimm out.

Wiley saw that Badger had thrown the ball, and his head dropped.

"Alas!" he muttered; "thus my fondest hopes vanish one by one. It has been thus ever since the days of my innocent boyhood on Nigger Island."

Mike Grafter smote Bob Gowan on the shoulder and yelled with delight, while Gowan seemed ready to collapse in a heap.

"Ha! ha! ha!" roared Grafter. "Ho! ho! ho! The wind changed suddenly, Bob. It's different now. They're all out. It's over, my boy. They won't have another chance like that. The game is just the same as finished."

"I dunno but you're right," admitted Gowan weakly. "That was awful! I'll never recover from it."

Frank congratulated Badger as the Kansan came in.

"The right man in the right place, Buck!" he said. "That was pretty work."

Wiley was silent now. An atmosphere of sadness had fallen on him, and his mouth was closed.

Perhaps no one present felt worse than Hobe Manton.

"Rotten! rotten! rotten!" he kept repeating. "If they'd tied it then they would have won. I've lost my money! I'm busted."

"It looks that way," said Dent Frost.

"And we've lost something on your advice," muttered Necker sourly.

The ninth inning was a swift one. O'Neill held the Merries down, but in turn Frank did not permit a single one of the three Outcasts to face him to touch the ball. All through the game he had done his level best, and the new curve had kept the great Outcasts from doing any hitting.

The game ended with the score one to nothing in favor of the Merries, who were wildly cheered by their admirers as the conquering heroes who had broken the wonderful streak of the Outcasts.

As the crowd was leaving the ground a sudden uproar broke forth. Two men were engaged in a hand-to-hand encounter not far from the home plate.

Pink Cassidy had stopped Hobe Manton and demanded the money promised him.

Manton promptly hit Cassidy, nearly knocking him down.

With a roar, Pink recovered and went at the gentleman pugilist, who immediately found that he had a real fight on his hands.

The uproar alarmed Frost and Necker.

"This is no place for us!" exclaimed Frost.

"Right!" agreed Necker. "Skip!"

They lost not a moment in getting away.

Two officers reached the fighting men and hesitated not a moment about using their clubs. Both chaps were stretched out and then arrested.

As the fighters were being dragged from the grounds Merry got a good look at one of them.

"Hello!" he cried. "So it's you, Manton! Well, you're in trouble, as you deserve. Lock him up, Mr. Officer; if you hold him long enough I'll have something in the way of a warrant to serve on him."

"Ye'll have plenty av chance, sor," said the policeman.

CHAPTER XX.

THE BITTERNESS OF DEFEAT.

The Johns Hopkins lacrosse team claimed the championship of the United States, yet in a fast game at Oriole Park, Baltimore, it had been defeated by Harvard, the score being four to three. One thing that made the pill doubly bitter was the fact that the Hopkins men had been inclined to believe before the game began that they would whitewash the chaps from Cambridge. As if to add to the bitterness, Hopkins made her three goals before Harvard scored at all, which led her players and their admirers to believe the game was safely won.

Then the tide turned. Hopkins made two goals in the first half and one early in the second half. This in spite of the fact that Harvard had kept the ball in the home team's territory the greater part of the time and had repeatedly seemed on the point of scoring. The fine work of the Hopkins' cover-point and the brilliant stops made by her goal keeper had checked Harvard time after time. At last the crimson scored and the back flow began.

Fred Fillmore, cover-point for Hopkins and captain of the team, had already recognized the fact that Harvard was a dangerous proposition. On the Harvard team were several old Hopkins players who added greatly to the strength of the boys from Cambridge. Their poor success in the early part of the game did not discourage them in the least, and they kept up the fast offense play of the team.

Harvard's greatest player was Herbert Onslaw, captain and first attack. Onslaw was swift, untiring, cool, and heady. He gave Fillmore no end of trouble, and the Hopkins captain gradually grew annoyed, for more than once he was tricked by Onslaw's rapid and clever playing. He realized that the crimson leader was showing him up in a bad light, and he was anxious to get even by turning the tables.

The Hopkins spectators were dismayed by Harvard's success in scoring, but they did not foresee the impending danger that was plainly discerned by Fillmore. The Hopkins captain decided to give more of his attention to Onslaw.

Shortly after Harvard secured her first goal she again obtained the ball, which, by good running and clever passing, was delivered to Onslaw, who rushed it into position to try for goal. The Hopkins goal tender spoiled the try and cuffed the ball away. A mix-up followed, and out of the scrambling players the ball was shot.

Onslaw seemed waiting in the proper spot for it, but Fillmore had chosen to hug him close. Instantly the Harvard captain started, but Fillmore started at the same time. Onslaw dashed toward the Hopkins goal. Fillmore was at his side and tried a body check. Onslaw crouched and came under Fillmore's hip. As a result, the Hopkins man was sent flying through the air and struck the ground heavily. He tried to get up, but fell over on his side and lay twisting on the ground.

The whistle sounded, and it was found that Fillmore's hip had been badly hurt, so that he could not then bear his weight on that leg. Although he insisted that he would be all right in a few minutes, he did not recover and was obliged to drop out of the game.

Lying on a blanket at one side of the field, Fillmore watched his team fighting desperately against the swift and determined Harvard men. His heart was filled with rage and bitterness, for, although his own attempt at body-checking an opponent had brought about his injury, he blamed Onslaw. When, a few minutes later, he saw Onslaw shoot the ball into the net he fairly writhed in mental pain, his injured hip being forgotten.

Hopkins still had a lead of one goal, and the spectators believed this lead would be held, for the second half was well along. A bunch of rooters cheered and cheered to urge the local men at their best efforts; but a much smaller bunch of Harvard admirers made much more noise.

Fillmore's eyes glittered as he watched Onslaw's swift and graceful movements.

"I'll settle with you some day!" muttered the injured captain of the local team.

He was inclined to be revengeful. Being a fine athlete, a handsome fellow, and the admired idol of his team, Fillmore was conceited and spoiled. He was a splendid player, but regarded himself as even better than he actually was. It had always filled his heart with fiery bitterness when Hopkins had gone down in defeat before the swift Canadians, who never failed to show their superiority when Hopkins met the champions from the North. It had been his ambition to develop at Hopkins a team that could hold its own with the Canadians, as well as defeat all opponents in the United States; but now he realized that unless the Baltimore lads could do better against the Cambridgeites, they would have very little show with the boys from beyond the northern border.

It must not be supposed from this that Hopkins was weak in any respect; instead of that, the team was faster than ever before in all the years lacrosse had been played in Baltimore. But the former Hopkins men on the Harvard team had coached their fellows to meet and offset the plays of the Marylanders, and Harvard had progressed fully as fast as Hopkins.

Therefore Fillmore was doomed to see the crimson players keep at it with such earnestness and skill that, three minutes before the time of the second half elapsed, another goal was made and the Southerners were tied.

But no one seemed prepared for what followed. Hopkins took the ball on the face-off, carried it down to Harvard's end, tried three times to score, lost the ball, saw it sail up the field, saw Onslaw take it in, and try to score, saw it driven back, secured, passed to Onslaw again, and then Onslaw sent it whizzing into the net!

Almost immediately the whistle sounded, and the game was over.

Fillmore fell back and covered his eyes with his hands, biting his lip to keep from cursing the fates. He was white as death, and a comrade who was near fancied he must be suffering fearful pain from his injured hip. It was, however, mental anguish whichdrove the blood from his face, bodily pain being entirely forgotten for the time.

"Onslaw did it!" he whispered, with blue lips. "He knocked me out on purpose! I'll get even with him if I live long enough! I'll find a way!"

It seemed that Fillmore's longing for revenge was destined to go ungratified for an indefinite period. Harvard played no second game with Hopkins that season, and Onslaw was a senior who would leave college before the two teams could meet again.

One warm spring evening Fillmore sauntered up McCulloh Street and paused at the steps of a students' boarding house, on which a number of young fellows were sitting. He was hailed by several of them and paused to chat with his particular chum, Tom Hackett, who played centre on the lacrosse team.

"Haven't seen you for several days to more than chirp at you," said Hackett. "Where have you been keeping yourself?"

"Home."

"Must be plugging hard. You missed lots of fun last night. Party of us went down to the Monumental. Hot show there this week. Say, there are actually some pretty girls in the bunch. One is a peach."

"Oh, they give me lassitude!" retorted Fillmore. "They're too cheap. Picked out of the slums. When you get to talking with 'em, and see just how coarse they are they make you sick. I've been seeing something more interesting. Speaking of dark-eyed girls, I'd like to show you one stopping over at my sister's, where I board."

"What's that?" cried Hackett. "Ah! so that's why you've been under cover lately! Ah-ha! The cat is out!"

"I suppose that has had something to do with it," admitted the captain of the lacrosse team honestly. "This one is something entirely different from the kind you were talking about. Better drop over and see her. There's another one there, a blonde; but she's been ill, and she's far from well now. The brunette and the blonde are great friends. The blonde is some distant relative of John Loder, my sister's husband. I should say she ought to be a daisy when she's well, for she's pretty now, although she hasn't any color. Got a bad cold last winter and had to go South. The brunette went with her. They're staying here in Baltimore until the weather gets settled so that the blonde can go farther North without danger."

"Oh, you sly dog!" laughed Hackett. "Supposed you were plugging, and you've been lingering near two pretty girls. Thought it strange you broke away so suddenly after practice the last few days. I suppose you'll find time to play Saturday?"

"You know I will. I'm not as far gone as that, although the black eyes of Inza have rather upset me."

"Inza—that's her name?"

"Yes. Hack, she's the most beautiful girl I have ever seen. She's a real queen, and no mistake. She's cultured, and she's traveled a great deal in this country and foreign lands. She's so sympathetic, too. You should see how she cares for Elsie."

"Elsie—she's the invalid?"

"Yes. She's a sort of invalid, although she won't acknowledge it, and she's the bravest little creature in the world. Inza told me that Elsie was very ill this winter, but she wouldn't acknowledge it to any one. Just drop round to-morrow evening and I'll present you to both girls, though I warn you not to get smashed on Inza. It won't do any good, and it may make you uncomfortable."

"Oh, I see; you're going to make a set for her yourself. Come,

come, Fillmore! I didn't think you'd go daft over any girl."

"Rot! I haven't. It's no use. I know better than that, old man. She's good company, and I like her; but she is the kind to hold a fellow off and wither him with her eyes if he gets a bit fresh. I wouldn't dare attempt to make love to her. I'd get a call quicker than lightning."

"And that makes her all the more interesting and attractive. Oh, yes it does! All the girls have been mashed on you, and you've turned up your aristocratic nose at them. Now you happen to find one who doesn't think you are the luminary of the world, and the result is that you're a goner. Well, well, well!"

"Not very well, thank you," returned Fillmore. "Don't get a notion that you're a Solomon. I'm playing my own game with the young lady of the dark eyes. She can't fool me a great deal, Tom. It's rather interesting sport. I'm taking care not to let myself get too far gone, for I know it's hopeless. She's engaged and soon to be married."

Hackett whistled.

"Engaged, eh? But then you know more than one engagement has been smashed. You might cut the fellow out. Who is he?"

"None other than Frank Merriwell, the former great Yale athlete."

Hackett whistled again.

"That fellow, eh? I've met some chaps who seemed to think him the wizard of the world. Let me see, hasn't he been touring lately with an athletic team and simply eating everything up that he came across?"

"Yes, he's been covering himself with glory in every department of sport. What do you think he's doing now?"

"Give it up."

"Organizing a lacrosse team, with the idea of going after the amateur championship of the United States. He wants a game with us. Of course we don't have to play him, but I understand he expects to have Onslaw and several other Harvard players on his team."

A third time Hackett whistled.

"What do you say to that? Do you want to play him, Fred?"

"I don't mind. His team will be easy for us, and it might give us a chance to rub it into those Harvard chaps some. Besides that, I've been thinking, if he really gets Onslaw, it might make an opening for me to even up with that duffer."

"Sure thing, old man! You've been pining for such a chance. But the success of Merriwell in other things seems to proclaim it possible that he will succeed at lacrosse."

"Don't be silly, Hack! Do you fancy a picked-up team can beat us? I guess not! It takes teamwork to play the game, and a team, in order to be great, must work together a long time. We're at our best now. If we were to go against Harvard again we'd white-wash 'em."

"I believe that."

"I know it. Oh, I don't fear Merriwell's team in the least. He'll have some dubs on it. One fellow is Bart Hodge, who is engaged to Elsie Bellwood, the invalid. She hasn't wanted him to know anything about her illness, and so it has been kept from him. She thought he would leave Frank, and she says Merriwell can't get along without Hodge as a catcher in all baseball games, so she kept her illness quiet."

"It's plain you're decidedly in favor of playing Merriwell's team."

"Rather."

"Well, I think what you say about it will go. Have you any positive reason to believe he wants a game with Hopkins?"

"Why, yes; Inza—or, Miss Burrage—told me he wrote expressing such a desire. She is anxious for us to give him a game."

"And that has a great deal to do with your feelings," laughed Hackett.

"Oh, I wouldn't mind beating Mr. Merriwell, just to take some of the confidence out of Miss Inza. It would please me to show him up before her."

"Go ahead. I think you can fix it."

"If I knew he'd have Onslaw I wouldn't hesitate. Just as soon as I find out Onslaw will play with Merriwell's team I'll inform Miss Burrage that we're simply waiting for a challenge or a proposition from Merriwell."

"That will be all right!" exclaimed Hackett. "I wouldn't mind getting against Mr. Merriwell at something and rubbing it into him. I'm tired of hearing him proclaimed the greatest all-round wonder the United States has produced."

"So am I. And Miss Burrage has an idea that he cannot be downed. She smiles scornfully when I hint that Merriwell has had luck and might meet with just as many defeats if his luck turned. Then Miss Bellwood is equally confident."

"Say, old man, I'm going to accept your invitation and come round to get a look at these girls."

"All right, but remember my warning about the black-eyed one. She'll take your fancy, but that won't do you any good."

"Oh, I don't know!" said Hackett teasingly. "I think I see through your little game. You're planning to get on the inside track and push Merriwell out. Better keep me away. I might steal a march on you, old man."

Fillmore flushed.

"I'm not worrying about that," he declared, as he rose to leave.

"You're hit hard," chuckled Hackett, also rising. "I'll walk down the street with you. This Inza must be a peach to upset level-headed Fred Fillmore after such a fashion."

CHAPTER XXI.

THE PANGS OF JEALOUSY.

illmore, who did not live in Baltimore, boarded with his sister, Mrs. Loder, on Calvert Street. He returned to his sister's home, his mind occupied with thoughts of lacrosse and Inza Burrage. It must be confessed that he thought more of Inza than of the game at which he had won fame among his college mates.

Reaching home, he found his sister and casually asked about the girls.

"They're in their room, Fred," smiled Mrs. Loder. "I don't think you'll see anything more of them this evening. Be careful, you bad boy! you're becoming altogether too interested in Miss Burrage. I'm afraid those eyes of hers have wrought havoc with your heart."

"Nonsense!" he laughed. "How foolish you are to get such a notion, sis. I like her because she's so bright and interesting. I'm not the sort of fellow to get broken up over any girl. They're all alike to me."

"Oh, I've heard youngsters like you talk before! You can't fool an old married woman. I've seen what was going on."

In vain he protested that there was nothing "going on."

"You can't fool me," she repeated. "Inza Burrage is handsome and fascinating, and you've been sticking to the house in a most amazing way since she arrived. Haven't you learned that she's engaged to a Mr. Merriwell?"

"Of course."

"She's in love with him, too, so it won't do you any good to waste your time. Don't get to mooning round her. She's aware that you are interested, and I think it's beginning to annoy her. I have a fancy that's one reason why both girls are sticking so close to their room to-night. They're keeping away from you."

"They don't have to!" he muttered, his pride touched and his cheeks hot.

Then he wandered off by himself, turned on the electric light in the little reading room back of the parlor, flung himself on a leather-covered Morris chair and studied for an hour. Finally his thoughts wandered from his studies and he dropped the book. His eyes had begun to smart and burn, and he turned off the light.

The doorbell rang. It was answered by a colored maid, and two young men entered. They gave the colored girl their cards, and she told them to step into the parlor and wait.

The sliding door between the parlor and the little room occupied by Fillmore was partly open. He caught a glimpse of the two visitors and saw that both were fine-looking fellows. One had dark hair and eyes. The other sat down where Fred could see him. The light fell full on his face, and the youth on the Morris chair noted its unusual strength and manly beauty. The longer he gazed at that face the more deeply he was impressed by a conviction that the young man was a person of great ability and force who was destined to make a mark in the world.

"This will be a great surprise for the girls," said the one of the dark hair.

He of the fine face smiled, and his smile was fully as wonderful as the face which it lighted.

"They will be more than surprised," he said.

A few moments there came a rustling on the carpeted stairs. With a rush that was little short of a run, Inza Burrage came down, followed a little later by Elsie Bellwood.

Inza, her eyes shining like twin stars, her cheeks aglow, entered the room. The youth of the fine face sprang toward her and she was clasped in his arms.

"Inza!" he cried, his voice hoarse with deep feeling.

"Frank!" she answered. "Oh, Frank! Frank!"

He kissed her again and again.

Fred Fillmore started up, feeling in his bosom a terrible sensation that he had never before experienced. He could not bear to see her held thus in those strong arms and kissed in that manner. In his heart something seemed ready to burst. For a moment he stood with his hands clenched, longing to rush in there and tear her from the man.

Then he turned away and fled with noiseless steps.

"That's the man!" hissed Fillmore, as he found his way to the rear of the house and ascended the back stairs. "That's Merriwell!"

He was astounded by his own emotions. He felt himself quivering from head to feet. Reaching his own room by way of the back stairs, he paced excitedly up and down.

"I'd like to punch him!" he huskily muttered. "Jingoes! what is the matter with me? It made me furious to see him kiss her. I didn't suppose anything could give me a feeling like that. What is the matter with me?"

He was somewhat dismayed over it. After a time he slowly murmured:

"By Jove! I am stuck on that girl! I didn't know it before. That's what ails me. If any one had told me I was hit so hard I'd felt like punching him. What am I going to do about it?"

There didn't seem to be much of anything to do, but his brain was awhirl, scores of wild fancies and ideas flashing through it. For a long time he paced up and down, gradually growing calmer. Finally he left his room and descended by the front stairs, whistling.

In a careless manner he strolled into the parlor, stopping short and ceasing to whistle in apparent surprise as he beheld the four persons there.

"I beg your pardon!" he exclaimed, starting to retreat.

Inza rose.

"Mr. Fillmore," she called.

"Miss Burrage," he bowed. "I didn't mean to intrude. I didn't know——"

"No intrusion," she assured. "Let me introduce you to Mr. Merriwell. Frank, this is Mr. Fillmore, Mrs. Loder's brother."

"Glad to know you, Mr. Fillmore," said Merriwell genially, as he grasped Fred's hand. "Miss Burrage wrote me about you. You're captain of the Hopkins lacrosse team, I think?"

"I have that honor."

"An honor it is," nodded Merry. "You are captain of the lacrosse champions of the United States at the present time."

Fillmore was then introduced to Bart Hodge.

He noted that an unusual tide of color had suffused the cheeks of Elsie Bellwood, and now, of a sudden, he realized that she, like Inza, was a wonderfully pretty girl. The two girls were of strongly contrasting types.

"Mr. Fillmore has been very good to us, Bart," said Elsie.

"Which places Frank and me under untold obligations to him," said Hodge. "I have only one fault to find with him. He should have written me that you were ill. It was a crime for you girls to keep it from me."

"I wanted to write," said Inza; "but she wouldn't let me tell you that."

"Why, it was nothing," declared Elsie. "I wasn't going to break up your trip just because I happened to be a bit out of sorts. I suppose the climate was too severe after spending the early part of the winter in the West."

"We wanted you to keep on with us," reminded Frank. "It was your own fault that you returned East when you did."

Fillmore was urged to sit down, and he accepted the invitation.

"Let's see," he said, "I believe Miss Burrage told me you were organizing a lacrosse team, Mr. Merriwell."

"It's practically organized," nodded Merry. "We're going to play a few games at the close of the college season. We've arranged for two games already."

Fillmore lifted his eyebrows in surprise.

"Well, you're a hustler!" he smiled. "Are you going to have some Harvard players on your team?"

"Five of them. Three were former Hopkins men."

"Will Herb Onslaw be one of the five?"

"Yes."

"I don't see how you induced him to play on a team where some one else is to be captain."

"Oh, that wasn't difficult. I think Onslaw's a very decent and modest chap."

"You don't know him!"

"It seems that you don't like Onslaw."

"Not much, for I know he's full of wind. He was dreadfully puffed up because Harvard happened to win from us. You know I was hurt in the game and did not play during most of the second half."

Hodge shrugged his shoulders and his lip curled the least bit. He detected the conceit in Fillmore.

"I know about that. It was very unfortunate," said Merry.

"Of course I'm not saying we'd won if I hadn't been hurt, but we had the lead when that happened. I think Onslaw was glad to see me go out of the game."

"He didn't appear to me like a malicious chap."

"Oh, I presume he's smooth enough. Sorry he'll not be with Harvard next year. I'd like to get against him again."

"Possibly you will. We'll give you a game right after the close of college, as soon as you like. I'd like to make arrangements for the game while in Baltimore. Of course, it's possible your team will not play us, but we're very anxious, and you shall have our first game together, if you'll take it."

"Why, I wouldn't be surprised if it might be fixed that way. Are you going to challenge us?"

"Hadn't thought of making it a challenge. Just fancied we might arrange a meeting, that's all. Still, if you think we'd better make it a challenge——"

"I don't suppose it will make any difference. How long will you remain in the city?"

"Until the day after to-morrow."

"Well, I'll introduce you to our manager to-morrow, and you can see what you can do. I'll urge him to make the game with you."

"Do! Who's your coach, Abercrombie?"

"He's one of them."

"Good man. No one in this country knows more about the game."

"Who'll coach your team?"

"We're going to have a Canadian."

"Oh!" exclaimed Fillmore. "You're going in for the real thing! Some day we'll put it all over those Canucks!"

"Perhaps so," admitted Frank; "but, to tell you the truth, I fear the players of this country will have to improve faster than they have to get away with the Canadians. We can trounce them at baseball; but at lacrosse and ice hockey they are going to keep the lead for some time."

"Don't you believe it!" cried the Hopkins captain. "Their day is coming right soon. I'll admit that they still outrank us, but the sport is comparatively new with us. We have not given it enough attention, and it hasn't become popular with the public. It deserves to become popular."

"It will," asserted Frank. "When people begin to realize what a pretty game it is they'll take to it. The public has to be educated up to a thing like that. Lacrosse has hardly any of the dangerous elements of football, yet it is exciting, and the open playing permits spectators to see almost constantly everything that is taking place. There is no more graceful game played."

"Why, you're a real enthusiast!" said Fillmore.

"Just as I am an enthusiast in all clean, healthy sports. I believe in such things, and I take hold of them with delight. I've seen lacrosse played in Canada, and the work of two well-matched teams up there puts us in the shade. However, let the public show the interest for lacrosse that it has in college baseball and we'll witness great advancement in the next few years."

"Have you played lacrosse yourself, Mr. Merriwell?"

"A little."

"It's a game at which practice counts for a great deal."

"Like baseball. Mere strength is of small matter in lacrosse. Speed, skill, nerve, and brains all come in. In this respect it has some advantages over football."

"Well, you can discuss all that to-morrow!" laughed Inza. "Just now I'm in favor of talking about other things. If you play the game here, Elsie and I will attend and root. Won't we, Elsie?"

"I wouldn't miss it for the world," answered Elsie.

"You'll see something that will give you small satisfaction," thought Fillmore; but he kept his thought to himself.

CHAPTER XXII.

OUT ON THE PIMLICO ROAD.

The following afternoon Frank and Bart took the girls out for a carriage ride. Although Elsie enjoyed it greatly, she soon became tired, and it was necessary to return with her.

On returning to the house they were greeted by Fillmore, who came out at once as he saw the girls being assisted from the carriage.

"Well, I'm glad we struck you this way," he said. "Been having a drive, eh? Hope you enjoyed it."

"It was delightful," said Elsie; "but I spoiled it by getting tired so soon."

"We're going to see 'The School Girl' to-night," explained Inza; "so we decided it was better not to weary Elsie too much."

"Oh, you've made arrangements for to-night, have you, Merriwell?" cried Fillmore. "I thought I might take you out to see some of the fellows this evening."

Immediately both girls expressed a willingness to give up the theatre, but neither Frank nor Bart would listen to that.

"Then," said Fillmore, "we can find Jack Branch this afternoon and fix it up about that game. Branch is our manager, you know. What he says will go, all right, all right. I know where to find him. He's out at Hastings', on the Pimlico Road. Hastings runs a road house. What say if we hike out there right away, Merriwell?"

"I'm willing," nodded Frank. "How'll we go?"

"Oh, any way. We can take a car, but, of course, it would be better to drive."

"Here's the team," smiled Merry. "We engaged it for the afternoon, and the afternoon is not more than half over."

"Good!" cried Fillmore. "Wait till I call Hackett. He's here with me."

Tom Hackett came out of the house when he was called. He

was introduced to Elsie and Inza and surveyed the girls keenly, but not offensively. He shook hands with seeming warmth with Frank and Bart.

"Powerful glad to know you, gentlemen," he said. "Fillmore told me about your arrival last night. Of course I've heard more or less concerning you at other times."

He was told of the plan to drive out on the Pimlico Road and immediately declared it would give him pleasure to go along.

"Wait a moment," said Fillmore, "and I'll be ready."

He then ran into the house and did some telephoning.

Soon the quartette was ready to start. As they drove away they lifted their hats to the girls, who had lingered on the steps outside the door. Fillmore noticed that Hackett turned to look back and fancied he did so to obtain another view of Inza.

It was a beautiful drive out along Mount Royal Avenue and through Druid Hill Park to the Pimlico Road. They chatted freely, their talk being mainly of such sports as must interest college men.

"What sort of a place is this road house we're going to?" inquired Frank.

"It's all right," answered Fillmore. "The fellows go out there often. Hastings knows how to use us. Occasionally we pull off a little scrap out there. He has a room fitted up for it, and I've seen some right good fights in his place. Not regular prize fights, you know, but bouts between amateurs. If you want the real thing, you'll have to go to the old Armory."

"I'm not at all particular about the real thing," confessed Merry. "Prize fighting is a bit out of my line."

"Seems to me I've heard that you were something of a boxer."

"Oh, I know a little about it; but what I know I learned for the purpose of being able to defend myself when necessary. I have a belief that every fellow should be able to do that."

"That's right, too," said Hackett. "Lots of fellows take lessons of Galway, at Hastings'."

"Who's Galway?"

"He's a boxing master, and a great fighter himself. He knocked out Johnny Neil at the Armory two weeks ago, and Neil had ambitions to meet Jeffries. When he gets mad he sometimes hammers a pupil. He hangs round Hastings' place the most of the time."

"If he didn't lush he'd be a wonder," put in Fillmore. "He has an awful wallop. Puts 'em all to sleep."

"I don't think Mr. Galway interests me," laughed Merry. "I shall take pains to keep clear of him."

In due time they arrived at Hastings' place. As soon as they appeared they were hailed with shouts of welcome from several young fellows, who were sitting on the broad veranda.

"There's Branch, Whisper, and the others," said Fillmore. "I telephoned before we started, and they're looking for us."

A colored man appeared and took charge of the horses as soon as they drove up. A few moments later Frank and Bart were shaking hands with the Hopkins men on the veranda, Fillmore introducing them.

Jack Branch, the manager of the lacrosse team, was a shrewd-faced, freckled chap, sharp-voiced and gimlet-eyed. He was a Connecticut Yankee, and had been appointed manager of the team on account of his natural shrewdness.

While Frank and Bart were chatting with their new acquaintances Fillmore and Hackett entered the house.

"It's worked well thus far," said Fillmore. "Now, if we can send Mr. Merriwell and Mr. Hodge back to their ladies with a jag on, I'll be satisfied. I'd like to show Merriwell up to Inza. He's going to take her out to the theatre to-night. We'll keep him and Hodge here for dinner and fill them up. Then we can take them directly to my sister's house and show them off in all their glory."

"You certainly have it in for Merriwell, all right," grinned Hackett.

"I have. Didn't I see him meet Inza Burrage and kiss her! She thinks he's perfection. She even told me he didn't drink; but I know better."

"Of course he takes something, but it's plain he's been telling her different. Is she straight-laced?"

"She thinks drinking debasing."

"A bit old-fashioned for a girl of to-day, eh?"

"It seems to be behind the times, but somehow I can't help respecting her for it."

"Why, I've heard you laugh about blue stockings more than once. You've told me you had no use for a girl who would not take a glass of wine and be jolly."

"I thought so; but Inza Burrage can be jolly without taking a glass of wine. The girl who drinks a little is all right to fool with, but I've concluded she isn't the sort to get smashed on."

"Then you are smashed on Inza Burrage? You admit it!"

"Between you and me, old man, something is the matter with me. When I saw Merriwell kiss her last night I wanted to rush in and take him by the throat. I got up to my room and decided to make him look like thirty cents to her. That's why I'm taking all this trouble. That's why I fixed it with Branch and the others to meet him out here. That's why I paid for the automobile that brought them out ahead of us. I had the auto waiting to start when I gave the word. Didn't you notice I wasn't in any hurry about driving here?"

"Sure."

"I didn't propose to arrive ahead of Branch."

"Well, while we're loading Mr. Merriwell let's not neglect Mr. Hodge."

"Hodge? Oh, of course not; but it doesn't make so much difference about him."

"Yes, it does."

"How's that?"

"I want to show him up to Miss Bellwood."

"Eh? Why——"

"You may have your dark-eyed peach—if you can get her; give me the other girl. She's the first blonde I ever saw who upset me, and she gave me the solar-plexus blow the instant I saw her."

Fillmore was astounded.

"What's that?" he gasped. "You don't mean to tell me that you consider her prettier than Inza?"

"That's just what I mean to tell you. She has the sweetest face of any girl I ever saw. In perfect health, I know she would be a hundred times prettier than Inza."

"Well, I admire your taste!" But the tone in which he uttered the words indicated that he did not admire it.

"That's all right. We can't all think the same. I'm sincere, old man. Give me Elsie, and you may have Inza."

The captain of the lacrosse team grasped his friend's hand.

"My boy," he breathed, "take her, with my blessing. Now we can work in unison and harmony. I'm delighted! Let's get those chaps filled to the brim to-day. That will be a beginning. Then if we can just put it all over them when we meet them at lacrosse—well, we'll be progressing. In the meantime, we may find still other ways of making them appear cheap in the eyes of their admiring ladies. Good luck to us! Disgrace to them!"

CHAPTER XXIII.

AT THE ROAD HOUSE.

Frank and Bart found their new acquaintances inclined to be a roistering set. This seemed quite unaccountable as far as Branch was concerned. To Merriwell the fellow from Connecticut seemed like almost anything other than a roisterer.

Frank talked with Branch about the game, and the Hopkins manager agreed that, unless something unexpected prevented, he would try to arrange it. He displayed a great amount of cordiality, but he chucklingly assured Merriwell that Hopkins would have a snap.

"We'll take chances on that," said Frank.

Terms were agreed upon. This was not difficult, as both managers knew the sport might not turn out a large crowd, and Frank was not inclined to be exacting. He was willing to play for pleasure, even if it cost him something.

"You see," he said, "I'm pretty near the end of my sporting trip. I shall leave for Old Mexico in the latter part of July."

"You're choosing a hot season for such a trip, aren't you?"

"Well, it's necessary. But you know they have all sorts of climates in Mexico. In some localities they have delightful weather the whole year round. Indeed, there are places where they never have such hot weather as you experience here. Baltimore is a fine place to bake in summer."

"Oh, Connecticut is good enough for me, then," grinned Branch. "We've had some mighty hot weather already."

Fillmore and some others joined them.

"Well, have you two fixed it all up?" asked Fred.

"As far as possible, I think," nodded Frank.

"I guess it's just the same as fixed," said Branch.

"And the game——"

"We'll pull it off if the committee don't kick up on us."

"Good enough! I've called a waiter, and he's bringing us a round of drinks. Shall we have them here?"

"That suits me," nodded Branch.

Frank and Bart exchanged glances.

A moment later a colored waiter appeared with a huge tray that was loaded with brimming glasses of beer.

"I didn't ask you what you would have, Merriwell," explained Fillmore. "I knew you were a good fellow, and, of course, you'll drink the same as the rest of us."

"I'm very sorry——" began Merry.

"Oh, come, come!" cried several. "You're with us, Merriwell! Of course you are!"

"But I don't drink beer," said Frank quietly.

"Why not?"

"It isn't good for me."

"Oh, rats! It's good for any man!"

"Do you mean to say you won't drink anything, Merriwell, old man?" asked Fillmore, as if greatly disappointed.

"You may bring me some gin," he finally said.

"Ah-ha!" they cried. "That's the talk! We knew he was a good fellow."

Merry turned to the waiter.

"Bring me some Old Tom in a bottle," he said. "I'll take plain water for a chaser; no ginger ale or anything of that sort."

Instantly Hodge took the cue.

"I think I'll drink gin, too," he said. "Make my chaser the same."

One of the students whispered to a companion.

"Hodge has to do everything just the same as Merriwell does it."

"If they stick to gin, we'll soak them both for keeps," the other whispered back.

The waiter disappeared, but soon returned with the bottle of Old Tom and the glasses.

As Frank poured a goodly drink Fillmore started up the song "For He's a Jolly Good Fellow," in which several of the others followed.

Hackett rose, holding his glass of beer aloft.

"Here's to Frank Merriwell!" he cried. "Frank Merriwell, a star of the first magnitude. May that star never grow dim."

"Thank you," bowed Merry smilingly. "You are exceedingly kind. Here is to you all, gentlemen. May you never be disappointed—unless you deserve to be."

They drank. Merry tossed off his drink at a gulp, barely wetted his lips with the "chaser," then tossed the remaining contents of the glass over his shoulder and the rail of the veranda.

Hodge made a wry face and did not touch his "chaser," which was carried away by the waiter.

Bart excused himself and followed the waiter inside.

"Here, Tom," he softly called.

"Yes, sar," said the waiter, pausing.

Bart whispered something in his ear, at the same time slipping a dollar into his hand.

The black fellow looked surprised and then grinned in a knowing manner.

"Yes, sir! Thank yo', sar!" he exclaimed. "I'll look out fo' it, sar— 'deed I will. Don't yo' worry 'bout that."

Saying which, he took the glass left by Hodge from the tray and drained its contents.

"I'll drink all yo' chasers, sar," chuckled the colored man.

Bart returned to the veranda.

Some one else ordered a round of drinks.

Frank and Bart took the same as before, while the others drank beer.

Black Tom carried away two "chasers" on his tray, but the moment he was inside and out of sight, he drank both, tossing one down after the other and smacking his lips.

"Dem chaps is slick," he said. "Plain wattah makes a fine chaser fo' gin. Yah! yah! Dis is a snap fo' Tom!"

Cigarettes were passed round by two of the college lads.

Frank and Bart politely declined. Fillmore took one.

"Don't you smoke, Merriwell?" he asked.

"Never."

"Why is that—on account of your wind?"

"That is one reason."

"Well, I don't smoke much myself. We're not supposed to smoke at all, but a cigarette now and then never hurts me."

"Possibly not."

"Do you think it does?"

"I can't say. You may not have a taste for them, but you can cultivate the habit."

"Oh, that's right; but when I find the habit growing on me I'll stop altogether."

"It's easy to say so."

"But not easy to do, I presume you mean. I never smoke unless I drink something. Two beers make me feel like it. You might join us for once."

"Wouldn't think of torturing myself. I dislike cigarettes. It's a cultivated taste, you know. I confess that one of those things would be certain to make my head feel bad, and it might upset my stomach."

"Well, you're queer!" cried Dick Whisper. "A chap who's knocked around as much as you have generally smokes."

"Most of them do," acknowledged Frank.

Bart also declined, and again one of the students reminded a companion that Hodge was bound to imitate Merriwell.

"Have a drink on me," invited Frank. "It's my turn."

They protested, declaring he was their guest and could not buy. But he insisted. He even threatened to stop and take no more drinks unless permitted to order. This brought them round and they gave in.

Black Tom was grinning in a manner that exposed every tooth in his head when he appeared with the drinks.

"Heah yo' is, gemmans," he said, with unusual freedom. "I hope yo' 's habin' a good time. Make yo'se'fs right at home. Anything else I can bring yo', gemmans?"

Fillmore glared at him.

"What's the matter with you, you black rascal?" he cried. "You act like you've been drinking yourself."

"Oh, no, sar! Nebber, sar! Boss don' 'low me to drink when I'm on duty, sar. I's just pleased to see yo' enjoyin' yo'se'fs. Yah! yah! yah!"

"Get out, you grinning monkey!"

"Yes, sar! yes, sar!"

But Tom waited in the background until the round had been disposed of, when he gathered up the glasses, carefully taking the "chasers" left by Frank and Bart.

"When yo' wants me again I'll be at yoah disposal, gemmans," he said, as he departed, giggling queerly.

The next time Black Tom appeared with an order he caught his toe on the doorsill just as he was coming out onto the veranda.

"Oh, Lordy!" he gasped.

Sprawling he went, with a great crash, beer and splintered glasses flying in all directions and bespattering some of the students.

"Oh, Lordy!" repeated the colored man, as he sat up and gazed around, his eyes rolling queerly and a look on his face that made the spectators roar.

"I's a-gwine ter git the old Sachet fer this!" he declared.

"What's the matter with you, you blundering, black scoundrel?"

demanded Fillmore. "Never saw you act so oddly."

"Somefin' sholy moved just as I was a-gwine teh step frough the do'," declared Tom, as he gathered himself up unsteadily. "Whoa, dar! It moved ag'in! Is de groun' shakin' ur nuffin'?"

"He's drunk!" declared Dick Whisper. "Hastings will give it to you, Tom."

"Dat's right, he will. He'll be hoppin' mad about de smash. But de flo' gave de funniest wiggle. Yah! yah! yah! It done tickle mah foot."

Then the negro went off into a spasm of laughter.

"You'll lose your place if you don't brace up, Tom," said Fillmore. "Here comes Mr. Hastings now."

"Oh, Lordy!" gasped the colored man, his manner changing with astonishing suddenness. "I's do' fo'!"

He made a scramble to gather up the waiter and some of the partly smashed glasses.

Suddenly he stopped.

"Yo' 's foolin' me," he said, with a grin. "De boss is done gone fo' de day. Said he wouldn't be back till to-morrer mawnin'."

"That explains your condition," said Hackett. "Go bring those drinks and clean up here, you tippling dog."

"Don't yo' be so pussunal, sar!" objected Tom, swaying a bit and looking offended. "I nebber done yo' no injury ner nuffin'. I's sho' sorry I spilled de drinks. I'll have them teh pay fo', 'sides payin' fo' the glasses I smashed. But I don' like teh be called nuffin' disgraceful. I allus tries teh treat averybody right, an' it ain't——"

"Oh, cut it out!" interrupted one of the collegians. "You're all right, Tom, when you are all right. Better bring that beer in steins after this. They won't break so easy."

Tom departed, stepping gingerly and lifting his feet very high. In a short time he returned with the drinks. Then he hastened to wipe up and sweep up the pieces of broken glass.

The boys began to sing, "When Good Fellows Get Together." They seemed to be feeling very well indeed. Merriwell and Hodge joined in, apparently feeling quite as well as any of them.

In the midst of the singing Fillmore found a chance to whisper in Hackett's ear:

"Merriwell is pretty well loaded now. Look at him. I don't believe he can stand much, and he's drinking gin as if it were water."

"Oh, we'll have him finished pretty soon," answered Hackett. "I want to soak Hodge just as much, but I think he can stand more than Merriwell."

A man appeared and informed them that they could not sit on the veranda and sing in that manner.

"What are you tryin' to do?" he growled. "Want to queer the place? There's people goin' by on the road. Come inside, all of yer."

"We resent that language, Morrisy!" exclaimed Fillmore haughtily, as he rose. "Speak to us in the proper manner to address gentlemen."

"That's right!" said Frank, also rising, and seeming a bit unsteady. "That's no way to talk."

"Oh, don't all you chaps go to gettin' on your high horses!" cried Morrisy. "You know me, an' I know you. If I've said anything you don't like, I apolergize; but you'll have to caper inside if you want any more drinks."

"Do you positively refuse to serve anything more out here?" asked Fillmore.

"Sure thing."

"Then, as you have apologized, we'll come in. Come on, fellows."

They all filed in and found seats round some tables in a cool and airy room. As another round of drinks was being served a man with huge shoulders and a thick neck came sauntering into the room, his derby hat cocked over one eye and a cigar canted upward in one corner of his mouth.

"Here's Husker!" was the cry. "Hello, Galway, old slugger! Come have a drink with us!"

The newcomer paused and surveyed the party critically.

"Well, now, you're a hot bunch, ain't yer!" he said. "You're certainly goin' it some. Tryin' ter drownd yerselves wid beer, hey?"

Fillmore hastened to Husker Galway and shook hands with him. Others rose and greeted him in a similar manner. In the pugilist's ear Fillmore whispered:

"I'm going to give you a knockdown to the chap I phoned you about. Get him into a bout and mark him up as much as you can. Give him a black eye or two, if possible."

"Does he t'ink he can scrap?"

"He thinks he can do anything and everything."

"I'll take some of der wind outer him in a hurry," promised Galway.

"This is our boxing instructor, Husker Galway, Mr. Merriwell," said Fillmore, introducing them.

"'Waryer!" said Husker, seizing Frank's hand.

For some reason Merry had prepared for just what followed. Something warned him that the pugilist would try to give him a grip that would make him wince, and therefore Frank proceeded to get the hold that he desired. When Galway tried to crush his fingers, Merry proceeded smilingly to close on the fighter's hand with a grip of iron.

"Delighted to meet you, Mr. Galway," he said, with that pleasant smile. "It really gives me great pleasure."

He gave the pugilist a grip that might have crushed the bones in another man's hand. At first Galway pretended not to notice it, but in a moment he tried to tear his hand away, the look on his face showing that he was in pain.

"Wot in howlin' thunder you tryin' ter do?" he snarled. "Leggo! Leggo of that fist!"

"I beg your pardon!" said Merry, in apparent surprise, as Husker seemed on the point of hitting him. "Evidently you—hic!—you don't belong to my lodge."

All the blood seemed squeezed from Galway's hand.

"Dat's the fin I broke on Pug Curran," said the pugilist, by way of explanation. "Was yer tryin' ter finish it fer me?"

Fillmore and the others were surprised, for they had seen the man cause dozens of people to wilt and beg while pretending to shake hands with them in an ordinary manner. The fact that Frank had checkmated the move and caused Galway to squeal was most astonishing to them.

Galway grew angry.

"You're too fresh, dat's wot's der matter wid youse!" he said, glaring at Merry. "You oughter have some of it taken outer yer!"

"Why, didn't I—hic!—didn't I beg your pardon?" said the young man, in surprise.

"Better beg it ag'in," growled the bruiser.

"Oh, very well!" exclaimed Merry hastily. "I'll do it!"

Husker fancied Frank was frightened.

Fillmore fancied Frank was drunk. He gave the pugilist a signal, and the latter grew more arrogant.

"Wot you need is a little t'umpin'," he said. "I'd like ter put on der gloves wid youse an' take some of der freshness outer yer."

"Would you?"

"You bet!"

"I'd rather not. I've heard about you."

"Oh, I didn't suppose you'd have der nerve. It wouldn't really hurt yer none, but it would do yer good. Der gloves are like cushions. A jab in der jaw is like a caress."

"Put them on with him, Merriwell!" cried Fillmore.

Taking the cue from their leader, the other students urged him to do so.

"Don't be frightened," said one.

"We've all been through the mill," declared another.

"You ought to stand what we can."

"I've heard you know how to box."

"Oh, go ahead! go ahead!"

Frank saw through the game now. For some moments he pretended to be anxious to keep out of it; but finally, of a sudden, with seeming drunken courage, he announced that he would put on the gloves with Galway.

The students shouted joyously.

"Now we'll see some fun!" they cried.

They did!

But it was not just the kind of fun they expected.

One of the rooms in the huge shed back of the road house was fitted up in a manner that plainly betokened the use to which it had been put more than once.

In the centre of the room was a spare platform. On four sides were seats. At the four corners of the open platform were stakes. The platform was inclosed by ropes.

Here more than one stiff fight had been pulled off as a boxing bout.

Hastings, the proprietor of the place, had no license to run affairs of the sort, but he had a pull with the police, and he had never been molested.

Men from Johns Hopkins, the Baltimore Medical College and sometimes youngsters from the City College frequented the place and witnessed the "mills" which took place there.

Of course Hastings had not escaped criticism. There had been complaints against him, but through it all he kept at his business and raked in the money the youngsters spent.

The boys followed Husker Galway and Merriwell out into the shed. Fillmore was in high spirits. He locked arms with Tom Hackett and chuckled softly over the affair.

"Merriwell has a beautiful bun on," he muttered. "He'll be a cinch for Husker. And Husker has taken the tip from me to cut him up and give him a black eye or two. Ha! ha! Won't he be a pretty bird to take back to Inza! She'll admire him, I don't think!"

"Wish Hodge was going to get his medicine at the same time," growled Hackett.

"Why don't you pick a fuss with him and do him up?"

"What are you thinking of? Didn't we bring him out here? We'll have to play the sympathetic. We must make them both believe we're very sorry over it."

"You're right, Tom. We've got to keep clear of the blame."

Husker Galway stripped down in a hurry, flinging off his clothes with the exception of such garments as were absolutely necessary to cover his nakedness.

Merriwell was more deliberate. He moved with a certain slowness and strained precision, as if he was doing everything with a great effort to appear cool and sober.

Hodge looked on indifferently, as if he took very little interest in the affair.

The students joyously selected a referee and timekeeper. They decided that the bout should be pulled off in rounds of three minutes each, although many were inclined to believe that the first round would be more than enough to end it.

A few of the reckless ones ventured to bet that Merriwell would last a whole round, getting even money on it. Two to one was offered that he would not last two rounds, and ten to one that he would throw up the sponge before three rounds were over.

Some of the boys seemed to have an idea that Husker would play with Frank for the first round, give him a cutting up in the second, and then, if Merry stood up for any more, proceed to put him out in the third.

One, who seemed well loaded with beer, staggered forward and clasped Merriwell round the neck, earnestly entreating him not to box.

"I'm 'shamed, old fel," said the maudlin chap. "'Tain't right! It's shame! You dunno w'atcher up against. You're a good fellow, but Husker is a slugger. He's offended; he's dangerous. I'm gentleman. Don't like to see him do you this way. Put on y'r coat an' come have a drink with me."

"Get out of the way, Ludley!" cried another. "You've got a peach! Go lie down somewhere!"

Ludley waved the other off with a hand that was limp at the wrist.

"Lemme 'lone," he said stiffly. "I'm friend to Merriwell. He's good chap. Whatcher want? Want to see him hurt? He's fine-lookin' chap. I hate to see fine-lookin' chap like him hurt, I do."

"You are very—hic!—kind, sir," said Frank. "I appreciate your extreme kindness, but I think I can—hic!—I can take care of myself. Don't worry 'bout me."

"Course he kin take care of hisself," said Galway. "Go jump off the earth, little boy."

Ludley shed tears.

"He's our ghest," he murmured thickly. "'Tain't right, boys—
'tain't right! You may think it's joke, but I shay it's shame."

"Why doesn't some one smother that fool?" growled Tom Hackett. "He always was an ass!"

Frank put Ludley aside and finished making ready. Some one
found him a pair of rubber-soled shoes, and these he put on.

Then they brought the gloves.

Instead of boxing gloves, such as are generally used for sparring, they were six-ouncers, the kind used in many prize fights.

"Hum!" said Merry, as he gravely surveyed the pair handed
him. "Aren't these a trifle light for a friendly go?"

"Oh, they're all right!" exclaimed several of the students. "We
box with them here."

"If that is so," said Merry, "I'll raise—hic!—no further objection."

Black Tom came unsteadily feeling his way out into the shed. He
scratched his woolly head and gazed in a dazed way at Galway
and then at Frank.

Suddenly he began to laugh.

"When yo' gwine teh ordah another round, gemmans?" he
asked. "I'll drink de chasers. Yah! yah! yah!"

Some one threw a wooden dumb-bell at Tom, and it struck him
on the head, bounding off.

"G'way dar!" cried the colored man indignantly. "Stop frowin'
dem peanut shells dis way!"

Hodge aroused himself and tied on Frank's gloves. As he did so,
he found an opportunity to whisper:

"They all think we're both loaded, Merry. This big bruiser thinks
so, too. When you undeceive him you want to do it by wading
into him and finishing the scrap."

"Come on!" cried Galway. "It takes you a long time ter git inter
gear."

"Don't be impatient, my friend," said Merry, floppily waving
one of the gloves at the bruiser. "We've got all the—hic!—all the
afternoon."

"Dat'll give yer a long time ter sleep," said Husker.

"Gentlemen," called the student who had appointed himself as
referee, "in the main bout to-day we have the great Husker Galway, heavyweight champion of the Pimlico Road."

He waved his hand toward Galway.

"His opponent is Frank Merriwell, all-round champion at anything and everything."

A wave toward Merry.

"The fight will be in three-minute rounds, with half-minute intermissions, both men to defend themselves in the breakaway. They will fight to a finish."

"Hoop-la! Yow! Yow!" yelled the students. "'Rah for Darby, the referee!"

The timekeeper had his watch in his hand. Suddenly he struck the gong that hung suspended at one side of the raised platform.

Galway strode forward to the centre of the ring.

Merry advanced with a shuffling, unsteady step.

"It's a shame to take the money!" muttered Fillmore. "Why, the fellow is all in now! Husker can put him out with one punch."

"Sure he can," agreed Hackett.

"But he won't."

"Why not?"

"He knows I want him to cut the fellow up, and he'll try to let Merriwell keep on his feet while he chops his face to pieces. I wonder if Inza will kiss him when she sees him to-night! Bet he'll feel so sore he'll drink like a fish after this is over. We must be careful not to let him get so drunk he can't show up before Inza."

Galway and Merry reached forth their hands and their gloves touched. Then they assumed the position of "on guard."

Merry put up his hands rather awkwardly.

Galway grinned.

"It's too bad, boy," he sneered; "but you'd be a plum pudding for any sixteen-year-old kid in Baltimore."

Saying which he reached over and tapped Merry lightly on the nose.

CHAPTER XXIV.

THE FINISH.

uch!" said Merry.

"Dat didn't hurt, did it?" asked the slugger, with an air of surprise.

"Not much."

"How 'bout dat?"

Husker tapped him again.

Merry didn't seem able to protect himself in the least.

"It's going to be a slaughter!" muttered Hackett. "I did hope he'd try to put up a scrap just to give us some fun."

The students cried:

"Brace up, Merriwell!"

"What are you doing?"

"Don't let him hit you that way!"

"Open your eyes!"

"Hit back at him!"

"You fools!" thought Bart Hodge. "It's plain you've planned to have lots of fun with us, but the laugh is coming the other way when this affair is over. You'll be the most surprised bunch of lobsters in Baltimore."

Galway danced round Merry. He came in and feinted, causing Merry to make a wild motion to parry. Then he laughed loudly, for it seemed that Frank had exposed himself.

The prize fighter resolved to show the youth up. To do so he kept working in and out and drawing Frank, as he supposed, into defenseless positions.

"Husker is fooling with him, Fred," muttered Hackett.

"Hope he doesn't fool too long. I think Merriwell is beginning to realize he hasn't any show. He'll be quitting."

Merry had divined Galway's purpose, and he was the one who was doing the playing. He was watching the fighter's every movement and sizing up his style. He saw how the man side-stepped, how he feinted, how he led and how he guarded. While this was going on Frank was planning his style of attack when the time should come.

Several times Merry rushed awkwardly just to see how the man defended himself. He led at Galway's head and his body. The man defended himself by parrying, blocking, and retreating.

Frank was not foolish enough to fancy Husker Galway an easy mark, but he counted on gaining some advantage by taking the man by surprise when he went into the fight in earnest.

Finally, as if by the rarest blundering accident, Merry landed on Galway's chin.

"Well! well! well!" cried Ludley, the chap who had displayed such a friendly feeling for Frank. "He hit him, then!"

"Could you see that?" sneered a student.

"Course I could! What's matter with you?"

Black Tom was scratching his head as he watched Merry.

"Nebber befo' has I seen nobody git loaded on de kind ob stuff he's been drinkin'," murmured the negro.

Galway was angered because he had permitted himself to be hit in such a manner.

"You couldn't do dat ag'in in a week!" he growled.

Frank seemed to try it, whereupon the slugger swung to land hard on Merry's body.

The blow was blocked, but it was done as if by chance more than skill.

The slugger's anger increased and he followed Merriwell up.

"Now he's going to get into him!" hissed Fillmore.

Merry managed to clinch, and he hung on when the referee tried to "break" them.

"Oh, leggo!" snapped Galway.

He tried to uppercut Frank.

"Break! break!" commanded the referee.

When they did break Merry unexpectedly shot his left to the slugger's chin, driving his head back.

Galway uttered a roar. His face flushed and he went after Frank like an enraged beast.

Merry ducked and went under the man's swing.

"Oh, the artful dodger!" exclaimed Jack Branch.

"He'll have to do something more than dodge in a minute," prophesied Dick Whisper.

Clang sounded the gong. The first round was over.

Fillmore was disappointed because Merriwell had not been damaged in the least in the opening round. He hastened to Galway's corner, speaking to the pugilist in a low tone.

"You haven't marked him."

"Plenty of time, young feller," said Husker. "I'll give him a black eye an' break his nose in der next round."

"Well, do something," urged Fillmore.

He fancied Merriwell would not observe that he took this occasion to speak to the pugilist.

Apparently Frank did not see it, but the truth was that nothing escaped his eyes. He knew now beyond question that the captain of the lacrosse team, who had pretended such friendship, was the one who had planned to have him beaten up by the slugger. Although his heart was hot with anger over Fillmore's treachery, he did not betray his feelings by any outward sign.

Hodge was attending to Frank in his corner, giving him a drink and mopping his perspiring face with a sponge.

"Don't fool around too long, Merry," he said guardedly. "I'm afraid you'll betray the fact that you're not half the mark they've taken you for."

"I'm not going to fool any longer," answered Merry. "I shall go after him now. I've fathomed his style of fighting, and I think I know his weak points."

Thirty seconds were quickly over.

Clang!

Galway rose instantly and advanced, while again Frank was slow about coming to the scratch.

The slugger engaged in earnest, going after Merry with the idea of quickly keeping his promise to Fillmore. He led at Merriwell's head.

The blow was skillfully parried, and out shot Frank's right.

Smack!

The blow sounded clear and solid, and it sent Husker Galway reeling.

"Oh!" cried half the spectators.

Merriwell followed the bruiser up with such swiftness that Galway was given no time to recover. Again Merry hit him—again and again, knocking him onto the ropes.

Fred Fillmore gasped with unspeakable amazement, while Tom Hackett's eyes threatened to pop out of their sockets.

No one could have been more astonished than Galway. He was surprised because the youth had been able to hit him at all, and he was still more surprised by the "steam" behind those blows.

"Yah! yah! yah!" laughed Black Tom. "I done thought it was bery strange dat gemman got so full on what he was drinkin'."

Galway recovered and rose from the ropes. His eyes glared and his face had the ugly look of a man infuriated to the point of some black deed.

"So you can hit?" he snarled, as he danced away. "Come again! Try it some more!"

Merry accepted the invitation, but the pugilist was on guard now, and it was not so easy to hit him. Besides that, Galway did some leading himself, and Frank had to look out for himself. The slugger reached Frank's chin, but Merry had leaped back, and the blow was light.

"Nearly got him then, Husker!" cried one of the students.

"Look out for that wallop! Look out for that wallop, Merriwell!" shouted Ludley. "He puts the best of 'em out with it!"

Frank was looking out for it. He knew the fighter had a dangerous left, and it was his hope to keep him from landing full and fair with one of those heavy swings.

Galway followed up. There was a bit of sharp sparring and then a clinch.

"Break!" yelled the referee.

They broke promptly enough this time, but again Frank shot out a lightning left and reached his antagonist's jaw.

"Look out for that in the breakaway, Gal!" warned one of the spectators.

"Great Cæsar's ghost!" came from another. "This is the real thing! It's no slaughter, after all!"

Bart Hodge laughed.

"You'll see the kind of a slaughter you did not expect," he declared.

The battle was a fast one now, for both men were at it in earnest. Frank received a number of blows, but not one landed in a way to do him any damage. He was on guard for the "wallop." Twice Husker tried to land with it, but both times his fist swept through the air, for the smiling youth was not there. Tom Hackett grasped Fred Fillmore's arm.

"What is the meaning of this?" he palpitated. "Merriwell is fighting like a wizard! He doesn't act as if he had ever taken a drink in his life. I thought he was loaded."

"So did I," admitted Fillmore. "He certainly is dazing me; but he'll get his medicine before long. Galway can stand all the punishment he's getting, and he'll land for fair in the end."

"Look at that! look at that! Merriwell has split his lip! He's bleeding!"

It was true. Frank had opened the slugger's lip, and Galway's teeth were covered with blood.

All this served to cause the pugilist to lose his head. Had he expected anything of the sort, he would have fought on coolly; but he had anticipated an easy victory, and the disappointment was too much for him. Thinking he would have plenty of sport by hammering Frank round the ring, he had readily consented to Fillmore's proposition. He realized at last that he was being used as a punching bag by the youth he had despised, and that was more than he could endure and keep his level. He was being "shown up" before the students who had admired him and regarded him as a wonder.

"Dern ye! I'll knock your head off!" he snarled.

Bart Hodge stood with his hands in his pockets, the remotest ghost of a smile on his dark face.

"This bunch will know more than they did when they started in on this little game," he thought. "Get into that big brute, Merry! End it in this round!"

Frank tried his best to end it, and he gave Husker Galway the severest sort of punishment; but the bruiser was tough, and, although he was very groggy, he managed to keep on his pins until the gong sounded.

The second round was ended.

Frank Merriwell was suddenly very popular with the students. They congratulated him on his success.

He paid little heed to them during the thirty seconds of rest.

Fillmore did not venture to speak to Galway now, for he knew that Merriwell was very wide-awake. Disgusted and disappointed, he lingered in the background.

"I believe Merriwell is going to whip Husker!" said Hackett.

"He can't do it," muttered Fillmore.

"He had him going in that round. The gong saved him."

"Galway was fooled. We've all been fooled! Perhaps the gong did save him. You'll see something different this next round."

Fillmore was disinclined to give up hope.

When the gong sounded next time Merriwell was up and met Galway in a twinkling. He lost no time in getting after the pugilist. Galway was wary at first, but Frank's success in hitting him twice stung him to a pitch that led him to rush and lunge.

Merry met him and they clinched.

Again in the breakaway Frank soaked the bruiser on the jaw, and this time it made the man reel.

Following up, Frank put his left to Galway's wind and his right to the fellow's head.

Galway went down.

"Ah!" cried the spectators.

But it was not a knockout. The referee began to count, but Husker snarled for him to "dry up" and leaped to his feet.

"You fool!" he grated. "No man ever counted me out, an' no man ever will!"

This bruiser had gladly taken upon his shoulders the task to "cut up" the supposed-to-be unsuspecting stranger. To him it was a pleasure in anticipation, and he had fully expected to make it a pleasure in execution. The fact that he was making a wretched mess of his wretched task bewildered while it enraged him. He saw before him the smiling, unmarked youth, wholly undisturbed and at his ease. Had that youth been a fighter with a reputation, Galway would have been prepared and would not have exposed himself with such disdain. Even now, after he had felt the force of Merriwell's skill as a boxer, he could not comprehend that this youngster was his master.

"You think you're some, don't ye?" he growled, as he cautiously advanced, Merry waiting for him. "Well, you're goin' ter git yours right now!"

Fillmore's fading courage revived. He saw that Galway was determined to retaliate, and he returned to the hope that the slugger might settle the matter with his dreaded "wallop."

"Wait a minute," invited Frank. "I want to tell you something. You tried to trick me and make an exhibition of me before these fellows. I don't know the cause behind your action, but you have failed. I have no particular feeling of hatred for you. I think I have satisfied you and the spectators that I am not the easy mark I've been picked up to be. I don't care to resort to the last extremity to end this business. I'm not a prize fighter. I am willing to call the matter off right here—I am satisfied."

"Satisfied, are ye?"

"Yes."

"Well, I ain't—not on yer life! I'll be satisfied w'en I puts you ter sleep, an' I'm goin' ter do it. Look out fer me! Either you squeal or I'll knock your block off!"

Frank said no more. As he had stated, knowing the low grade of the bruiser, he had no personal feeling toward the man; but now he found that there could be but one end to the encounter. Either he must whip Galway or Galway would whip him.

From that point the fight was fast and savage. Merriwell astounded every witness save Hodge by his cleverness in blocking, guarding and getting away. He remained on the defense some time, leading the slugger to think him frightened at last. Then he landed fair and full with the force of his body behind the blow, and there was a crash as Galway fell.

A hush followed.

Then the now sober referee stepped forward, leaned over the prostrate bruiser, and, marking each numeral with a stroke of his index finger, began to count:

"One—two—three——"

Galway stirred and partly lifted himself.

"Four—five—six——"

The pugilist rose to his hands and knees.

"Seven——"

Husker lifted his hands from the floor.

"Eight——"

He brought up his left foot and planted it.

"Nine——"

He staggered to his feet before the final word could be uttered.

It was a display of sand, and, although the fellow was an ordinary prize fighter, Frank could not help admiring him for it.

But Merry realized that it would not do to let his admiration of the fellow's grit hold him in check. It was all the more apparent that there could be only one termination of the encounter.

Merriwell closed in.

Galway side-stepped and rushed. His ponderous left swung through the air with an upward movement.

It was an effort to land the "wallop" on Frank's jaw.

The youth was not there.

The swing seemed to throw Husker Galway off his guard. Before he could recover Frank came in. With a straight, clean blow, the champion all-round athlete of America sent his opponent down with a shock that jarred the platform to its very foundations.

It was all over. The referee counted ten in his most deliberate manner, but the prostrate slugger did not even move a muscle. Then, when his gloves were removed, the victor joined in the efforts to restore Galway, paying little heed to the profuse expressions of admiration and the flow of congratulations from the students.

At last he sat up, supported by one of the students, and his eyes sought the face of the youth who had caused his downfall.

"Young feller," he said, "you delivered the goods. I didn't believe it was in yer; but I'll back you against anyt'ing on two legs dat stan's! You're der real stuff!"

CHAPTER XXV.

CAUGHT IN THEIR OWN TRAP.

Although Fred Fillmore was among the first to congratulate Merriwell, he found an opportunity to slip out of the shed while efforts were being made to restore Husker Galway.

Hackett followed him.

"I've got to have a drink!" exclaimed the latter. "I want something to brace me up after that."

"Just what I'm after," said Fillmore. "That was enough to drive any one to drink."

They found their way to the bar and both ordered whisky, regardless of the fact that they had been drinking beer and an abundance of that.

"What do you think of it, Fred?" asked Hackett, his hand unsteady as he poured his drink.

"I can't think!" confessed the captain of the lacrosse team. "Husker Galway knocked out—by him!"

"And he was jagged when the scrap began."

"Was he?"

"Wasn't he?"

"I don't believe it."

"But—but he appeared to be."

"I know he did."

"Then you think——"

"He fooled us."

They looked at each other. After a moment or two, Hackett nodded slowly.

"I reckon that's right," he said. "He fooled us. But he must be a tank, for he drank as many as seven big slugs of Old Tom gin."

"So did Hodge."

"Yes."

"Well?"

"Well, Merriwell may have braced up after getting into the scrap. Perhaps that was what sobered him."

"What sobered Hodge?"

Again they looked at each other blankly.

"It's too much for me," admitted Hackett. "I give it up. But I never dreamed Merriwell could fight like that, even if he didn't take a drink. Why, why, Fred, he knocked out the champion of the Pimlico Road and a man who might easily be the champion of Baltimore!"

"Don't I know it? You don't have to tell me! I'd bet my life Husker could hammer the head off him—before I saw this. I can't believe Merriwell did it!"

"Well, let's drink up. Here's to drown our disappointment."

They tossed off the drinks.

"I haven't taken a drink before this term," said Fillmore dolefully, "and I did so to-day to pull those dubs into the trap. If any one peaches on me, I'll get a raking over."

"You can't get much of a raking, for wasn't Branch in the bunch? He's the one who will get the raking. He'll lose his job."

"He doesn't care, for the season is pretty nearly over, and he graduates, so he doesn't want the position again. That's how I induced him to get onto the band wagon to-day. We're not going to take Merriwell and Hodge back to their ladies in the shape we expected."

"Unless we get them into a mess with the whole bunch and all jump on them."

"Can't do that. The boys won't stand for it. Some of them are gone on Merriwell now. They thought it would be a joke to get the great athlete out here and put him up against Galway; but they'll see no joke in mobbing him. It won't work. We're baffled to-day, old man, and we may as well throw up the sponge."

"But there's another time coming," muttered Hackett.

"We'll have to give Merriwell that game. I hate him! I thought I hated Herb Onslaw, but I hate Merriwell worse. I'd like to get a rap at him."

"You might be able to in the game."

"That's right," nodded Fillmore. "More than one fellow has been knocked out with a lacrosse stick while playing. No one could prove I did it intentionally. It would give me lots of satisfaction. It's the very chance I've been praying for with Onslaw."

"Onslaw will be in the game, too."

"So Merriwell says, but we're not sure of it. I hope he is! It would delight me to get even with both chaps in one day. Yes, we'll have to give Merriwell the game."

"Let's drink another and get back before we're missed."

Their faces were flushed and their tongues thick. Already they had taken as much as they could stand, but the time had passed when they could gauge their capacity. Once more they drank whisky, and both staggered a little as they left the bar.

They met the students, accompanied by Merriwell, Hodge, and Galway, coming from the shed. To their surprise, Galway showed no resentment toward his conqueror.

But he gave Fillmore a vicious look, although he said nothing.

The slugger was determined to "blow" the crowd. He insisted that it was on him.

Frank and Bart could not refuse without appearing caddish, so they accepted the man's invitation, although they now ordered ginger ale.

"What?" cried several of the students, in astonishment.

"Ginger w'ot?" gasped Galway. "Oh, say! dat's a joke. Ye're foolin'!"

"No," said Merry. "We have had quite enough to drink. I make a practice of stopping when I have enough. I always order ginger ale or sarsaparilla at that stage."

"I would meself," grinned Galway, looking very hideous with his bruised face and split lip; "but w'en I have enough I can't say sarsaparilla."

In vain Frank and Bart were urged to drink something stronger; they persisted in their determination to take nothing but ginger ale, and ginger ale they drank.

On the other hand, although they already had too much, Fillmore and Hackett again drank whisky.

A short time after that both these fellows were in a wretched condition. They insisted on returning home, and Merry, thinking the open air would do them good, besides wishing to get them away from the road house, ordered the team hitched up.

It was necessary to lift Fillmore and Hackett into the carriage. Hodge looked after one, while Frank took care of the other.

It happened that neither chap betrayed himself directly, although both mumbled things which were suggestive of their feelings over the outcome of the encounter.

"Shay!" Fillmore finally exclaimed, seizing Frank's arm and looking into his face wonderingly; "shay, Merriwell, how'd ju do it?"

"Do what—defeat Galway?"

"No; how'd ju drink all that gin an' keep shober? Tha's what puzzlesh me. Musht be reg'ler tank, Mer'well."

"I didn't drink any gin," laughed Frank. "That's the secret of it, my boy. I never drink intoxicants."

"Oh, shay, come off! I shaw you take five, shix, sheven drinks— more'n that."

"Sho did I," put in Hackett, bracing up. "You're ri', Fred, ol' man—I shaw him do it. Reg'lar tank, tha'sh ri'."

"You did not see me take a single drink of gin," declared Merry. "When you insisted that we should drink something, gin was brought for us, with water on the side. We drank the water and left the gin. Black Tom drank the gin, and I hope it does not cost him his position."

"Wha'—wha'—wha'——" gurgled Fillmore, in a dazed way. "I don't think I jusht undershtand ju. How wash that?"

"We drank the water, which looked the same as gin, and left the gin, which was brought with it."

Hackett was sitting on the back seat with Hodge. He reached forward and jabbed Fillmore in the back.

"Ol' man," he mumbled, "we're a pair of eashy marks, that'sh what we are! We've been fooled. We started to get thesh fellersh full an' have fun wish them, an' they played it on ush. I want to go die shomewhere!"

Fillmore was even more disgusted than Hackett.

"Next time you pick out two chaps as easy be sure you do not make a mistake," advised Hodge.

Frank laughed over it.

"I fancied you were planning something for us," said Merry, "and so we turned it on you. It's all right, fellows. No hard feelings. We're able to stand the joke."

"Joke's on ush," said Hackett.

For some time Fillmore rode in silence. They had reached Druid Hill Park.

Suddenly the captain of the lacrosse team flew into a drunken rage.

"Anybody can keep shober 'f he drinksh water!" he snarled. "That washn't smart! I 'fuse to ride with a man who drinksh water! It'sh dishgrace! Lemme out! I'll take car home! Lemme out!"

"Don't be silly," said Frank. "You're not going home now, either of you. You're not in condition to go home. We'll take you to the Belvidere with us and get you straightened out. You don't want to show yourselves in this condition. What will your sister think, Fillmore? What'll she say? Keep still!"

"I'm all ri'! Guess I know when I'm all ri'! Needn't think you're only shober person on earth! I'm shober—perfec'ly shober. But I've been inshulted! I've been basely desheived! I won't ride 'nozer inch wish you! Lemme out!"

"That's ri', Freddie, ol' man!" joined in Hackett. "I'm wish you! Le'sh git out an' walk."

"Shtop thosh horsesh!" commanded Fillmore, starting to rise.

Frank pulled him back on the seat.

"I tell you to keep still!"

"I tell you go to thunder!" snarled Fred, as he tore from Merry and flung himself from the carriage.

He fell sprawlingly, but gathered himself up directly and was on his feet when Merry stopped the horses.

"G'wan!" cried the unreasonable chap. "Want noshing to do wish you!"

Hackett tumbled out.

"G'wan!" he echoed. "Noshing to do wish you at all!"

He joined Fillmore and feebly tried to brush the dust from his friend's clothing.

"What are we going to do about it, Hodge?" asked Frank.

"Let the blamed fools go," answered Bart, at once. "Why should we bother with them? They've fixed themselves the way they planned to fix us."

"I suppose that is true, but they're intoxicated, and I can't leave them this way."

In vain he tried to reason with Fillmore and Hackett. They took to the nearest walk, arm in arm, and reeled away. Merry drove along as near them as possible, hoping they would change their minds and decide to get back into the carriage.

"Show that you can take a joke as well as anybody, fellows," he urged. "Come, get in here again."

He was invited to go to a most disagreeable place, and the Hopkins men kept on until they came out of the park and boarded a street car.

Then, of course, Merry had to give up.

Befogged by drink, Fillmore went straight to his sister's home, taking Hackett with him. On entering they encountered Inza and Elsie, and thus, through their own folly, exposed themselves to the girls in much the same condition in which they had intended to expose Frank and Bart.

CHAPTER XXVI.

BEFORE THE GAME.

The game of lacrosse between Hopkins and Merriwell's team was arranged, no objection being raised to it by the committee of athletics at the college.

This was the way the two teams lined up on the field at Oriole Park:

THE MERRIES.	JOHNS HOPKINS.
Wilkins, In home.	Brisbane, Goal Guard.
Morgan, Out	Delano, Point.
Onslaw, st attack.	Fillmore, Cover point.
Thatcher, 2d attack.	Lowe, st defense.
Merriwell, 3d attack.	Kellogg, 2d defense.
Vernell, Centre.	Mowry, 3d defense.
Gamp, 3d defense.	Hackett, Centre.
Hunter, 2d defense.	Woodin, 3d attack.
Wilson, st defense.	Grimes, 2d attack.
Starbright, Cover point.	Whisper, st attack.
Ready, Point.	Pierce, Out home.
Hodge, Goal Guard.	Zanger, In home.

Merry got his team altogether and put in some earnest practice before appearing in Baltimore. As he had expected, he was able to get five Harvard men to play with him. Vernell, his centre, was from Yale.

The day of the game in Baltimore was cloudy in the morning, but toward noon it cleared up and the sun shone forth from a blue sky. There was a light breeze blowing, and this promised to be most refreshing, as hot weather had prevailed for more than two weeks.

The Baltimore baseball team was playing away from home, so it was an easy matter to secure the park.

The great surprise of the day was the crowd that turned out to witness the contest. Never before in the history of lacrosse at Baltimore had there been such a gathering at a game. The stand was well filled, and the bleachers to the right, which happened to be near one of the goals, were packed.

Not all the spectators were from Baltimore, however. On the bleachers there was a gathering of Yale and Harvard men, who for once mingled like fellows of the same college. Such a game was destined to do more to promote good-fellowship between the two universities than many anonymous ten-thousand-dollar contributions for that purpose.

The leader of the team opposed to Hopkins was a Yale grad. With him were Morgan, Gamp, Starbright, Ready, and Hodge, all former Yale men. Vernell, who played centre for him, was still in Yale and on the Yale lacrosse team. The other players were Harvard men.

So Yale and Harvard met on the bleachers. They sat side by side and locked arms. They laughed and joked and cheered together. They united in singing the songs of the two colleges. First it was "Boola," then "Up the Street." "Bingo" was followed by "Fair Harvard."

The people in the stand clapped their hands and showed their delight over the singing. A little bunch of Hopkins men cheered repeatedly, but their cheering was weak and almost ludicrous in comparison to the cheering for a Yale or Harvard team on their home fields.

In the stand sat Elsie Bellwood and Inza Burrage, both thrilled by the joy of it.

"Oh, Inza!" breathed Elsie; "isn't it grand! Isn't it just splendid to be at a game like this and see Frank and Bart on the field once more!"

Inza was no less moved.

"It's like old times," she answered. "Oh, the sweet, old days!"

Then she softly hummed:

"Oh, the days that have vanished forever—
The sweet, sunny days of the past!
They'll come again back to us never,
They were happy—too happy to last!"

"But there are happier days in store for us all, Inza," said Elsie. "I feel it—I know it!"

"I believe that, also," nodded Inza. "Still, I often think of the days when we first met. I think of Fardale, and it seems so far—so very far away! I think of our visits to Yale, and somehow that seems long, long ago."

"What a splendid-looking lot of fellows!" exclaimed Elsie. "Aren't they, Inza?"

"Yes; but I see one who looks finer in my eyes than a thousand like the others on the field."

"Oh, fie! I don't believe you're looking at the one I see."

"I don't believe so, either."

"I hope not."

"So do I. There, Elsie, we're both satisfied. Hear the Harvard cheer. Isn't it a splendid sound?"

"I like the Yale cheer better."

"I love them both. Look, there go the two captains—there goes Frank!"

The captains and some of the officials were holding a consultation near the centre of the field. It was soon over, and the referee placed the ball in the centre of the circle.

The two teams spread out and lined up in regular order. The game was about to begin.

Vernell was a clever man at centre. He waited until Hackett placed his stick, after which he quickly placed his in such a position as to balk the effort he fancied the Hopkins man intended to make.

The whistle sounded.

Hackett attempted to draw the ball, but with a snap Vernell defeated him and obtained it, quickly passing it to Merry, who was in position to take it.

Merry scooped it as Mowry came in on him.

Mowry tried a "check up," but was a second too late, and Frank got away with the ball, although the Hopkins player was right on him.

Merry was forced to pass, and he sent the ball to Onslaw with a quick "tip."

Lowe attempted a check with his stick, but Onslaw turned in such a way that the move to balk him failed.

Wilkins was in position to try for a goal, but Delano was clinging to him like a leech.

Onslaw found himself pocketed between two of the Hopkins men, and he ventured a pass to Wilkins.

Delano darted in and knocked the ball out of Wilkins' stick.

It went to Fillmore.

The Hopkins captain was on the alert. Like a cat he scooted the ball from the ground, avoiding Morgan, and darted out to one side, where he made a long pass to Woodin.

Woodin went flying toward the Merries' goal, running like a deer and managing to keep clear of Gamp.

Starbright left his man and darted across to intercept Woodin before the Hopkins third attack should reach a dangerous position.

Woodin passed to Pierce, but Pierce failed to take the ball in the air. It bounded away with him after it and Ready pressing him.

Pierce managed to scoop it up, but Ready pressed him so hard that he could not turn toward the goal. In this predicament Pierce made a throw over his head. Either by rare judgment or accident, he sent the ball into Zanger's stick, and Zanger made a quick snap for goal.

Hodge blocked the ball, but Zanger followed up and drove it in again.

"Goal!" was the cry.

In truth, Hopkins had made a goal in astonishingly quick time, and there was cause for the Baltimore students on the bleachers to cheer with delight.

"Oh, wasn't that terrible!" breathed Elsie Bellwood. "Why did they let them do it?"

"Because they couldn't help it, I think," answered Inza, as she watched the players of the two teams changing sides.

"I'm afraid these Hopkins men are going to win with ease," said the girl with golden hair.

"I'm not afraid of it," retorted Inza. "One goal will not win this game."

"But, you know, Fred Fillmore has told us right along that no picked-up team in the country could defeat Hopkins."

"Which he believes," nodded Inza. "But you mustn't think Frank is foolish enough to bring a weak team here to meet the champions of the United States. Don't worry, Elsie. You'll see something different before the game is finished."

In spite of Inza's confidence, it was not long before the situation began to assume a graver aspect, for, although Vernell again got the ball, which was carried down to Hopkins' goal, Brisbane barely stopping a score, the Baltimore players got in and carried the sphere up the field, kept it in the vicinity of the Merries' net for fully three minutes and finally drove it in.

The Hopkins cheer sounded louder and more exultant than ever.

"It's just as I feared!" exclaimed Elsie.

"Wait, wait," repeated Inza.

As the players were shifting sides Hackett spoke to Fillmore:

"A regular snap," he laughed.

"I'm afraid it's too easy," retorted the Hopkins captain.

Fillmore was watching for his chance to get at Onslaw or Merriwell. He felt that such a chance would come in a scrimmage before the game was over, and he hoped Merriwell would be the man he could land on. He was satisfied that the game would give him opportunities to show Frank up as a very ordinary lacrosse player.

On the next face off Hackett baffled Vernell and secured the ball for his own side.

Then it seemed as if the locals were going to add another tally right away. Woodin himself carried the ball through, avoiding man after man, and sent it whizzing waist-high at the net.

It was one of the most difficult throws for a goal guard to stop, but Hodge managed to check it and send the ball off to one side, where he hoped Ready or Starbright would secure it.

Ready tried, but Pierce's body checked him, while Whisper came in and scooped the ball.

Right up to the net dashed Whisper. He fancied he would make a goal without trouble; but Hodge was there again. The ball fell in front of the net not ten feet away.

An instant later there was a general mix-up of the players of both sides, all scrambling for the ball. Hodge himself secured it, detecting the opportunity and leaving the net to do so. He could not carry it far, but he sent it up the field to Merry.

Merriwell caught the ball handsomely and was off like a deer.

Mowry tried to close in on him, but Frank actually ran right round the Hopkins man, holding his stick so the ball could not be knocked out of it.

He found Kellogg ready for him. Apparently, Kellogg would force him to make a pass.

In some manner, Frank turned aside and went round Kellogg.

Lowe missed him by yards.

Fillmore saw his opening. He was swift on his feet, and he did not believe any one could carry a ball round him as Frank had carried it round Mowry and Kellogg. He came in to stop the captain of the opposing team.

Apparently, Frank was intending to dodge to the left, although he made a bluff of bearing to the right. Fillmore smiled a bit to think the man should fancy he could be deceived in such a manner. Then Merry turned quickly to the left; he leaped to check him.

But, to his dismay, the turn was only a feint on Merry's part, for he shifted and went leaping to the right, passing round the captain of the local team with the same ease that he had passed the others.

He was now in position to try for goal, and he sent the ball whizzing into the upper left-hand corner of the net.

"Goal!" was the cry that went up.

The Yale and Harvard men on the bleachers united in a cheer for Merriwell.

Fred Fillmore was astonished and enraged. He realized that Frank had made a sorry spectacle of him at a time when he had hoped it would be the other way. He knew two girls in the stand were rejoicing, and he ground his fine, white teeth together in impotent rage.

"Next time I'll break his head with my stick rather than let him dodge me that way!" he muttered.

Almost instantly he decided that it would not do to attempt such a thing in the open. It might be done in a scrimmage or general mix-up, but to do it in the open would be to invite criticism and to run the risk of being put out of the game by the referee.

"Well, this is not wholly one-sided!" shouted a Yale man on the bleachers.

"Not while Frank Merriwell is in the game," cried another.

The eyes of Inza Burrage were glowing and she could scarcely keep from cheering herself.

"Didn't I tell you, Elsie!" she cried. "I knew what would happen! Both Frank and Bart are playing splendidly. Bart kept Hopkins from scoring that time, and then Frank made a goal for his own side."

Elsie had brightened up, but she was quivering, while the color came and went in her cheeks.

"It's awfully exciting!" she murmured. "I didn't think it would be so exciting!"

"It's a beautiful game," said Inza; "and not enough is made of it in this country. The United States should not permit Canada to hold such a long lead in such a fine game."

"Fred Fillmore didn't stop Frank that time."

"Hardly!"

"I wonder why he dislikes Frank so? I know he does dislike him."

"Of course he does. He tried to lay it onto Frank when he and Tom Hackett came home intoxicated after that trip to the road house out on the Pimlico Road. I didn't believe him; I knew he was lying. He and the other fellows tried to get Frank and Bart full, but they were fooled, and Fred has been holding a grudge ever since."

"I think he would hurt Frank, if he could."

"I have an idea that Frank can take care of himself."

Hopkins had hoped to keep the visitors from scoring, and the whole team was rather sore over the success of the Merries.

Following this there was quite a period during which neither goal was in imminent danger. Hopkins took the offensive and kept it up, but each time the ball drew close to the Merries' net some of the defenders sent it away.

The home team grew more and more persistent. Woodin rushed the ball down the field repeatedly, or made beautiful passes to the vicinity of the visitors' goal.

Finally the locals closed in for a united attack, and both Hodge and Ready were kept busy.

During the five minutes of play that followed in the first half Hopkins made another try to score; but Frank's players succeeded in baffling the attack.

Finally the whistle sounded.

The first half ended with the score three to one in favor of the locals.

CHAPTER XXVII.

A HOT SECOND HALF.

"I haven't found the opening, Tom," said Fillmore, in a low tone, as he and Hackett rested during intermission. "It will come, though."

"Shame they got that goal!"

"That's right, it was a shame. Know how it happened?"

"Why, Merriwell just run right round the whole of you fellows."

"I turned my ankle just as I was jumping to check him," lied Fillmore. "If it hadn't been for that he'd never got past me."

"I thought it was remarkable you should let him dodge you that way."

The Harvard and Yale students were singing in chorus when the players returned to the field. They sang:

"For Merry's a jolly good fellow,
Merry's a jolly good fellow,
Merry's a jolly good fellow,
Which nobody can deny."

"Wouldn't that make you sick!" growled Fillmore. "Merriwell gave Harvard more trouble than any other ten Yale men when he was in college, yet here are those Harvard chaps joining the Yale gang in singing his praises."

The teams lined up, and once more Vernell proved his skill at centre by drawing the ball from Hackett, much to the disgust of the latter.

The first half had been lively; the second half was hot. Both teams went into it fiercely, straining every nerve. Up and down the field flew the ball. Woodin made some splendid runs. Fillmore distinguished himself by taking the ball out of Morgan's stick just as Dade was on the point of trying for goal. At times it was difficult to follow all the rapid plays.

Still it was some time before either side forced the goal guards to sweat. Hodge was the first one compelled to work hard, and he made five difficult stops in rapid succession, causing the spectators to cheer him loudly.

Frank laughed softly.

"Good old Bart!" he muttered. "I knew I had picked the right man to guard the net. Reckon Onslaw knows it now."

Onslaw had advised Frank to use Wilson.

It was Ready who passed the ball to Thatcher.

Thatcher tried to advance it, but was pocketed by two of the Hopkins defenders. Neither Morgan nor Wilkins was in position to take the ball, so Thatcher was compelled to pass it back to Merriwell.

It was a poor throw, for Mowry was nearer the ball and seemed sure to get it.

How Frank covered ground so fast no one seemed able to tell, but, running like the wind, he thrust out his stick and took the ball just as Mowry was on the point of catching it.

A yell of delight went up from his many admirers.

"Wake up, there, you fellow!" shouted a man. "You didn't catch it, did you! Ha! ha! ha!"

Kellogg came at Frank, but Merry easily avoided him, holding his club high and swaying it as he ran.

Lowe, however, managed to force Merry off to one side.

Frank passed to Onslaw.

A moment later there was a grand scrimmage in front of the Hopkins goal, in which a number of men of both teams were engaged. Fillmore was in it, and he found his opportunity. He smashed Onslaw across his bare shins with the stick, and the Harvard man went down.

The whistle blew.

Fillmore protested regret. Onslaw said nothing. His shins were rubbed and patched up and he re-entered the game.

Not three minutes later there was another scrimmage, for once more Frank secured the ball and ran with it to a position where he could try for goal. Brisbane stopped the ball and drove it away. Players of both teams went after it and there was a mix-up, Merriwell being in the midst of it.

Fred Fillmore got into it. They saw a stick sweep through the air. The blow, as it landed on a player's head, was heard in the stand.

Again the whistle blew.

Frank Merriwell was prone on the ground with his scalp cut open.

Fillmore had a broken stick, and he was bending over Merriwell, proclaiming his regret.

Inza Burrage started up, but she saw Frank rise to a sitting posture, and she sat down again, although her face was deathly white.

"Fred Fillmore did that intentionally," she exclaimed. "They should put him out of the game!"

Frank's injury was quickly dressed. A bandage was tied about his head, and he continued to play.

"What's the matter with Merriwell?" yelled a delighted Yale man.

"He's all right!" answered a hundred voices.

"They'd better put that Hopkins stiff out of the game!" shouted still another man.

Fillmore was warned by the referee, and the game was resumed. It was Herb Onslaw who finally shot the ball into the net.

Hopkins was now only one goal in the lead. The local players fought hard to hold that lead.

The ball was sent into the territory of the Merries, but it did not remain there long. Starbright shot it back, and Frank took it.

They could not stop him. He carried it down and shot for goal.

Brisbane stopped it, but it fell at his feet.

Wilkins was at hand, and he scooped it into the net.

The score was tied.

Never had Fillmore and his fellows been more desperate. They had fancied the game safely in their hands; but now they saw it slipping through their fingers.

It was no use. Again the Hopkins players saw the ball go into Merriwell's possession, and again they did their level best to keep him from reaching a position where he could try for goal.

But, swiftly dodging man after man, Merry wove his way through them toward the net and the anxious goal keeper.

Brisbane was nervous. He feared he could not stop the ball. That fear aided in his undoing.

He did not stop it.

Merry cast it deftly into one of the upper corners of the net, and his team had taken the lead.

After that Hopkins seemed to slump. Had the game lasted a few minutes more the Merries would have added another score. As it was, it finally ended four to three, just as the game with Harvard had finished.

The moment the game was over Frank Merriwell walked up to Fred Fillmore.

"You failed in your trick to-day, just as you failed at Hastings' road house," he said. "I don't know how you happened to be chosen the captain of the Hopkins team. You can play lacrosse, but you are a dirty fellow."

"Be careful!" muttered Fillmore. "Be careful what you say!"

"I am very careful. I am going to remain over a few days in Baltimore, and I shall try to see you again while I am here. If I meet you in a convenient locality I promise to give you something in return for the crack on the head that you gave me to-day. That is all."

That very night Fred Fillmore caught a train at Union Station, bound for New York. He was not anxious to meet Merriwell again.

CHAPTER XXVIII.

ELSIE BELLWOOD'S RESOLVE.

"How are you feeling to-night, Elsie?"

"No better."

"That's too bad, dear! I'm so sorry!"

Inza Burrage placed her arm lovingly about Elsie Bellwood and drew Elsie's head down upon her shoulder. They were in their room in the home of John Loder, in Baltimore. It was evening.

"I'm so sorry!" repeated Inza sympathetically, as she softly patted Elsie's pale cheek. "What seems to be the matter?"

"I'm tired, tired. I seem to be tired all the time now, Inza. I can't get rested."

"You'll be better to-morrow, dear," declared the dark-eyed girl cheerfully; "I'm sure you'll be better to-morrow."

"I don't know," sighed Elsie. "I fear not. Each day I've thought I would be better the next, but I improve so slowly it is very discouraging. It doesn't seem that I'll ever be well and strong again, as I used to be."

"Oh, but you will—of course you will! You're much better than you were in Virginia."

"I'd be dead now if I hadn't improved at all," returned Elsie, with a faint smile. "I used to feel so well. Inza, you're wasting your time staying by me this way. I appreciate it, oh, so much! But, I know how you must feel. You are well and strong and full of life. You make me feel guilty over keeping you in like this. I feel that I am——"

"There, there!" exclaimed Inza laughingly, placing a soft hand over Elsie's lips. "I won't listen to such nonsense! Are you not my dearest friend! It's a great satisfaction to me if I can do anything for you, as I know how much you have done for me in the past and how much you would do now if you had the opportunity."

"But you would be with Frank a great deal more if you did not feel it your duty to stay here with me. I am robbing you of that pleasure. It is not right. You had a letter from him in the last de-livery to-day."

"Yes."

"And I had one from Bart. Dear Bart! They have been very suc-cessful with their lacrosse team, and now they are coming back from their trip."

"And Frank must leave for Mexico in a very few days. He wants me to go with him."

Elsie started a little, and her face seemed to take on an added shade of pallor.

"To go with him?" she murmured.

"As—as Mrs. Merriwell."

Slowly Elsie lifted one not quite steady hand to her cheek.

"I am glad," she finally said, in a voice that was very low. "You will go with him, Inza?"

"Are you ready for the marriage?"

"Am I ready?"

"Yes, Elsie. I know Bart has urged you. You know it has been our plan to be married together—to have a double marriage. Frank wants it; Bart wants it; I want it. When will you be ready?"

Elsie did not reply immediately. It seemed that she was think-ing. In truth, she was summoning her strength.

"It will be a long time before I am ready, I fear," she finally an-swered. "You must not wait for me, Inza."

"Oh, Elsie, that would spoil everything! Oh, we must wait! I shall insist upon it."

Elsie turned and looked into the dark eyes of her companion.

"Inza," she said, "I may not be married for a year—I doubt very much if I shall. I may not be married then. It is not right for you to wait longer. Frank has asked you; he is impatient. Too many times something has arisen to delay your union with him. Through it all your love has been constant and his has never changed."

"Oh, no matter what happened, my love for Frank would re-main the same."

"You have been tried as with fire. There is no reason why you should permit anything to longer delay the consummation of your happiness and his. It would not be right to Frank if you did permit anything. You must marry him and go with him to Mexico for your wedding trip."

"But why won't you make it a double wedding? I do not under-stand——"

"When the boys were here in Baltimore I talked the matter over with Bart. He almost insisted that I should set a date. He wanted us to get together and agree on a date. I said no."

"But why—why? I can't understand why!"

"Don't fancy for a moment, Inza, that you love Frank more than I love Bart. It is not that my feelings have changed, but I have been ill and——"

"You are much better now. At times you are quite strong for a little while. Why, you attended the lacrosse game with me."

"And was ill for two days after. I tried not to let you know how ill I was. I did not wish you to think me spleeny, Inza."

Inza laughed musically.

"I know you too well to think anything like that," she said. "I have known you to endure too much. Oh, no, no, no! you are not spleeny! Anything but that!"

"I never knew my mother to remember her well," said Elsie. "My father told me lots about her. My mother was for many years a semi-invalid. If she seemed pretty well for a day or two, she was ill for weeks after. Father adored her. He told me that never was there a sweeter or more patient woman. He told me I was like her as he knew her when they first met. Even as a little girl I bore a remarkable resemblance to my mother. One old-fashioned picture of her was precisely like a picture I had taken, with the exception that there was a difference in our dresses and the way our hair was arranged. Father often said it was his prayer that I always remained well and strong.

"In every other way save in health he hoped I would exactly resemble my mother. I've meditated often on his words. I used to fear that some time I would become an invalid, the same as mother. That fear has grown upon me. It has taken a firm hold of me, and I cannot shake it off. Something seems to tell me that I shall never be wholly well and strong after this. A young man burdened with an invalid for a wife has a millstone about his neck, continually dragging him down. If he is a man of ambition and ability his life may be ruined. He can never rise as he would if he had a wife to cheer, encourage, and stimulate him to his best efforts. I believe Bart was meant by fate to become a great man. As his wife, if I were an invalid, I should hold him down. Therefore, Inza, I have resolved not to marry him—now."

Elsie had spoken earnestly, sincerely, from the bottom of her heart. She meant the words she uttered. There was no shamming about it; she was not posing. She really feared she would become an incumbrance upon Bart Hodge, and, for that reason and that alone, she was not ready to marry him. On her part it indicated a most remarkable attitude and most astonishing self-sacrifice. Few girls, loving a man as she loved Hodge, would have paused to consider—would have firmly held the cup of happiness back—out of consideration for his future.

In these days it is seldom a girl thinks that she may make or mar the man whose bride she is to be. As a rule, the one thought of the girl is to gratify herself and her selfish desires for comfort, ease, position, and happiness. Not one girl in a thousand hesitates to marry a man through fear that she may become a burden to him.

For years Inza had known Elsie to be generous, unselfish, and self-sacrificing to a wonderful degree; but now it seemed to Inza that her dearest friend was carrying her self-denying inclination to a mistaken extreme, and of this she attempted to convince her.

Elsie listened to Inza's argument, but it did not alter her determination.

"My dearest friend," she said softly yet firmly, "I am not strong enough now to pass through the excitement and strain of preparing for such a wedding. It would overtax me, even were I willing to place such a burden on Bart's shoulders. But you must not permit me to delay your own happiness and that of Frank. You must marry him now."

This Inza was extremely loath to do.

"It ruins our plan, which we have talked over so many times," she murmured regretfully. "Does nothing ever transpire in this world as we plan it?"

"I'm afraid few things come out just as we wish them," answered Elsie; "yet we should be happy. I am sure all will be well in the end. Promise me that you will not put Frank off longer."

It was no simple task to induce Inza to agree to this, but finally, by her gentle persuasion, Elsie succeeded. Immediately a sweet smile illumined her face.

"I am so glad!" she breathed. "Both you and Frank will be very happy together."

"But you, Elsie—how about you?"

"Don't think of me. I am all right here, where I have a good home and kind friends."

"Bart——"

"It will be better for him than it would be if he found himself tied to an invalid wife. It is my love for him that has led me to this resolution. I have written him, explaining as well as possible the situation, although I have not told him that I am putting off our union for his sake. Promise me, Inza, that you will not tell him this. Let him think, if he will, that it is on my own account that I ask the delay."

164

Again Inza flung her arms round Elsie.

"You are the dearest, sweetest girl in all the world!" she exclaimed; "but I cannot believe that your fears for your own health have any foundation. You have been so strong and well! It will all come out right in time, and we will be together again, you as Bart's wife and I as Frank's. We'll have jolly times, as we have had in the past. Oh, but we have had such splendid times, haven't we, Elsie?"

"Surely we have. No matter what may happen to me now, I shall always remember the past with unspeakable pleasure and be glad I have lived."

They fell to talking over old times and the many scenes and adventures through which they had passed since the wild night when Captain Bellwood's vessel was wrecked on Tiger Tooth Ledge, near Fardale. They laughed lightly as they spoke of misunderstandings and jealousies, now happily forever at an end.

Then, as was natural, they began to talk of Inza's trousseau and plan it, and both were very deeply engaged in this and very happy over it. Finally they paused from sheer exhaustion.

"One thing has made me a bit unhappy," Elsie finally observed.

Inza looked at her quickly.

"You mean——"

"Frank's unfortunate trouble with Fred Fillmore. Fred is Mrs. Loder's brother. At first she didn't know why he left Baltimore so suddenly after the lacrosse game; but I think he has written her, placing the blame on Frank."

"Frank was not in the least to blame!" exclaimed Inza quickly. "They were just foolish boys, both of them. Fred thought himself in love with me, and I had to hold him at a distance. He must have been crazy, else he would not have tried to knock Frank out in the game by hitting him over the head. No one could blame Frank for being angry and threatening to settle with Fred the next time they met. That was why Fred left Baltimore. There was no need for him to do so, for I would not have permitted Frank to quarrel with him."

A little later Elsie said:

"I think I'll go to bed now, Inza. I need rest. If I could only rest so I would not feel tired in the morning!"

Inza remained to assist Elsie. The girl with the blue eyes and the sweet, pale face sank back amid the pillows with a sigh.

"I'm so glad, Inza," she breathed—"so glad all your dreams are going to be realized. You will be very, very happy, and I shall be happy because you are."

Inza kissed her.

"Always thinking of others, you unselfish child!" she exclaimed. "What a world this would be if there were more like you in it! I am going down to the library for a book I am reading, dear. I will return soon."

Lightly she descended the stairs. The library was dark as she stepped in, but she pushed a button and turned on the electric lights. At the same moment she detected an odor of tobacco smoke. The flood of light showed her a person standing near the centre of the room, his feet quite wide apart, smoking a cigarette.

"Fred!" she exclaimed, startled; "Fred Fillmore!"

CHAPTER XXIX.

FRED FILLMORE'S ADVANCES.

The young man regarded Inza with a peculiar look. His face was flushed and his manner unnatural.

"Good evening, Miss Burrage," he bowed, with cool self-assurance. "This is a great pleasure, I declare."

She detected something odd in his speech, and, being quick of wit, decided at once that he had been drinking. He wore a blue coat, light trousers, tan shoes, outing shirt and no waistcoat. His necktie was carelessly knotted. The evening was almost oppressively warm.

Inza caught her breath.

"You startled me," she confessed.

"Did I? I beg your pardon. I couldn't seem to find the button myself, although I should know where it is. Had I been able to find it I'd turned on the lights for you."

"Oh, but you didn't know——"

"I knew you were coming."

"You did?"

"Yes."

"How?"

"Perhaps I heard your footsteps," he answered evasively. "Perhaps I know the rustle of your garments. I assure you the sound to me was like the rustle of an angel's wings."

A shadow came to Inza's face.

"When did you return to the city?" she asked.

"I arrived an hour ago."

"You have seen your sister?"

"Not yet. There was some one here I longed to see far more than her. My desire has been gratified."

"How did you get into the house?"

"With my own key, which I carried with me when I left."

He held the key up.

"Mrs. Loder knew you were coming, I suppose?"

"Not through me."

"Then you had better see her at once. She was much distressed because you left so suddenly without even bidding her good-by."

"You know why I left. I did it for your sake."

"For my sake?" cried Inza, in great surprise.

"Yes."

"I don't understand you."

"You know I had trouble with that fellow Merriwell."

The dark eyes of the girl flashed.

"'That fellow Merriwell!'" she exclaimed. "I do not like the manner in which you refer to him."

"I beg your pardon."

"You had better!"

"I couldn't help saying it. You know I had trouble with him."

"Which was your own fault."

"Perhaps you think so, but I assure you that you are mistaken. If he had acted like a gentleman that day he accompanied us to Hastings' on the Pimlico Road all would have been well."

"'If he had acted like a gentleman!'" Once more she quoted his words. "Frank Merriwell always acts like a gentleman. It is natural for him."

"I presume you think so, but the fellows in that party universally agreed that he behaved like a cad. Why, he pretended to drink with us, but he took water instead of gin."

"He told you at the start that he did not drink, but you insisted. You tried to force it upon him. Why? Because you had arranged a miserable scheme to make him ridiculous. You hoped to get him full and then to pit him against a prize fighter and a slugger. You thought you were fooling him, but he fooled you. That is why you say he did not act like a gentleman. Shame on you, Fred Fillmore! It was you who behaved like anything other than a gentleman."

She was aroused and he was beginning to feel the sting of her scorn.

But, strange as it seems, he liked it!

Why?

Because, with her cheeks flushed and her eyes flashing indignation, she was far handsomer than ever before in his eyes, and he had thought her the handsomest girl in all the world. He felt his blood taking fire as she stood before him glowing with indignation in her defense of Frank.

"I don't blame you for thinking that," he said. "Of course he told you anything he pleased, and you believed him."

"He never told a lie in all his life!"

"Is that so? A second George Washington, it seems! I'll not attempt to undeceive you."

"It would be quite useless."

"If I had remained in Baltimore I'd felt it necessary to give Mr. Merriwell all that was due him. A quarrel with him would have made your position here in my sister's home far from pleasant, and so I saw fit, on your account, to leave the city. I longed to smash his face."

"You tried to smash his head on the field in the game, and you did give him a scalp wound."

"That was an accident."

"It was not!" denied the girl positively. "I was watching closely, and I saw you strike him over the head with your stick."

"Had I done it intentionally the referee would have put me out of the game."

"He warned you. You did not tell the truth when you protested that it was unintentional. Frank was angry. You know you skipped from Baltimore after the game because you did not dare remain here and face him."

He laughed, snapping his fingers.

"Of course he impressed you with that idea. He is a great boaster. I left the city for the reason I have stated. I remained away as long as I could. Your eyes have haunted me, Inza. I have thought of you by day and dreamed of you by night. I could not forget you, even though I tried. I became desperate. At last I felt that I must see you again, and here I am. The real truth is that I'm in love with you, Inza—madly in love with you!"

In vain she tried to check this declaration. He spoke swiftly, intensely, passionately, his own eyes fairly burning with the intensity of his emotion. His voice shook and he felt himself all aquiver. He advanced toward her, but she flung up a repulsing hand.

"Keep away!" she exclaimed, falling back. "Are you out of your senses?"

"Perhaps I am," he hoarsely admitted. "I believe I am. Only one person in the world can restore me to my normal condition, and you are that one, Inza."

She would have retreated to the door by which she had entered the room, but, stepping quickly in her way, he prevented the movement.

"Don't go!" he entreated. "At first I felt it was folly to even think of you; but I could not help it, and I had to think. The more I thought the more desperate I became. I've known plenty of girls in my day, but never one who has thrown a spell on me as you have. I began to consider coming here and telling you everything. That seemed folly, also. I said I would not. Then I began to fancy myself a coward unless I spoke. I grew more desperate. I fought against the influence that was drawing me to you, but I could not overcome it. Finally I rushed for the train, without preparation, without further hesitation, and here I am. Don't be afraid of me. I want to marry you, Inza! My mother has promised to set me up in business as soon as I graduate. When my father died he left a fortune in trust for me. I am not a poor student with no prospects ahead of me. I can support you. I——"

She stopped him at last.

"Mr. Fillmore," she said, "it is useless for you to go on. Stop! I am to be the wife of Frank Merriwell. I am engaged to him, and we are to be married very soon."

"I hope not!" he cried. "I hope I'll never live to see that! You can break the engagement with him."

"You must be deranged to think I would do such a thing. My poor boy, don't deceive yourself. I love Frank Merriwell, and I do not care for you."

"Don't call me 'poor boy!'" he panted. "That hurts! I've been pitying myself until I realized I was a fool and that the only thing for me to do was win you from him. That I will do, somehow! I must, for I am one who has his way. You don't know the blood of the Fillmores. My father before me was a man who always had his own way. He started out a poor boy, but he resolved to be rich, and he became rich. All his life when he wanted a thing he found a way to obtain it. All my life I have been the same. I want you, and I'm going to have you! Heaven and earth shall not prevent me!"

Inza knew he was in a dangerous mood, but she was not one to hurt a person's feelings needlessly. The fact that she had aroused in his breast such a passion was enough to cause her to treat him as kindly as possible. A short time before she had been full of scorn, but now she repressed this and held it in check.

"Let me reason with you," she said. "You must understand the absolute hopelessness of your love, as you call it. Perhaps it is not love at all. It must be infatuation. In a little while you will forget me, or, if you remember, you will be thankful that you did not succeed."

"Never!"

"Oh, yes, you will! You are too young to marry. You have not yet made a start in the business world. I am older than you. You should not marry for some years to come, and then you should choose a wife some years younger than yourself."

"That's all rot! There's not much difference in our ages—not enough to raise the slightest barrier between us. Even if you were old enough to be my mother, I'd love you just the same!"

She could not refrain from smiling a bit at this, for it struck her as ridiculous.

"Don't laugh at me!" he exclaimed. "I'm no boy! I'm twenty-one!"

"Gracious! You'll soon be growing decrepit and senile."

"Don't laugh at me!" he repeated. "It hurts!"

"I don't want to hurt you, but I want to make you understand. What you wish can never be."

"If Merriwell were out of the way——"

"Even then it could never be, for I do not love you."

"You might—you might in time! I'd make you love me! I'd find a way!"

"You could not. You can't make a girl love you by commanding it. You'll simply succeed in causing her to fly from you."

"If you fly from me, even as Apollo pursued Daphne will I pursue you."

"Have you forgotten what happened when at last Apollo overtook Daphne? He did not succeed in his desires, for she was changed into a laurel tree, and his reward was bitter disappointment."

"How much more bitter would have been his feelings had he seen her captured by another! As Apollo was wounded by Cupid's dart thus have I been wounded. Inza, listen to me, I beg! Put off your marriage with Merriwell for a time. Your feelings toward him may change. Perhaps—perhaps——"

"It is folly for you to dream of such a thing."

"Then let me enjoy the sweet hope of folly for a time. Frank Merriwell is going to Mexico soon. Wait until he returns, and then, if you still——"

"You do not understand. Fate has caused us to put off the event more than once."

"But your plans are not coming out as you had intended. There will be no double marriage, for Elsie cannot——"

"How do you know about this?"

"How do I know? I'll tell you. After entering this house I was making my way to my room. I had to pass the door of the room occupied by you and Elsie. The door was a bit ajar. I heard you talking, and I could not help pausing——"

In a moment her anger rose again.

"So you listened! You played the eavesdropper!"

"I couldn't help it, for I heard you speaking of Merriwell. That name stopped me in my tracks. I beg a thousand pardons. I heard you say you were coming here for a book, and I scudded down the stairs to be here when you came, in order that I might see you and speak with you."

Inza had hoped to convince him of his folly without being harsh, but now she was again aroused. To her his action seemed mean and despicable.

"Fine business eavesdropping at the door of a room and listening to the confidences of two girls!" she cried, her face flaming. "I did not wish to hurt you, but this confession of yours has filled me with unspeakable contempt. If there is anything I detest it is a person who plays the sneak!"

He started as if struck in the face. It is possible he had not realized how contemptible his action would appear in her eyes, else he would not have told her he had listened.

"Don't!" he cried.

But she had decided that to be merciless with him would be the greatest kindness.

"I want you to understand how hopeless your case is," she said. "If I had never seen Frank Merriwell I could not care for you! If you were the last fellow in the world I could not care for you! You repel me!"

He lifted his hand, his fist clenched.

"Don't!" he exclaimed hoarsely.

"I want you to know the exact truth, so you will not deceive yourself longer."

He stood still, his eyes fastened on her. Silence fell between them.

She was the one who broke this silence.

"Now you know; now you understand," she said. "This will end it."

"No!" he declared. "This is not the end! It is the beginning!"

"If you annoy me——"

"I'll never give up! I'll win you from him—or I'll kill him!"

Fillmore fairly hissed the final words, and his face took on a look that frightened the girl.

"How would that help you?" she demanded. "You would make me loathe you, and you would send yourself to the chair."

"But I'd have the satisfaction of knowing he had not secured you. He never shall! I'll kill him first!"

CHAPTER XXX.

TRUE LOVE'S TELEGRAPHY.

Two days later Frank Merriwell and Bart Hodge stepped off the Congressional Express at Union Station, Baltimore. They took a cab and drove directly to the home of John Loder. They had planned a surprise for the girls, and a happy one it was.

Happening to look from the window, Inza saw them get out of the cab in front of the door.

"Elsie," she cried, "Elsie, Frank and Bart are here! Come—come quick!"

She ran down the stairs and Elsie followed as swiftly as possible. There was no waiting for any one else to answer the ring at the doorbell.

Frank stepped in and caught Inza in his arms, kissing her.

"Oh, Frank!" she murmured, as she clung to him; "oh, Frank, I'm so glad!"

Bart's face was aglow as he saw Elsie.

"Here we are!" he said, attempting to be commonplace in his manner. But a moment later he was imitating Merriwell's action.

"Bart!" whispered Elsie; "dear Bart!"

Five minutes later they were seated in the parlor, but they were still greatly excited over the meeting.

"You're a pair of bad, bad boys!" said Inza. "Why didn't you let us know you were coming?"

"Oh, we thought it would be jollier to give you a surprise," answered Merry. "We didn't know we'd be able to get here so soon. Canceled our last lacrosse game and the team disbanded. Met with only one defeat, and that was in Canada. For a fact, those Canadians can give us points at some things."

"Lacrosse, polo, ice hockey, and such sports," nodded Hodge. "But we lost our game with them by only one point, and we did defeat one Canadian team. Beyond question, we had a team that could walk away with anything in the United States."

"And is that the end of your tour?" questioned Inza.

"Yes, it's all over," answered Bart regretfully. "We've had a royal good time."

"We've had a royal good time," echoed Frank; "but now we're going to work."

"Our day of play is over," sighed Hodge.

"It's Mexico for me, with very little delay," said Merry. "The Central Sonora Railroad is under construction, and it's my duty to be on the ground."

"But we're going to take you with us, girls," declared Bart.

"Then you are going, too?" asked Elsie quickly.

"We've talked about it. Frank wants me to go. You know how we're going to take you."

Elsie shook her head, sadly yet firmly.

"I couldn't take the trip," she said. "It would be too much for me—now."

A shadow came to Bart's face.

"Why, Elsie——"

"Please, please don't urge me, Bart!" she entreated. "You know I'd be glad to go, but you cannot know how disappointed I am because I cannot."

"I'll have to talk to you alone," said Hodge grimly. "I'll have to get some foolish notions out of your head, little girl."

"I hope you can!" cried Inza.

"Leave it to me," he said.

Inza was doubtful if he would succeed, but she did not tell him so. She hoped he might, but she knew Elsie had quite made up her mind on that point.

"We have but a day or two to spend in Baltimore," said Frank. "You must go out to dinner with us, girls. What do you say to dinner at the Belvidere? At nine this evening I am to meet some friends at the University Club. Before that I am yours to command."

"I'm another," smiled Bart. "The Belvidere looks good to me. Eh, Elsie?"

To his surprise he saw that her face was colorless and her figure drooping.

Inza noted this and flew to her friend.

"The excitement, the shock has upset her!" she exclaimed. "You should have let us know you were coming."

She knew what to do to restore Elsie, but the delicate girl with the golden hair was quite weak and exhausted as she lay amid the pillows with Bart Hodge, repentant and anxious, hovering over her. Hodge was conscience-stricken.

"It was my fault!" he declared. "I suggested to Frank that we should give you this surprise. Oh, I'm sorry, Elsie—I'm sorry! I didn't mean——"

Forcing a faint smile, Elsie lifted her hand and gently pressed her fingers over his lips.

"No one is to blame," she said. "It was fine of you to wish to give me pleasure by such a surprise. But you see how weak I am. I can't go out to dinner to-night. Oh, what am I good for in the world anyhow?"

Bart was deeply touched by this cry which came from her heart. His fine, dark eyes glowed with tenderness and love.

"Don't—don't speak that way, sweetheart!" he murmured entreatingly. "I never dreamed you were like this, or I should not have left you."

But Elsie, with the unselfishness which had always marked her as the rarest and noblest of girls, retorted:

"I didn't wish you to know, for I felt that it was right that you should be with Frank, and I would not rob you of one moment of pleasure."

"She'll be all right in a few minutes," said Merry encouragingly. "We must have that dinner at the Belvidere."

"I'm afraid you do not understand, Frank," said Elsie. "I overdid when you were here last. I made a mistake in attending that lacrosse game, and it set me back. Oh, I'd love to go to dinner with you and Inza and Bart at the Belvidere, but I dare not attempt it."

Hodge was now more troubled and distressed over Elsie's condition than he seemed. Had she not understood him so well, she might have fancied him unsympathetic; but between them there was that mental telegraphy which seems to unite the hearts of all true sweethearts, and she knew that, manlike, while he did not betray the softness of a woman, his emotions were even deeper than her own.

Elsie turned to Inza.

"You must go out to dinner with Frank," she said. "Yes, I insist upon it."

"And I will remain here with Elsie," said Hodge. "That is best."

In this manner it was arranged.

"Whom do you meet at the University Club to-night, Frank?" asked Inza.

"Some Yale men. I'll cut it out if you wish. Have you anything you'd like to do——"

"Oh, no! I wouldn't have you fail to meet your friends for anything."

"Then I'll bring you back here after we've had dinner. There'll be plenty of time."

"And you'll find me here," said Bart.

Suddenly Merry stepped to the portières which separated the parlor from the reading room. With a sweep, he flung them back and stepped between them.

"Hello!" he exclaimed. "I thought there was some one behind these curtains."

He had found Fred Fillmore standing there in a threatening attitude.

Angered at being thus discovered, Fillmore aimed a swift blow at Merriwell's face. Like a flash of light Merry caught the fellow's hand, gave it a twist and locked his other arm round Fred's. With his free hand Fillmore attempted to strike again, making a sweeping blow at Frank's head.

Merriwell pressed downward sharply and firmly on the hand of the imprisoned arm, and Fillmore's blow stopped before he had reached Frank, while a cry of pain broke from his lips.

"I wouldn't repeat the trick, Fillmore, if I were in your place," said Merry quietly. "You'll simply hurt yourself by it. If you attempt to kick me on the shins I shall use still more pressure on your arm."

The baffled fellow glared sidelong at his master.

"Curse you!" he hissed.

"Save your curses. You know they have a way, like chickens, of coming home to roost."

"Let go!"

"In a moment. I didn't know you were in the house, but I fancied some one was listening behind these curtains."

"I have a right to do what I please in this house. You are an intruder here! You'd better get out!"

"You have a right to do what you please anywhere if you behave yourself. I did not intend to touch you, but you struck at me, and I was compelled to defend myself. The last time you struck at me I was unprepared and could not defend myself. I have a little scar on my head now."

"I wish I had brained you!"

"I can't understand your folly. It doesn't seem possible that you can hold a silly grudge because you and Hackett failed in your little trick to get me full at Hastings' road house and have me hammered by a paid ruffian. That can't be the reason why you hate me so intensely."

"It isn't."

"I thought not. I've never done you harm, and I have no desire to harm you. Miss Burrage and Miss Bellwood have been stopping beneath your sister's roof——"

"Which you seem to forget."

"If they had not been stopping here I might be inclined to handle you without gloves. Let's not make more of a scene before them. Miss Bellwood is not well. I shall be in Baltimore a day or two. If you wish to see me, call at the——"

"No, Frank—no!" cried Inza. "For my sake—and Elsie's! Fred is unreasonable; he's out of his senses. Please consider us!"

"Of course I will," said Merry quickly.

"Of course you'll be glad to hide behind petticoats!" panted Fillmore. "But petticoats cannot protect you. You are my enemy, and I hate you! When a Fillmore hates he's never satisfied until he crushes!"

"Don't bring disaster on yourself through your unreasonable and unwarranted hatred."

"Don't give me advice, but look out for yourself!"

"I think I can look out for myself."

"You're very self-confident, but you're not the smartest chap in the world, and you'll find it out."

"I'm afraid you have been annoying these girls."

"No!" declared Inza quickly. "Anything he might do could not annoy us."

This seemed to enrage Fillmore. He ground his white teeth together and attempted to break from Frank with a jerk. A slight pressure on his arm caused him to desist.

"Go ahead!" he groaned; "go ahead and break my arm!"

He had been caught with a jujutsu hold.

"You think you're smart, I suppose!" he went on pantingly. "Just because you happened to get this hold on me I presume you fancy you are a great master of the art of jujutsu. Bah! You'd be a baby in the hands of one who actually knew something about it."

"We're not discussing that," said Frank. "I was forced to this to defend myself without getting into a disgraceful fight with you here in the presence of the girls."

"You may have a chance to defend yourself before you leave Baltimore," declared Fillmore significantly.

"I presume you mean that you are going to force me into a fight. Well, forewarned is forearmed. I'll try to be ready for you."

"See that you are!"

In vain Inza tried to interpose and pacify Fillmore.

"You can't blame me," he said. "You know why I hate him. I have a right to hate him!"

"You are not gaining favor in my eyes by such disgraceful behavior."

These words from Inza's lips were enough to open Merry's eyes to the true situation. His faith in Inza was absolute, but he knew Fillmore had been trying to pay her attentions. This and the fact that Mrs. Loder was Fillmore's sister made the matter most embarrassing.

Merry saw at once that it would be necessary to take Inza from that house as soon as possible.

"Please, Fred," entreated Elsie; "please, for my sake, don't make any more trouble here!"

"All right," he said. "Let Merriwell release me. I'll make no more trouble—here."

Instantly Frank set him free.

"Take my advice," he said, "and make no more trouble anywhere. It can do you no good."

"I want no advice from you!" snarled the infuriated fellow, moving his wrenched arm to make sure it was not seriously hurt. "All I have to say to you is: Look out for yourself!"

With which he turned and hurried away.

CHAPTER XXXI.

THE UNSEEN LOVER.

Shortly after Frank and Inza departed Fred Fillmore left the house. Elsie watched him run down the white steps and hurry away along the street.

"He means to make trouble for Frank, Bart," she said, turning to Hodge. "He's a desperate fellow."

"What's the matter with him?" asked Bart. "Is he crazy?"

"He's quite lost his head over Inza."

"I thought that was about the size of it."

"That was the cause of all the trouble in the first place. He fell to hovering round Inza, and paying her attention. She never encouraged him in the least, for she is no flirt. Of course she treated him well, for we are in his sister's home. When Frank appeared he was jealous. That's what led on to that affair at the road house."

"Well, he'd better not fool with Frank Merriwell, for he'll regret it if he does. Frank will not harm him unless forced into it. What has he been doing lately?"

"Just watching constantly to get a look at Inza. He's quite lost his senses over her. And he drinks, too, Bart. He seems to be full almost all the time. He actually proposed to Inza the night he returned here, forcing her to listen to him."

"Oh, he did, eh?"

"Yes."

"She wrote Frank nothing of it."

"No, for she knew it would do no good, and she did not wish to make trouble. She has been thinking he might get over his unreasoning infatuation, but I think he grows worse and worse every day."

"Inza will soon be Mrs. Merriwell, and that will settle Mr. Fillmore."

He led Elsie back to her seat amid the pillows, taking care to see that she was perfectly comfortable.

"There, little girl!" he laughed, his eyes shining as he looked at her; "there you are. I've been a scoundrel! What you need is the right kind of a doctor, and I'm the doctor! You never let me know you were more than a trifle indisposed. Why should you be ill? It's all nonsense! Sweetheart, we'll have the color back to your cheeks in short order. Oh, yes we will!"

She smiled on him.

"You're so encouraging, Bart, dear!" she breathed. "Truly you make me feel better."

"I hope to make you feel so well that you'll agree to carry out the plan we have spoken of so many times. Are you willing to see Frank and Inza reach the consummation of their happiness and leave us behind?"

"I have to be willing," she said. "We must wait, Bart, dear."

"I've waited so long, Elsie—so long!" he exclaimed, in a low tone that was deep with feeling. "And now the time has come. Elsie, my own, why do you put it off?"

"Because I feel that it is right."

He had her hand imprisoned in his. She was leaning against one of his strong arms and looking up into his dark eyes, where she saw a world of tenderness and devotion.

"Don't you love me the same as you did?" he asked anxiously.

"What a foolish question, you big, silly boy! I love you more than ever before. You don't understand—you don't know how much I love you!"

He thrilled as he heard her speak these words with lips that knew not insincerity or deceit. He had trusted her fully, completely, and he was certain she trusted him in the same degree. Between them there was no shadow of doubt, for "love cannot dwell with suspicion."

"Elsie," he urged, all palpitant with the intensity of his yearning for her, "be mine—my own little wife—and I'll guard you and tenderly care for you until you are well and strong again. My strength shall be yours. I'll bear you over all the rough places in life's pathway. I'll shield you from every chill breath of the world. You shall be, as you have been, the star of my ambition. With you near me, I'll be encouraged and spurred on to do great things in the world. The knowledge that you trust me fully will forever guard me from my weaker self and keep me strong and true."

Young though he was, he instinctively knew that the greatest evil that can befall a man is to be doubted or distrusted by one he deeply loves. The knowledge that a beloved one is absolute in her faith and trust in him has kept many a man true and faithful and exalted, even above his natural self; while doubt, suspicion, and distrust has ruined thousands who were naturally upright and honorable. A man with a conscience that makes him worthy to be called a man is repelled at the thought of betraying one who has proved that she loves and trusts him fully.

Bart Hodge had once been wayward and willful—even weak at times; but the friendship and trust of Frank and Elsie had fortified him against temptation and made him strong and manly in every way. He was worthy of Elsie's love, even though she was a girl among ten thousand.

"Bart, dear," said Elsie gently, "I have thought it all over, and I know it would be a mistake for me to attempt to pass through the strain and excitement at this time. I beg you not to urge me. As you love me, do not insist. I hope the time will come very soon when I shall feel ready to take your name. When that time comes I'll be the happiest and proudest girl the sun ever shone on."

A sigh of disappointment and resignation came from his fluttering heart.

"Man proposes and woman disposes, to alter an old saying," he smiled regretfully. "I've waited, and I can wait longer. It seems that I'll have to."

He kissed her as he spoke these words.

"You dear, good boy!"

"You'll find me ready when you are, sweetheart," he declared. "I shall not go to Mexico with Frank."

"Oh, I wouldn't prevent that for anything!" she cried. "If you have planned——"

"My plans must be altered, that is all. I'm going to be near you until you are yourself again, little girl."

"And then——"

"And then I'll positively decline to be put off any longer, Miss Perversity."

"I hope you do not think I am perverse."

"I think you are the most bewitchingly perverse little body in all creation; but your very perverseness charms and fascinates me. Girl, you were bewitching in health and strength; but by my life, you're a hundred times more so now! Why, I just long to do something to shield and protect you. It makes me feel a hundred times stronger than usual to see you pale and weak. You had the face of a flower, but now you have the face of an angel!"

"Oh, Bart, you're too extravagant in your flattery!"

"It's no flattery, Elsie, dear."

But of a sudden she saw a cloud stealing over his face as he

181

gazed upon her.

"What is it?" she asked, quick to feel every changing mood of his.

"Oh, nothing—nothing," he answered; but after a moment he embraced her and held her as if fearful that she would slip away from him.

It was in truth this fear which had found lodgment in his heart. For the first time he had been seized by a feeling of apprehension lest he might lose her ere she could become wholly his. What was this strange weakness that had come upon her and clung to her in spite of everything? Always she had seemed a bit ethereal, as if not wholly of this world; and now a singular, terrifying fancy took hold of Bart. It seemed to him that some envious lover of the spirit world had laid claim to her and was seeking to win her from him. His active fancy pictured this unseen lover slowly but surely drawing her to him.

As this fancy ran through his mind Bart was silent, but of a sudden he hoarsely cried:

"He shall not have you!"

Elsie was startled.

"Bart!" she exclaimed.

"He shall not have you!" repeated Bart. "You are mine! I'll not let him take you from me!"

"Are you losing your reason?" she asked.

"No, no, Elsie! You are mine! Look, sweetheart, I seem to see a demon, a spirit, or something that is striving to wrest you from me. That is why you are weak and you do not grow stronger. Elsie, you love me! Fight against this unseen power that is seeking to part us—fight it with all your remaining strength! Will that you shall grow strong. If you do not, dearest girl, I'm afraid the monster may conquer! Fight, Elsie—fight for your life and for my love!"

Never had she seen Bart in such a mood. He clung to her as if fearing he would lose her at once if he relaxed his hold.

"Bart—dear Bart, it is a silly fear. Shake it off."

"Promise me you will fight against him!" urged Hodge huskily.

"I promise."

"Then make up your mind to get well and strong as soon as you can. It's the only way. Throw off this weakness. You must, dear Elsie—you must!"

She repeated her promise, but still he could not get over the feeling of apprehension and dread that had assailed him.

CHAPTER XXXII.

THE PRICE OF A LEG.

red Fillmore boarded a car and sprang off at the Auditorium. He went directly to the box office, where he made certain inquiries that led him to take another car, which he left and walked briskly to the Rennart Hotel.

"Please send my card up to Mr. Hashi," he said to the clerk.

Ten minutes later he was received in one of the rooms of the hotel by a suave, smiling little Jap, who did not look particularly formidable, yet who had the movements of a panther coupled with that animal's grace.

"What can I do for you, most honorable sir?" inquired the Jap.

"You are Mr. Hashi, the great Japanese master of jujutsu, I believe?"

"I have that humble honor, most respected sir."

"You can break a man's bones as if they were pipe-stems?"

"It is true, that which you speak. If such should be my wish, noble sir, I could swiftly obtain its accomplishment."

"You are giving exhibitions here in Baltimore, and thus far you have by your art defeated all who have ventured to face you on the stage."

"It is with accuracy that you have made this statement. Such has been my exceeding good fortune."

"Do you want to make some money?"

"It is for that purpose, highly intelligent sir, that I am traveling in your most interesting country."

"I'll give you five hundred dollars to break a man's arm!" cried Fillmore.

Hashi smiled blandly.

"Such an accomplishment may not be obtained unless the opportunity occurs. Even then it may not be secured without much trouble making of extreme seriousness, wise and respected sir."

"But it might be done in a contest? You might do it if you were matched against another man."

"It might then by accident be made to appear."

"That's it—that's the idea!"

"But five hundred dollars—the amount is small in its exceedingness, discreet sir."

"Five hundred dollars—it's a good price. I will undertake to arrange it for you to meet this man I wish injured. If you break his arm, I'll give you five hundred."

"Is this to be accomplished on the platform in the view of the audience?"

"Oh, no; I won't want you to do it in the theatre. I intend to arrange a private meeting."

"In what place is this to be, distinguished sir?"

"In a club."

"When do you bring it about?"

"To-night."

"It is extremely soon."

"No time is to be lost. Will you do it?"

"Five hundred dollars—the amount does not to me appear a sufficient sum. Your generosity should increase it when you apprehend the trouble which may after it occur. If I should be placed in the arrest and prevented from my engagement at the theatre fulfilling it would to me be a misfortune."

"There is no danger of anything of the sort. Can you break a man's leg?"

This seemed to be an afterthought on the part of Fillmore.

"It is in no degree a difficult accomplishment to obtain, distinguished sir."

"Then that's what I want—that's what I want!" cried Fillmore. "A man can't walk into church to be married with a broken leg."

"The remuneration should be exceedingly larger, accomplished sir. For an arm five hundred is extremely insufficient. For a leg one thousand would be the smallest amount I could humbly accept."

Fillmore thought a moment. He did not have a thousand dollars. In his pocket there was something more than six hundred, and five hundred of this he had obtained by skillfully raising a check given him by his mother.

"I'll go you!" he suddenly cried. "A thousand dollars if you break the man's leg."

"I should humbly expect the money in advance, generous sir."

"And then give me the throwdown! What if you failed to make good? What if you could not do the trick?"

"Hashi has the modest honor of never making of his promises a failure. If I give you my word and you give me the required opportunity, you may rest in dependence on it that I shall accomplish the matter."

"That sounds first-rate, but you don't know the man I am going to pit you against. He has a reputation."

Hashi smiled confidently.

"It makes not a difference who he may be."

"You'll find him a hard nut to crack."

"Do you mind mentioning his honorable name?"

"His name is Frank Merriwell."

The Jap continued to smile.

"Somewhere in your interesting country I have heard of him. Is it not that he is a what you call athlete?"

"That's the fellow. He claims to be the champion amateur athlete of this country. He is conceited and overbearing. He knows a little something of everything. He thinks he knows all there is to know about jujutsu."

Hashi's smile had a pitying flavor:

"It is a thing of remarkability that those who the least know about the art are ones that think nothing more there is left for them to attain."

"That's him!"

"Against him you must have a great enmity, honorable sir."

"I hate him! It would give me joy if you were to break his neck!"

"A thing that might be done with great ease of accomplishment."

"Will you? What's your price?"

Still smiling, Hashi shook his head.

"Respected sir, it is not money enough you can make advancement to bring me to that."

"I'll give you anything you ask! I'll raise the money somehow!"

Still the Jap shook his head.

"A broken limb will make amendment, but a broken neck remains fatally so."

"That's what would suit me! Then he would be out of my way forever."

"And should it become known of our talk here, the money could unto me no good bring, for a severe punishment of death would come unto us both. No, respected sir, no, no. A broken limb—yes; a broken neck—no!"

"Then it is settled, you are to break his leg to-night. What time are you through with your exhibition at the theatre?"

"I come at the advancement of the program, and it is before nine that I am quite ended."

"That's all right. Leave the theatre as soon as possible. I'll be waiting for you with a carriage, and we'll drive directly to the University Club, where we shall find Merriwell."

"How, respected sir, will it then be arranged?"

"I'll find a way. Leave it to me. I know a number of college fellows who will be there. I'll tip them off to be on hand. It should be easy to bring about a meeting between you and Merriwell. He tried jujutsu on me. If necessary, I'll insult him and say you can show him up."

"It will be better, I would humbly suggest, to draw him into the contest without his suspicions arousing by the process of the insult. Let it seem that it shall be a friendly affair from the commencement. That is what it should not be difficult."

"That's right if you'll do your part."

"You may depend on it that I am reliable if you pay me the advancement."

"I'll give you a hundred down and the rest as soon as you do the job."

Hashi smiled as he shook his head.

"It will not be a matter for considering unless I am in reception of five times that before starting."

The Jap had gauged Fillmore, and he was determined to get every dollar possible out of the fellow.

In vain the young rascal argued; Hashi continued to smile and remained firm. Finally Fillmore was compelled to yield or give over his dastardly plan.

"All right," he said; "but there will be trouble if you fail me."

"Let me humbly urge, respected sir, that you have no need to use the threat. Be waiting at the stage door. If the opportunity is found for me, I shall earn from you the money that has been justly agreed upon."

Fillmore left the Rennart in high spirits.

"A broken leg will block this marriage for a time," he muttered. "It will give me an opportunity to make further plans and carry them out. Ah! Mr. Merriwell, you don't know the kind of an enemy you have in me! I'm fighting for haughty, black-eyed Inza, and I'll fight to the finish!"

CHAPTER XXXIII.

AT THE UNIVERSITY CLUB.

here was an unusual gathering of young college men at the University Club that evening. Word had been passed round that Merriwell would be there. He appeared shortly before nine o'clock, accompanied by Hodge. Maurice Spaulding, a Yale man, hastened to greet him.

Frank and Bart surrendered their hats to the darky checker and followed Spaulding into the reading room. Immediately several Yale grads hastened to greet them. After this, they were introduced to other club members and visitors.

The Yale men gathered in a group, with Merry and Bart in their midst, and chatted of such things as interested them all. They were very proud of Merriwell and the athletic record he had made.

"It will be a long day before Yale sees another leader like him!" cried Spaulding enthusiastically. "You made plenty of enemies in your day, Merriwell, old man. I believe my cousin Wallace was one of them."

"Wallace Spaulding—is he your cousin?" asked Frank, in some surprise.

"I regretfully confess that he is," grinned Maurice. "Wallace regarded himself as the real thing in his college days, and, as far as things go, he was."

"I don't see how you've kept up in athletics as you have since leaving college, Merriwell," observed Henry Harriman. "Most chaps take a slump unless they go into professionalism. Of course there are exceptions."

"And Merriwell is a shining star among the exceptions," nodded Cutler Priest.

"Hail to the all-round amateur champion of the United States!" cried Vincent Carroll. "What's the secret, Merriwell, old chap?"

"Never let up," answered Frank quickly. "That's the secret of success in most things."

"Is that your motto?" questioned Harriman.

"One of them," answered Merry.

"But you've had some things besides athletics to occupy your time and attention since toddling out into the world," observed Raymond Harrow. "I understand you're in the mining game."

"Somewhat," admitted Frank. "Still I find a chance now and then to drop everything and go in for baseball and kindred sports."

"Well, let's all go take something," suggested Carroll. "Merriwell used to be a cold-water crank, I understand; but, of course, he's broken the pledge since he began to ramble from Old Eli's fireside."

"On the contrary," said Frank, "I've kept it the same as ever. That's one secret of my success, only there is no secret about it. Be temperate, fellows—be temperate."

"Oh, I am!" protested Carroll; "I'm temperate, but I'm no total abstainer. A total abstainer is not a temperance man. Temperance means moderation, and unless you use a thing with moderation you have no claim to temperance. Got you there!"

"Your argument cannot be overthrown," admitted Frank. "Therefore I'm willing to be classed among the cranks."

"Oh, but come have something with us!" they urged.

"I'll do that," he laughed; "but it will be something nonintoxicating."

Hodge was treated with the same cordiality, and the entire party crowded in before the little bar.

Frank and Bart both drank ginger ale.

"Here's to Merriwell, the pride of Yale in the old days and the pride of Yale to-day!" cried Carroll, holding a glass of beer aloft. "May his star never grow dim!"

"That's the talk!" they cried. "Drink—drink it down!"

Some one ordered another round.

"Here's to Hodge!" cried Spaulding. "Merriwell's right-hand man at Yale and his loyal backer ever since. If there's any baseball on the Golden Shore, I'll expect to see Bart Hodge doing the backstopping when Frank Merriwell fans the batter with the double-shoot."

"You expect to see it!" laughed Harrow loudly. "You'll be fanning yourself in another country."

"Blasphemer!" exclaimed Spaulding. "Go to! You seem to think every one is traveling the same road you've taken."

They left the bar and entered the billiard and pool room, where some of the club members were amusing themselves.

Two young chaps had lately entered the billiard room. They were Bob Ridgely and Martin Manners, known to some of those in Frank's party.

Manners brought Ridgely up.

"How are you, Harrow," he said familiarly. "Looking for a victim? I understand you're a shark at billiards."

"Not looking for a game to-night," answered Harrow.

"Perhaps some of your friends are?" said Manners, in the way of one inclined to "butt in." "I've been told Frank Merriwell would be here to-night. They say he's a shark at everything, even billiards. I'd like to try him a go."

He looked straight at Frank as he made this challenging remark.

"Mr. Merriwell—Mr. Manners," said Harrow.

"Er—I beg your pardon, what name?" said Merry.

"Manners is his name."

"Quite remarkable," said Merry quietly. "Haven't heard that name in some time. How do you do, Mr. Manners."

"What do you say, are you good for a hundred points?" asked Manners. "I'd enjoy beating the great champion at something."

"I beg to be excused this evening," said Frank. "I didn't come here for billiards or anything of that sort, but to meet these friends of mine."

Ridgely laughed and pulled at Manners' arm.

"No go, Mart," he said. "Better look for some one fast enough to make it interesting."

Hodge was angered at this insolence and felt like expressing himself, but Maurice Spaulding picked it up.

"This club is supposed to be for gentlemen!" he exclaimed.

"It's supposed to be," drawled Ridgely; "but I see the rules are not enforced."

"Cad!" growled Carroll.

"Oh, take a little joshing!" cried Manners. "The great Merriwell, who is champion at everything, ought to stand a little fun. What's the matter?"

"I hear he's a gone-by," grinned Ridgely. "He's been playing baseball with schoolboys of late and trying to keep up his reputation that way."

It seemed that Spaulding would strike the insolent fellow, but Frank caught Maurice's arm.

"Never mind him," he said. "I'm always stirring up soreheads. I don't know what he has against me, and I care less."

The entire party seemed highly incensed by the words and behavior of Manners and Ridgely, but the latter continued to insist that it was nothing but a joke.

"I'd back Merriwell myself," he averred. "That is, I'd back him in his own field. I wouldn't put him up against professionals. It would be folly to back him against Jeffries in the ring."

"Don't mind him," said Harriman. "Some one will settle him for insulting guests of the club."

"But I haven't insulted any one," persisted Ridgely. "Some silly persons might put an amateur against a professional. What would Merriwell or any other amateur do against a professional wrestler like Americus?"

"They say Americus is going to show up Hashi, the jujutsu chap, to-morrow night," said Manners.

"What's that?" exclaimed the voice of a newcomer. "Well, I'll bet five hundred dollars that Americus or any other man in Baltimore can't get the best of my friend Hashi. If there is any one here who thinks he can handle Hashi—well, here's Hashi to give him the chance."

The speaker was Fred Fillmore, and he was accompanied by the Japanese master of jujutsu.

"'Ware, Merry!" hissed Hodge, quick as a flash.

Instinctively he knew there was something in the air. He felt it like an electric shock. Frank did not need the warning. He, too, felt a sudden tightening of his nerves.

Fillmore swaggered into the room. His face was flushed and his manner seemed to indicate that he had been drinking heavily.

The Jap who followed him was smiling serenely.

A number of those present had seen Hashi's performance at the theatre, and they recognized him instantly.

The billiard players paused and regarded him with interest. The others were no less interested.

"Who says Americus can handle Hashi?" demanded Fillmore. "Americus is all right in his class, but he'll overstep himself if he accepts Hashi's challenge and goes after the hundred dollars offered to the wrestler of less than two hundred pounds who can handle this little master of jujutsu. Why, Hashi can break Americus in two, if he wishes; but he's a harmless little chap, and it's likely he'll be content with flinging Americus over his head and across the stage."

As he said this Fillmore placed a hand on the shoulder of the Jap, who continued to smile and look innocent.

"Gentlemen," said the Hopkins man, "it gives me great satisfaction to introduce my friend Hashi."

The jujutsu master bowed in his politest manner, murmuring:

"It inexpressible pleasure gives me the honorable gentlemen to humbly greet."

"You see Hashi is very modest," laughed Fillmore.

"Keep your eyes open for tricks, Merry," whispered Bart. "There is something behind this, sure as fate."

Frank nodded the least bit.

"Hashi has taken to the warpath," explained Fillmore. "He has heard a great deal of talk about jujutsu being a fake. The Sun today contained a letter from some duffer who claimed that there was nothing to the Japanese art of self-defense and that any ordinary American athlete could defeat a Japanese expert. It has angered him somewhat."

"Indeed meek confession I must speak that it has incensed me to the great extremeness," put in Hashi.

"No one would ever dream it from his everlasting smile and his soft speech," muttered Raymond Harrow.

"The critic of the Sun didn't have the nerve to sign his full name," said Fillmore; "but I have a fancy that I know who the man is."

"We are honored to meet Professor Hashi," said Maurice Spaulding.

The Jap bowed very low, after his manner.

"The honorableness is fully upon me," he asserted. "I am quite overcome in your august presence."

Vincent Carroll laughed softly.

"He has a fluent way of expressing himself," he observed in an aside to Cutler Priest. "Seems to take great satisfaction in articulating big words."

"It is the way of his countrymen," nodded Priest. "In Japan they have no personal pronouns, but apparently Hashi has picked them up in this country, for he uses them."

"The professor is a particular friend of mine," Fillmore went on, "and I am interested in seeing him maintain his reputation. He is looking for some of these great American athletes who think they can defeat him."

"It's coming, Merry!" muttered Bart softly.

Frank was calm and unconcerned. Apparently Fillmore had not observed him since entering the club; but Frank knew the fellow had a keen pair of eyes. This seeming oversight on Fillmore's part was enough to convince Merry beyond doubt that the visit was premeditated in full expectation of encountering him there.

He knew Fillmore had listened behind the portières at John Loder's and heard of the engagement to meet certain Yale grads at the club.

"Did you read in the papers about the American wrestler who repeatedly defeated a Japanese jujutsu expert in Omaha and other Western cities?" inquired Henry Harriman.

Fillmore laughed.

"Of course we read it, all of us," he answered. "I showed the reports to Professor Hashi. He says the Jap was no expert."

"Honorable attention give," murmured Hashi, "and I will complete explanation make. No one ever a full master of the art can become who does not unto it give the long and faithful attention. Acquirement of it may not be obtained with the exceeding great rapidity. Since in your distinguished country the art has appeared, many there must be who it seek to teach that have not ever at all learned it in its uttermost completion. Therefore thus discredit upon it is contumely heaped, which should not ever be the proper condition. The pretending one in the West who has been much defeated by the honorable skillful American athlete was not of the art completely the full master."

"That's about the size of it," nodded Fillmore. "The Jap who was put to the bad in Omaha was a faker. Hashi is ready and eager to demonstrate that no American wrestler can defeat him, and no ordinary athlete has a ghost of a show with him. He is most disgusted with the Americans who learn a little jujutsu and think they know it all."

"It is even thus true, augustly honorable sirs," bowed the Jap.

"I presume," said Spaulding, "that jujutsu is regarded in Japan as the proper mode of self-development?"

"Leniently pardon my humble correction, beneficent sir," said Hashi. "Jujutsu is not what in your bounteous country you know as the excellent art of self-development. That is where the unfortunately grave error makes presentation. Jujutsu is not the physical culture; it is the exceedingly efficient manner of self-defense. Boxing done in your expansive country is for the self-defense much extremely more than for the physical culture. In Japan jujutsu is of the same nature. Continuation of practice may much increase the participator in physical development; but it is not that end solely that it is in use brought."

"This gives me a new idea of jujutsu," confessed Spaulding. "Why, most of the teachers of it in this country speak of it as a system of physical culture."

"That's just where the mistake comes," said Fillmore. "As Hashi says, practice of it cannot help improving the one who practices; but it is not regarded in Japan in the light of an exercise for physical development solely. It is chiefly taught that the one who acquires it may be able to defend himself against a less skillful, even though a stronger, opponent."

"We're finding out all about jujutsu, Merry," said Hodge softly.

"But not learning anything new," said Frank.

Suddenly Fillmore seemed to discover Merriwell.

"Hello!" he muttered.

Frank regarded the fellow calmly.

"Here, Hashi," said Fillmore, "you have the fortune of beholding one who regards himself as the champion athlete of this country and has somehow won considerable recognition of his claim."

The Jap bowed very low.

"Augustly deign to let my bewildered eyes find resting upon the famous one," he urged.

Fred jerked his thumb toward Merry. It was a gesture calculated to irritate Frank.

"Behold him, professor."

Hashi smiled, but there was the least touch of incredulity and contempt in that smile.

"I am greatly overcome in his honorable presence," he murmured.

"Here's a chance for you to prove your claim that you are more than a master for any athlete or wrestler that weighs not more than two hundred pounds."

"How would you generously suggest that such may come about?"

"Challenge him! His name is Merriwell. Challenge him!"

Fillmore laughed, as if considering it a great joke.

The face of Bart Hodge was dark and frowning.

"Here it comes!" he muttered again.

Hashi advanced a little and surveyed Frank more fully.

"I humbly confess my exceeding admiration at beholding one so grandly famous," he purred. "Believe me greatly overcome in your august presence."

"What claptrap!" said Hodge. "Out with it and show your hand! Nobody is fooled by this slick game."

Hashi looked surprised, but said:

"Wonderful much pleasure it would give if the excellent honorable American athlete would condescend to meet me in the contest of skill."

"All right," said Frank promptly. "Where shall it be?"

Fred Fillmore was somewhat surprised by Merry's prompt acceptance of the smoothly delivered challenge. He had fancied it would be necessary to drive Frank into it through ridicule.

Frank was not pleased. He was dressed in evening clothes, and he had no desire to meet Hashi; but he had understood from the first that it was a scheme to force him into the meeting in some manner, and therefore he decided to meet the schemers halfway.

"The sooner it is over the better," he thought.

Martin Manners and Bob Ridgely were somewhat disappointed. They were friends of Fillmore, and it had been arranged that they were to join in the ridicule of Merry in case he declined or seemed reluctant to meet the Jap.

Hashi had been told by Fillmore that it might be no easy matter to draw Frank into the snare, and he, also, was somewhat surprised.

"It is the exceeding great honor you are beneficently willing to bestow upon me?" he questioned.

"If that's the way you look at it," nodded Frank.

"You'll get all that's coming," muttered Hodge.

"I know where we can pull it off," laughed Fillmore quickly. "There's a private gymnasium near the Diamond on Howard Street. That will be a fine chance."

"Well, well!" cried Spaulding; "it seems that we're going to have an entertainment not down on the bills."

"'Rah, 'rah!" cheered Harrow. "This is the kind of stuff to suit me!"

The Yale men were enthusiastic, and to a man they expressed their confidence in Merry.

"Do your best with him, old man," urged Spaulding.

"Without doubt I'll have to," nodded Frank.

Merry knew he was going against "the real thing." He was not one of the scoffers at jujutsu, although he held that the Japanese art alone was not enough to make a man complete master of other men.

Now it happened that for many months Merry had been perfecting his knowledge of jujutsu, which he had first picked up during his trip round the world. In Japan he had learned much of the art, the secrets of which were well guarded at that time. It was this knowledge that had enabled him on many occasions to overcome assailants far heavier and stronger than himself, greatly to their dismay and chagrin. At Yale he had practiced it, although he had not called it jujutsu at that time.

Frank was not conceited enough to fancy himself the equal of Hashi in the knowledge of all the Japanese methods; but there was another thing that promised to make Merry the equal of the Jap. Frank was a wonderful wrestler, and a scientific boxer.

He had even learned the French method of boxing with his feet. Every muscle in his body was splendidly developed, but his mental development quite equaled his physical. Therefore he would not be confined in his encounter with Hashi to one style or system of offense and defense. He hoped to baffle the Jap by his knowledge of the Japanese acquirements, and to this he added the hope of defeating him by accomplishments of a sort in which Hashi was not proficient.

In his heart Fred Fillmore was exulting.

"Worked him easy!" he mentally cried. "Hashi will do the job! He'll swear it was an accident. Instead of making preparations for your wedding to-morrow, Mr. Merriwell, you'll be resting in Johns Hopkins Hospital with a broken leg."

"How do we reach this gymnasium?" asked one of the party. "I presume we're all invited to witness this set-to."

"Hashi wants you to come along," nodded Fillmore.

"As far as I'm concerned, you're all invited," said Merry.

"Call carriages!" cried Spaulding. "Leave it to me, gentlemen. Let me see, how many want to go?"

He quickly found out the number and hastened to order carriages for them.

A short time later people on the street were surprised to see many carriages collect before the University Club. Those who watched observed a number of chatting, laughing, well-dressed young men leave the club and enter the carriages, which rumbled softly away over the asphalt.

"Something doing somewhere," commented one of the watchers.

Frank, Bart, Spaulding, and Harrow were in one of the carriages.

"This is a queer affair," commented Spaulding. "I don't know what to think about it."

"I do," declared Hodge.

"Eh? You do?"

"Yes."

"What do you think?"

"It's some sort of a put-up job."

"You mean——"

"Fillmore and the Jap came to the club for the purpose of bringing this affair about. Fillmore and Merry had a little trouble some time ago. You know Fillmore struck Frank over the head in the lacrosse game at Oriole Park."

"That's a fact!" exclaimed Harrow. "I'd forgotten about that."

"They had a little trouble shortly after we arrived in the city this afternoon. Mark what I say, that fellow has engaged Hashi to make a holy show of Merry. He thinks it will be an easy thing to do."

"Well, I didn't see through the thing!" confessed Spaulding. "I thought it was purely accidental. If I'd thought it was a put-up job I'd surely had something to say to Mr. Fillmore. How did you happen to agree to it under such circumstances, Merriwell?"

"What was the difference?" said Frank. "If I'd spoken up and declared it a scheme more than one present would have fancied me a squealer."

"I suppose that is so."

"Besides, I must confess that I was not a little annoyed, and I felt a desire to teach that Jap a lesson. I hope I may be able to succeed. I'll wager that Fillmore has promised him money if he makes an exhibition of me."

"Frank," said Bart, "behind this there is something more than the mere desire to show you up."

"What do you mean?"

"Take my advice and be on your guard every moment. You know what things may be done with these bone-breaking Japanese tricks."

"I know very well."

"If that Jap wished and he could catch you just right, he might injure you for life."

"Would he venture to do that?" cried Harrow.

"Fred Fillmore would be delighted to have him do it."

"This affair seems more serious than I suspected," said Spaulding. "Are you certain you can handle him, Merriwell?"

"No man can be certain of his ability to handle another who is a stranger to him," confessed Frank.

"But you had no hesitation about agreeing to meet him. I fancied you felt fully confident."

"I give you the assurance that I shall handle him if it is in my power."

"Don't worry; he'll do the trick," asserted Hodge, whose confidence in Frank was solid as the everlasting hills.

It was not a long drive from the club to the gymnasium on Howard Street. They left the carriage and ascended a flight of stairs.

In a dark corner on the stairs stood a fellow who seemed waiting for something. As Frank passed, this person seized his arm.

"One moment, Merriwell!" he whispered.

It was Cutler Priest.

"All right, Hodge," said Frank, for Bart, not recognizing Priest, had turned quickly.

"Merriwell, you're in danger!" whispered Priest. "I came over from the club in the carriage with Manners and Ridgely. Both had been drinking. They were shooting off their chin. Fillmore planned this whole affair."

"As I thought," said Merry.

"He's paid the Jap to do you up."

"This simply makes my suspicion an assurance."

"But, from some things Manners let drop, I feel sure that it is not the intention to simply defeat you. The Jap is going to break your bones."

"Do you know this?" asked Frank, his heart burning with indignation.

"I'm dead sure of it. You are going to be maimed. Better not go into it. Keep out of the dirty trap!"

"Keep out?" laughed Frank, and there was something terrible in the sound of that laugh.

"Yes."

"On the contrary, I'll go into it, and Fillmore's paid tool had better look out for himself. He may get a portion of his own medicine!"

CHAPTER XXXIV.

AMERICAN AGAINST JAP.

Stripped to sleeveless sweaters, trousers and light rubber-soled shoes, Frank and the Jap faced each other on the huge mat spread on the floor of a seldom-used room above the gymnasium.

The spectators stood around, feeling a thrill of excitement. One and all they seemed to anticipate something unusual.

Hashi still smiled. Frank was calm and grave.

Fred Fillmore found it difficult to control his features to hide an expression of eager satisfaction and malignance.

"This is my time to triumph!" he thought. "Merriwell walked into the trap like a lamb going to the slaughter. While he is recovering from a broken leg I'll be perfecting my plans to steal Inza Burrage from him. I'm bound to have her! She shall be mine!"

Hodge was watching Fillmore, and the expression on the fellow's face made Bart long to hit him.

"Is the honorable gentleman quite prepared?" gently inquired Hashi.

"Quite," nodded Merry.

They crouched and moved toward each other. Hashi held himself on the alert, waiting and expecting his opponent to attack with a rush.

It is a feature of jujutsu to seem to yield before the first rush of the enemy, but to turn the attack to the undoing of the assailant, actually causing him to use his own force to aid in his defeat. Therefore Hashi was a bit disappointed when Merry failed to come after him in the style of most American wrestlers.

"I must provoke him to attack," thought the Jap.

Aloud he observed:

"The honorable gentleman seems exceedingly overcome by vastly much timidity."

It was now Frank's turn to smile.

"I haven't observed you making any headlong plunge," he retorted.

"I would humbly refrain from alarming you greatly more, discreet sir," said Hashi.

"That is indeed very considerate of you."

"Well, well!" cried Fillmore, with a mocking intonation; "I do believe Merriwell is frightened!"

"I don't see the professor displaying amazing courage about coming to a clinch," laughed Spaulding.

"That's his style."

"Perhaps it's Merriwell's style."

Frank and Hashi circled slowly. At last, tired of waiting, the Jap reached out swiftly as if to get a sudden hold on Frank; but he drew back instantly and waited again.

Merry knew it was an effort to lead him on.

Twice Hashi repeated the movement, and once he came near falling into Frank's clutch, for Merry made a lightning snap at his wrist and barely missed.

Finally Hashi came still nearer. Suddenly he felt a hand close on the back of his neck. Merriwell had caught him before he could prevent it.

He knew now that Frank could move with such swiftness that light itself seemed barely faster.

Hashi shot his own hand up and tried to secure a hold on Frank's wrist, with the intention of seeking a certain nerve with his fingers and robbing the American youth of strength in that arm.

Frank read his intention and prevented it by his manner of maintaining his hold, at the same time closing on the professor's arm at the shoulder.

Hashi twisted and snapped away barely in time to prevent the American from finding one of those paralyzing nerves.

He continued to smile, but he understood that Merriwell was inclined to meet him at his own game.

A moment later Frank secured another hold on the Jap. Instead of coming at Hashi, he drew the yellow athlete toward him.

Then there was a grapple.

"Ah!" cried the spectators.

Hashi sought to get one of Frank's hands in a certain manner. Being baffled, he changed instantly and tried to bring himself into a position of advantage by twisting Merriwell's arm behind his back. Again he was defeated.

In the meantime Merry had continued to seek to secure a hold on the little man, finally obtaining it. They went to their knees together.

Hashi broke Frank's hold. As they came up, the Jap again sought to twist Frank's arm behind his back. He was prevented in this, and he clasped Merry's body behind, getting him round the waist. Frank slipped down, reached up and closed his fingers in a lock about the back of Hashi's neck. Hashi's waist lock held, but Merry went over, sending the heels of the Jap in a half circle through the air. Hashi landed flat on his back, with the American full upon him.

It was a clean case of a wrestler's trick being baffled by another trick, and the Jap was down.

A shout went up from the spectators.

Fillmore looked astounded and dismayed.

But the Jap did not let Frank rise. Instead of that, as Merry was getting up, Hashi caught one of his legs.

Fillmore caught his breath. He knew what that meant, and he was satisfied now that Hashi had permitted Frank to bring about the fall in order to obtain this opportunity.

Frank seemed warned just in time, for he gave a squirming whirl that brought him round facing in the opposite direction and prevented the Jap from securing the leverage he desired.

"Let go of that leg!" he commanded.

But he did not wait to see if the Jap obeyed. He did not dare risk it. Instead of waiting, he dropped in such a manner that his free knee was driven into Hashi's wind.

That broke the fellow's hold.

Fillmore saw this and breathed a curse of dismay.

Hodge was stirred up.

"What did he try to do, Merry?" he palpitated.

"Oh, nothing," smiled Frank. "These jujutsu men never recognize a fair fall. To them it means nothing to be thrown flat on the back. He was trying for another hold, and I had to check him."

The Jap was breathing with difficulty. For some moments the smile seemed a sickly one, but he maintained it, even as the Japanese soldier smiles in the face of intense suffering and death.

Fillmore gave Hashi water and hovered over him.

"You failed!" he whispered.

"Sufficient is the time, honorable sir," answered Hashi softly. "I nearly made accomplishment."

"Look out! I'm afraid you led him to suspect. He'll be on his guard."

"Nothing can save the agile gentleman when I obtain the sufficient hold," declared the Jap.

Merriwell was warmly congratulated by Spaulding and the others.

"That's only the beginning," he said. "The little man let himself go over that he might get his hold on me. He is recovering, and he'll be very dangerous after this."

Hashi rose and took his place on the mat.

"Will the honorable gentleman athlete again give me the exceeding pleasure?" he invited.

Frank stepped out.

"The professor has peculiar ideas of pleasure," laughed Harrow. "I wouldn't regard it as much sport to have the wind driven out of me in such a manner."

Again the American and the Jap crouched and advanced with the greatest caution. Again Frank finally tried for the neck hold, but this time Hashi avoided it.

"Get him! get him!" hissed Fillmore.

"I'll get you some day!" muttered Hodge.

Hashi was disappointed because Frank would not attack after the American fashion. Once both secured a hold at the same moment, but instantly both broke, each realizing that the hold of the other was dangerous.

They were like crouching panthers.

"Get his arm!" mentally cried Fillmore. "If you can't break his leg, break his arm!"

Suddenly there was a mix-up. The movements of the combatants were swift and sudden. They grappled, broke, grappled again, twisted, turned, writhed. Frank saw and baffled each effort on the part of Hashi to get his fingers in contact with some paralyzing nerve. In return the little man repeatedly defeated Merriwell's strategic moves.

Suddenly Hashi went down, catching his arm with a twisting lock about Frank's right leg near the knee.

"He has him!" thought Fillmore. "Now he'll break the fellow's leg as if it were a pipestem!"

Instantly Frank stooped and seized the shoulder of the Jap, his grip being one of iron as he drove his thumb into a certain spot. Had he not located the spot accurately Hashi would have broken his leg in a twinkling. As it was, he found a nerve that completely paralyzed the yellow man's whole arm and rendered him helpless to exert the leverage on the imprisoned limb which must have crippled Merry.

No cry of pain escaped the vicious little man, but his hold was broken in a twinkling and Frank was free.

Merry knew now what had been attempted. The mere warning had not fully proved to him the dastardly purpose of his enemy; but now there was no doubt about it. He laughed aloud.

"Now the Japanese whelp gets his medicine!" grated Bart Hodge.

He had heard Merriwell laugh like that before, and he knew what usually followed.

Frank seized his opponent and lifted him from the floor, giving him a fling that sent him clear of the mat and slam against the nearest wall.

One thing practiced by the Japanese is the art of falling. Hashi was jarred, of course, when he collided with the wall, but he fell to the floor and sat up smiling in his usual bland manner.

That smile, however, was the mask which concealed the intense rage and chagrin which he felt. He knew now that the American was well up in the art of Japanese self-defense, besides being master of the American style of wrestling.

Hashi felt that he would be disgraced if he permitted Frank to defeat him. Besides, he would not earn the five hundred dollars.

But the disappointment of the Jap was not equal to that of Fred Fillmore.

"Fiends, take him!" whispered the young rascal. "Is he going to let Merriwell do him up?"

He had fancied Merriwell's action in hurling his antagonist against the wall would end the struggle; but vicious hope had new birth in his heart when he beheld the smiling yellow man pick himself up from the floor.

"The honorable gentleman is very skillful," purred Hashi, toddling back to the mat.

There was a steely glitter in Frank's eyes as he regarded the tough, little rascal.

"Wait a moment, Hashi," he commanded.

"Respected sir, yours to command," said the Jap.

"I am onto your trick now," said Frank. "I know what you are trying to do. Jujutsu teaches a man how to break limbs. The hold you had on my leg would have crippled me if I had not moved quickly to prevent it. But a leg or an arm is not the only thing that may be broken by such a method."

"Oh, respected sir——"

"You may as well cut out the respected sir! You tried to break my leg. It is no more difficult to break a neck. I warn you to hold up. Don't try that trick again if you respect your neck!"

"That's the talk, Merry!" cried Hodge.

"The honorable gentleman is so greatly suspicious!" murmured Hashi.

"Now come ahead," invited Frank, stepping to the very centre of the mat. "I shall defend myself at any cost to your limbs or life."

"Curse him!" whispered Fillmore.

Some of the spectators clapped their hands.

"This was to be a friendly trial of skill," said Maurice Spaulding.

"Of course it was!" cried Cutler Priest.

Hashi hesitated. For a moment his eyes left Frank. They met the eyes of Fillmore, and there he saw a command for him to go on.

"The honorable gentleman is wonderfully skillful," said the Jap. "I congratulate him upon his excellent skill, and his hand I would shake."

Was it possible that the Jap acknowledged himself beaten?

Frank was not duped, although he accepted the hand extended. He was prepared when Hashi instantly tried to obtain the arm lock which would have rendered him helpless.

Merry had a grip of steel, and he exerted it suddenly, crushing the fingers of the Jap.

Hashi was baffled again. Even though it seemed that the American would take his hand off, the little man did not wholly lose his persistent smile.

When he had baffled his antagonist, Frank suddenly changed his method and caught the fellow in a wrestling grip. Together they went to the mat, where Merry obtained a half-Nelson hold.

As Hashi felt his head bent under him and realized he must quickly go over upon his back, he flung his feet straight up into the air, and, using his head for a pivot, attempted to spin out of the hold like a top.

Merry anticipated that.

With his free arm he caught the Jap about the waist and checked the spinning. Then he promptly turned Hashi over flat and fair upon his back.

"Great—great work!" cried the spectators.

Merriwell was up, cool and unruffled.

Fillmore longed to leap out and deal Frank a blow.

"No use!" he thought despairingly. "No use! The miserable Jap can't do it!"

Hashi's smile clung, but it had lost its confidence and self-assurance.

"The honorable gentleman has the way in which to mix wrestling and jujutsu," he said, as he rose. "In this excellent manner he is using two arts against one. It is not an eminently fair test of one competent style against another."

"Ha! ha! ha!" laughed Spaulding. "He confesses himself beaten!"

"I beg the august gentleman's respectful pardon," said the yellow man. "I was humbly seeking to elucidate why I have the unfortunate success encountered."

Then he again stepped toward Merry.

"Why, he's the kind that never gets enough!" exclaimed Raymond Harrow.

"What do you think about your Japanese wizard, Fillmore?" asked one of the witnesses.

Fred attempted to answer, but his voice was husky and his words choked in his throat.

One more lightning trick did Hashi attempt. He did it without apparent preparation or thought, hoping this change of method might take Frank off his guard.

Frank baffled the attempt, seeming to read the Jap's very thoughts. He went in for another wrestling hold, but Hashi slipped away. The Jap tried to work Frank's movement by securing a hold that would turn it against Merry; but this trial again brought about his undoing. Merry secured a hold and hurled Hashi over his head.

The Jap fell sprawling on the mat, sat up, rose quickly, bowed low and confessed:

"One art against two is not sufficient. The wrestler alone I will humbly undertake to defeat; but the wrestler who has also the accomplishment of jujutsu is indeed too much."

Fillmore's scheme had failed.

Now Frank turned on the rascal.

"Next time you hire a tool to break my leg he'll not escape as easily as this one has," he said.

"What do you mean?" snarled Fred, his face pale.

"I mean what you heard me say. I was warned. You thought I had been led blindly into the trap. Fellow, you had better have a care! If you annoy me further I'll not bother with your tools, but I'll reach for the fountain head of the trouble. That is all I have to say."

"You're crazy!" sneered Fillmore.

But suddenly he found himself looked on with aversion by Merriwell's companions, who began to mutter among themselves. Their black looks and ominous behavior alarmed him.

"I believe the fools are going to jump on me!" he thought.

Fear overcame him, and he made haste to get out of the room and the building, leaving Hashi to follow when he would.

Although he had not broken Frank Merriwell's leg, Hashi had the five hundred dollars.

CHAPTER XXXV.

THE OLD HOME.

The town of Bloomfield was agog. Strange things were transpiring there, and gossip was busy.

Old Jacob Worthen, the richest man in town, known to be a miserly old curmudgeon, came knocking along the wooden sidewalk with his crooked cane.

Several of the villagers saw him. In a body they left the steps of Lem Briggs' grocery store, where they had been loafing and blocked the sidewalk.

"How de do, Mr. Worthen?" said one. "Fine day ter-day."

"Haw!" said old Jacob. "That reminds me, Cy Jones, I've got a little note of yourn that runs out next Tewsday. I s'pose ye'll be reddy to pay. I need the money."

"'Cordin' to what I hear," said another of the group, "you can't be needin' money much jest now, Mr. Worthen. They do say you've sold the old Merriwell place."

"Sold it!" snapped the richest man in Bloomfield. "I had to give it away. Best place in this town, too; but it's hoodooed. Been a constant outset to me ever sence it came inter my hands. Then stories about it bein' ha'nted ruined its valoo. Didn't nobody want to buy it, an' I couldn't keep a tenant on it. Yes, sir, I hed to give it away."

"Who bought it?"

"One of them smart city lawyer chaps. He bought it for another party, too. S'pose if I'd knowed who wanted it I might 'a' got a thousan' or so more fer it."

"Well, who was it that wanted it?"

"Old Asher Merriwell's nevvy. Mebbe some of ye remembers him? Ruther smart-lookin' young chap last time I saw him."

"Why," said Cy Jones, "I heerd he lost all his money an' was poor."

"Guess that was right time you heerd abaout it. His guardeen speckerlated and lost everything. Sence then, though, the boy run acrost his father. You've heerd about him—gambled a good deal. He went out West somewhere an' found some rich mines. Well, he died, an' them mines went to the boy. They do say he's got more money'n he knows what to do with."

"Well, what's he goin' to do with the old place?"

"Fix it up fer his home, I s'pose. He's got a crew of city workmen tinkerin' away there now an' a nigger—some one old Asher hed—kinder lookin' after the place."

"Well, well, well!" mumbled one of the old gossips. "Will wonders never cease! Beats all creation how fortenit some folks be. Now looker this boy. Lost every dollar he hed in the world, hed to leave college an' go ter work, an' nobody ever s'posed we'd ever hear from him ag'in. Now here he turns up rich as mud an' is comin' back here to make a spread. I've spent sixty-seven years right here in Bloomfield, an' I ain't never hed no chance in the world. It's all luck—all luck."

"Go on, Bill Kimball!" exclaimed old Jonas. "You've allus bin too lazy to draw your breath. You've spent your life a-loafin', an' you complain you ain't never hed no chance. Now the town's helpin' ye, when you might be comfortable well off an' able ter take keer of yerself."

"Ain't never had no chance," persisted Kimball doggedly. "Don't you talk to me, Jonas Worthen! You was born to have luck."

"I started out in the world jest as poor as you did."

"Well, I'm glad one of the Merriwells is comin' back to the old place," said Lem Briggs, the storekeeper. "Is he merrid? I s'pose he is, or else he wouldn't be havin' the place fixed up."

Later in the day Bill Kimball was walking past a fine, old house amid some elms, about half a mile from the village. He stopped to stare at the house, where men were at work, when an ebony-faced young negro came from the stable and strolled out toward the road.

"How de do?" saluted Kimball. "I kinder guess I know you. Ain't you Toots?"

"Dat's my name, sar," said the negro smilingly. "Why, bress mah soul! I believe yo' is Mistah Kimball. I's po'erful glad teh see yo', Mistah Kimball."

"Well, I'm glad to see you back here, Toots. What's goin' on? Workmen slickin' all up round the old place, hey?"

"Kindah makin' it presentable, sar."

"What are you doing here?"

"I's de ovahseer, sar," was the proud answer. "Yo' know Mistah Frank has done bought de ole place, an' he's gwine teh make it his home."

"When is he coming?"

"Day after to-morrow, sar. To-morrow dey's gwine teh decorate de church."

"Hey?" squawked Bill Kimball. "Goin' to what?"

"Decorate de church."

"What for?"

"Fo' de weddin'."

"Weddin'? weddin'?" gasped the old man. "Is there goin' to be a weddin'?"

"Yes, sar; Mistah Frank is gwine teh be married."

"Good land!" said Kimball, fanning himself with his straw hat. "That'll be news for the folks! Who's he goin' ter marry?"

"Handsomest gal in de worl', sar—Miss Inza Burrage. Brack eyes, rosy cheeks, an' de sweetes' mouth you ebber see. Ki-yi! It'll sho' be a swell affaih fo' dis town."

"Landy massy!" spluttered Kimball. "Won't that stir the village up! Be they goin' to settle down here?"

"Not now, sar."

"They're not?"

"No, sar. Dey're gwine teh be married heah an' give a pahty in de old home to a lot ob deyer frien's. Den dey're gwine off ter Mexico, where Mistah Frank has one of de berry riches' mines in de worl'."

"But they're comin' back?"

"Sho', sar. Dis is gwine teh be deyr home. Mistah Frank alwus did mean teh hab dis fo' his home when he was married. He's engaged me reg'ler fo' teh obersee de ole place. Next year I 'spects he'll mak lots ob changes an' alterations an' repairs. He says teh me, says he: 'Toots, when I come back from Mexico I's gwine teh hab some fine horses an' keep a prime stable, mah boy. Yo' knows mo' about horses dan anybody I ebber seen. I's got teh hab yo teh look after dat stable an' de ole place. Name yo' price, Toots, an' I'll 'gage yo' fo' life.' Ki-yi! Dat's de sort of job teh fall into."

"Well, well, well!" said Bill Kimball.

"Yes, sar, I's bery well satisfied, sar. Mistah Frank is de fines' gentleman ebber drew a bref. I knows him well, sar. He's a prince, sho'. Some day yo'll see one of de fines' estates right heah dat can be foun' anywhere in de country."

"Well, I must git along back inter the village," said old Bill. "Won't the folks talk when they hear all about this!"

He hobbled away as fast as his old legs could carry him.

CHAPTER XXXVI.

THE WEDDING.

xcitement in Bloomfield was at fever heat. Scores of visitors were in the town. The old hotel was filled to overflowing. Nearly all these guests were young men and women, and a pleasant, jovial lot they were.

Of course, the members of Frank's athletic team were present to the last man. Besides these there were others who had been his chums and comrades in college. Bink Stubbs and Danny Griswold were together again, fussing in their old, friendly way. Dismal Jones had turned up from somewhere, as long-faced as ever, quoting Scripture to fit all occasions. Grog Carker appeared more rabid in his socialistic views than in the old days, and equally easy to lead into prophesying the coming of the "great earthquake that should overturn the social conditions of the whole world."

A surprise that delighted every one was the appearance of Jack Diamond and his handsome wife, Julia, bringing with them a little Diamond somewhat more than a year old. Jack had "crossed the pond" to make a visit in Virginia and arrived just in time to hasten to Bloomfield for the wedding.

Barney Mulloy came on from the West, and his brogue seemed not a whit changed, while his wit and good nature remained quite as infectious.

It was the day before the wedding. A select party assembled at the station for the purpose of meeting Inza, who was to arrive on the afternoon train, accompanied by Winnie Badger, with Buck Badger and Bart Hodge as escorts.

Frank had reached Bloomfield earlier in the day.

As train time drew near a closed carriage that was quite unfamiliar in the village drew up beside the station platform. The curtains at the carriage windows were drawn. The carriage was drawn by two fiery horses. On the seat sat the driver, a wide-brimmed hat slouched over his eyes, while his features were almost wholly hidden by a profuse mass of whiskers.

Some of the people on the platform observed the driver closely. One man walked past and surveyed him. This man hastened to join some of the loungers.

"Say!" he exclaimed, in a hoarse whisper, "I bet ten dollars that feller's wearin' false whiskers!"

"Git out!" retorted several. "What makes you think so?"

"I seen Sile Levitt wear whiskers jest like them in the play over to the Four Corners Schoolhouse last winter."

"You're luny! What would that man want to wear false whiskers for? He ain't in no play."

Another carriage appeared. Mr. and Mrs. Diamond left it. They had come to meet Inza.

The train whistled in the distance.

In a few moments it whistled for Bloomfield station. It came rushing up to the platform and stopped. Inza and her companions were on board.

In the midst of the excitement the door of the strange closed carriage opened and a pale-faced young man stepped out. He fixed his eyes on Inza, who had descended from the train. She was dressed in a brown traveling suit and was acknowledging the merry greetings of the friends who had met her.

Bart Hodge had hastened away to look after the baggage.

The villagers were staring agape.

"Gosh!" exclaimed Bill Kimball, who had reached the station barely in time to see the passengers descend. "That's her—that stunnin' gal in brown! She's got black eyes, an' Toots told me she was black-eyed and the handsomest gal in the world. That's her!"

"Who's that pale-faced feller that's jest got out of that kerriage?" asked a young chap, turning his quid of tobacco in his mouth. "He's actin' almighty queer."

The person referred to was approaching Inza from behind, stepping softly. He was unobserved by the friends who surrounded her. Of a sudden he stepped forward, flung his arms round her, caught her from her feet and turned to dash with her toward the carriage. The door was open. The driver had his whip poised.

Inza screamed.

The man who had seized her flung her into the carriage and leaped after her, jerking the door closed with a slam.

The whip in the hands of the driver whistled through the air and cut the horses.

Away they leaped.

The astounded people on the platform had seemed dazed, but

now they awoke and shouted.

Buck Badger, who had sauntered after Hodge, turned at Inza's cry. He saw her flung into the carriage and saw the desperate man leap after her.

"The old boy's to pay!" cried Buck, his hand going to his hip. "That's whatever!"

Two strides brought him to the edge of the platform. As the horses turned toward the street beyond the station something bright glinted in the hand of the Kansan. This thing was leveled and a spout of smoke burst from it.

The sharp report of a revolver added to the excitement of the moment.

With that report one of the horses gave a convulsive leap and fell to the ground, dragging the other horse down. The uninjured animal was so entangled in the harness that he could do little damage kicking. The carriage was overturned.

Men rushed to the spot. From the upset carriage they dragged Inza Burrage, somewhat hysterical, yet practically unharmed. Likewise they pulled out the young chap who had tried to carry her off in such a crazy manner. He had been stunned, and made no resistance.

It was Fred Fillmore.

The village constable came bustling up while men and boys were at work extricating the uninjured horse.

"What's this mean?" he demanded. "Who's guilty of breakin' the law here? Somebody's goin' to git arrested."

"I opine there's your man, officer," said Buck Badger, pointing at Fillmore. "He's either a criminal or a lunatic, and either way he should be taken into custody. That's whatever."

Hodge tried to reach Fillmore.

"The whelp!" he cried. "He——"

The constable seized the desperate young man.

"I arrest you in the name of the law!" he cried.

"Where's the driver?" was the cry.

But the wearer of the false whiskers had found an opportunity to slip away and improved it.

* * * * *

The little church was beautifully decorated and fragrant with flowers. It was well filled. There was a hush. The organ began to throb and a thrill ran over every person present.

Down one of the aisles slowly advanced the minister, carrying a little book in his hands. At a distance behind him came Frank Merriwell, looking handsomer than ever before in his life, accompanied by the best man, his bosom friend, Bart Hodge.

Merry's heart was beating high with the mighty exultation of the grandest moment of his life. He turned with Bart and followed the minister toward the altar.

Suddenly the sound of the organ changed. The music became the "Wedding March."

Down the centre aisle came a vision of loveliness, Inza Burrage in snowy white, with her veil flowing round her. She was somewhat pale, but never had she looked sweeter, and a more bridelike bride-to-be the sun could not shine on.

She was followed by a pretty girl friend, who was acting as bridesmaid. Elsie Bellwood was not there. That was the only thing that marred the occasion.

As Inza approached the altar Frank stepped out and met her.

A splendid couple they made. Many an eye grew dim as they stood there hand in hand and the minister began the ceremony.

No one dreamed what was to happen.

The ceremony had progressed until the minister was on the point of pronouncing Frank and Inza man and wife, when there came a startling interruption.

A wild-eyed youth dashed down the aisle.

"Hold!" he shouted. "I forbid this marriage!"

It was Fred Fillmore, who had somehow managed to escape from custody. The poor fellow was insane in his desire to stop the wedding. Indeed, drink and his passion for Inza had quite upset his mental poise.

Of course, his appearance created consternation, and Inza nearly swooned.

It happened that the constable and two deputies were close after Fillmore. They reached the church as Hodge, Badger, and Browning rushed Fillmore down the aisle to the door.

"Let me have him!" cried the officer. "I bet, by gorry! he don't git away from me ag'in!"

"I should say you had better take care of him!" exclaimed Hodge, in disgust.

Although the wedding had been thus interrupted, Inza bore up bravely and the ceremony continued.

* * * * *

That night there was a merry reception and wedding feast in the old home at Bloomfield. Frank and Inza were supremely happy, and their friends were sharers of their happiness.

That day had seen the crowning triumphs of Frank Merriwell's career.

In truth, Fred Fillmore was mentally unbalanced. It became necessary to place him in a private sanitarium, although the examining physicians announced that there was a fair prospect that he might recover in time.

THE END

Lightning Source UK Ltd.
Milton Keynes UK
UKHW041114130920
369836UK00002B/8